HISTORY OF THE MODERN MUSIC OF WESTERN EUROPE

Da Capo Press Music Reprint Series
GENERAL EDITOR
FREDERICK FREEDMAN
VASSAR COLLEGE

HISTORY OF THE MODERN MUSIC OF WESTERN EUROPE

BY R. G. KIESEWETTER

Translated by Robert Muller

New Introduction by Frank Harrison,
Oxford University

DA CAPO PRESS • NEW YORK • 1973

Library of Congress Cataloging in Publication Data

Kiesewetter, Raphael Georg, Edler von Wiesenbrunn,
1773-1850.
History of the modern music of western Europe.

(Da Capo Press music reprint series)
Translation of Geschichte der europäisch-abendländischen oder unsrer heutigen Musik.
Reprint of the 1848 ed.
1. Music—History and criticism. I. Title.
ML160.K48 1973 780'.9 74-140375
ISBN 0-306-70089-1

This Da Capo Press edition of
History of the Modern Music of Western Europe
is an unabridged republication of the first
English edition published in London in 1848.
A new introduction by Professor Frank Harrison
has been prepared specially for this edition.

A Subsidiary of Plenum Publishing Corporation
227 West 17th Street, New York, New York 10011

Manufactured in the United States of America

INTRODUCTION
by Frank Harrison

The author of this book was an amateur musical historian — but an amateur only in the sense of maintaining life by other means than professing musical history. In aims, methods and achievement he was not only professional, but ranks as a pioneer in a new professional field. His biographer has called him a forerunner of musical *historismus*[1]. *Historismus,* one supposes, connotes not only the activity of writing history but also an anticipatory concept of the effects and reactions of written history upon people and thus upon events. Kiesewetter's views about musical *historismus* make him an interesting figure in musical historiography (*i.e.*, the history of musical history), independently of his important contributions to what is now called musicological knowledge.

Raphael Georg Kiesewetter acquired his musical training — in keyboard, flute, singing, bassoon, guitar, thorough-bass and counterpoint — chiefly from private teachers. His higher education was in philosophy and law, to a level sufficient to qualify him for a

1. Herfrid Kier, *Raphael Georg Kiesewetter (1773-1850), Wegbereiter des musikalischen Historismus* (Regensburg: Gustav Bosse, 1968) [= *Studien zur Musikgeschichte des 19. Jahrhunderts,* 13] The writer of this Introduction is much indebted to Kier's clearly organised and informative book.

series of administrative posts in the Austrian war office, whose picture collection he founded. He is mentioned (as "Kösswetter, bass, now court councillor") in a Beethoven conversation-book as a frequenter, apparently about 1805, with Beethoven, J. M. Vogel and others, of evenings of music-making, eating and punch-drinking at the home of one "Frank from Prague." Viennese music-patronage was shifting in the early nineteenth century from princelings like F. P. and J. F. M. Lobkowitz to lesser aristocracy and higher government servants, and music performance was moving from palaces to town-houses and the assembly-rooms of music societies. In February, 1809, Kiesewetter was among the "fine bass-singers" participating in concerts at the home of Marianne von Rittersburg. He seems to have used his enforced free time during the French occupation of Vienna in that year for intensive work on musical theory. In November, 1812, he sang in a mammoth performance of Handel's *Alexander's Feast* (with Mozart's additions, and under the title of *Timotheus, or the Power of Music*) organised by J. F. Sonnleithner, member of a family prominent in Vienna's music. Inspired by the success of performances by five hundred and ninety persons — all amateurs except the winds and double-basses — before audiences of nearly five thousand in the Imperial Riding School, Sonnleithner promoted the idea of a "Society of the Friends of Music of the Kingdom of Austria," which was duly founded and given statutes in 1814. From 1821 to 1843 Kiesewetter was its vice-president and was active in many of its affairs, including the acquisition of library materials and of an important collection of musical instruments.

Around 1816 he began to exercise his talents for organising and directing performances, and also to develop an interest in music of a kind which was not performed in the usual concert-giving routine. His program for the only Friends of Music concert he himself conducted (January 7th, 1816) was drawn from the then standard repertory: Beethoven's Second Symphony (1802), a duet from Paër's *Sofonisba* (1796), Moscheles's variations *La Marche Alexandre* for piano and orchestra (1815), two choruses from Salieri's *Les Danaïdes* (1784), the finale from Cherubini's *Élisa* (1794) and a symphony from Méhul's *Ariodant* (1799). Kiesewetter's idea for "historic" concerts was derived partly from the example of London's annual series of "Ancient Concerts," where no music less than twenty years old was heard. Something of the thought behind this limitation was revealed by the writer of a review of the "State of Music in London" in *The Quarterly Musical Magazine and Review* for 1827 (pp. 72-3):

> The Concert of Ancient Music is established to preserve not only the works of certain masters, but the style of executing those compositions which have been handed down by tradition from the authors themselves. It should seem then that very much the same selections must be made from year to year or these two principles must be in a good measure relinquished. . . . If the performance of such *chef d'oeuvres*, (of which be it recollected it is the specific object of these concerts to embalm the remembrance) be given up, and the compo-

> sitions of a later age (e.g. of Haydn and Mozart) substituted, the utmost danger would attend the experiment; because it must be obvious that the style must also be changed as we approach our own times — and the tradition would gradually be lost.

The main ingredients of the twelve programs of the London Ancient Concerts in 1827 were Handel (about 42%) and English glees and madrigals (about 11%). The pre-eighteenth-century composers represented were Wilbye, Locke, Purcell and Corelli, and the only Bach item (given in the program without initials for the name) was J. C. Bach's aria "Confusa, abbandonata" from his opera *La Clemenza di Scipione* (1778). Kiesewetter was also prompted to the idea of his "historic" house-concerts (which he ran from 1816 to about 1845) by the Berlin Singakademie, which in 1827 revived J. S. Bach's *St. Matthew Passion* under Mendelssohn. He was also aware of the performances and publications of sixteenth-century music in Paris by Alexandre Choron, who in 1827 built a hall to accommodate two hundred performing students of his *École de musique religieuse*. The programs of Kiesewetter's concerts, compared with most similar enterprises of that time, were both epicene and sophisticated. One of his earliest programs has J. S. Bach's *Jesu meine Freude;* the following items were performed on November 10th, 1822:

Palestrina	Motet *Exaltabo te* à 5
Biffi	Psalm *Notus in Judaea* à 3
J. S. Bach	*Kyrie* à 5
Caldara	Motet *Caro mea* à 2
Durante	Psalm *Beatus vir* à 4
Jomelli	*Magnificat* à 4

Schütz's *Christmas Oratorio* was done in 1829; the repertory also included works by Victoria, Marenzio, Benevoli, Carissimi, A. Scarlatti, Fux, Hasse, Leo, Marcello and Pergolesi.

Kiesewetter's first systematic researches into musical history were in Petrucci's prints (he thought the 1503 print was the first), and this led him to write about lost performance traditions of Western music. He published in the *Allgemeine musikalische Zeitung* in 1820 an article with the title "Ueber den Umfang der Singstimmen in den Werken der alten Meister, in Absicht auf deren Auffuhrung in unsrer Zeit" ("On the compass of vocal parts in works of the old masters, in the context of their present-day performance"). His second publication, a lengthy monograph entitled *Die Verdienste der Niederlaender um die Tonkunst* [Amsterdam: 1829] *(The Contributions of Netherlanders to Music)* is acknowledged as a landmark in western musical historiography. The question it set out to answer was the subject of a competition organised by the relevant section of the Royal Netherlands Academy of Arts and Sciences. Before publication, Kiesewetter added to his monograph (which won the gold medal and was published in a volume with Fetis's silver medal-winning essay) an appendix taking into account Baini's research on Dufay, whom Kiesewetter saw as the head of the first Netherlands school, whereas in the monograph itself Okeghem (there Ockenheim) was regarded as the earliest outstanding Netherlands composer. Kiesewetter's monograph and Fétis's essay were the first important modern contributions to regional research in musical history.

As this writer has observed elsewhere, Kiesewetter's monograph

> put an end to the prevalent notion that the Italians had been the musical preceptors of all Europe. He showed that the Roman and Venetian schools of the sixteenth century took over the style of their Netherlands predecessors, and thus put the achievements of Palestrina in a new perspective.[2]

Some of the music examples at the end of Kiesewetter's monograph (Fétis did not give any music examples) were taken, with acknowledgement, from Burney and Forkel, and one of the Ockeghem (*recte* Josquin) examples is credited to his learned and helpful friend, the Abbot Maximilian Stadler. Kiesewetter himself transcribed items by Busnois, Regis, Josquin, Tromboncino, Cara and Aaron.

Kiesewetter's handling of accidentals in these pieces illustrates his characteristic probity of scholarship. In Forkel's transcription of a Gafori example he put a cross over notes he thought should be sharpened in performance; in his own transcriptions he used a cross or an asterisk to distinguish original from added accidentals. In remarks on this subject appended to his transcription of Palestrina's hymn *Jesu corona virginum*, he expressed concern that his additions of accidentals might affect the sense of the composition. He felt, however, that this was worth the risk, since an editor's decisions were aimed at giving the enquiring amateur a palatable score — better an occasional

2. Frank Ll. Harrison, "American Musicology and the European Tradition," in: Frank Ll. Harrison, Mantle Hood and Claude V. Palisca, *Musicology* (Englewood Cliffs: Prentice-Hall, 1963), 28.

mistake than that the user should be faced with "unintelligible melodic lines, revolting to the musical sense, and ear-splitting modulations." In any case, he observed, a doubter could try out his own ideas, since the original content was still discernible. In the foreword to the catalogue of his anthology of polyphonic music from the tenth century to the early eighteenth (*Galerie der alten Contrapunctisten* [Vienna: 1847])[3] he described in equally strong terms how without supplied accidentals "the most beautiful and noblest conceptions of the master become unintelligible, even quite horrible, in performance," and defended his aim of remedying their seeming severity "according to the demands of a wholesome ear." From this side of the nineteenth-century plainsong revival and present-day acceptance of modal chord-usage it is clear that a "wholesome" ear was exclusively a contemporary western-tonality-oriented ear, whose preconceptions, understandable in Kiesewetter's time, still influence much current practice concerning accidentals in editing pre-sixteenth-century music.

The present reprint is one of two existing translations of Kiesewetter's *Geschichte der europäisch-abend-ländischen oder unsrer heutigen Musik*, published by Breitkopf & Härtel in Leipzig in 1834, with a second edition in 1846; there is an unpublished French translation by Auguste Bottée de Toulmin. Nothing seems to be known of Robert Müller, the translator of this English edition, beyond such facts

3. Kiesewetter's collection of scores went to the National Library in Vienna, and was of great service to his nephew, A. W. Ambros.

as are deducible from his Introduction — that he was a professional musician and had himself consulted many of Kiesewetter's authorities. Though Kiesewetter in 1847 expressed the opinion that Burney's *General History of Music* (4 vols., [London: 1776-89]) was still the only work deserving the name of History of Music, since Forkel's was left unfinished, he felt that his own *History* had a different aim:

> It is in no sense [he wrote to Bottée de Toulmin] the complete and final History which in spite of the valuable works of Burney and Forkel all musical experts eagerly await. My work is moreover not merely the summary whose aim is indicated in the title. It is not written for people who are already well versed in this field of literature, but for the needs of musicians, teachers and amateurs — people who usually vegetate in the deepest ignorance for want of a suitable work which operates at their level and brings them closer to historical fact. This is not an eleventh book made out of ten preceding ones, but it is in a certain sense a "first," because of its plan, its point of view and its opinions, in which it may perhaps be too daring and different. There are, if I am not mistaken, in no branch of historiography so many false traditions, so many sacrosanct authorities, so much credulity and so little critical approach as in the sphere of music; it is imperative that voices be raised if only to stimulate honest doubt and to suggest other views. Whatever may happen, I am ready to become a martyr to my love for truth. I am not at the risk of sacrificing a great

> reputation: *moriatur unus pro populo*[4] ["let one man die for the people"— a semi-jocular reference to the forecast of Jesus's death by the high-priest Caiaphas, reported in St. John's gospel].

Kiesewetter's plan, whose originality he so clearly recognised, involved the division of nine centuries of western musical history into time-segments named according to their dominant creative figures. This idea of organising music history in terms of retrospectively assessed heroes has been influential in western musical historiography until very recently. The heroes, nevertheless, have not stayed the same. At present Hucbald and Guido have less significance than in Kiesewetter's layout, while the century which on these terms could be called the "epoch of Leoninus" was not for him "distinguished by the name of any particular individual." The high status he accorded to the Neapolitans Leo and Durante was partly justified by his percipient comment that Bach and Handel "began and ended their own particular epoch." Kiesewetter modified the hero-approach inherent in what he modestly called his "circle of vignettes" by adding, in a "review of epochs," lists of those he considered the outstanding composers, teachers and writers of each epoch.

The value of Kiesewetter's researches in medieval music, compared to the writings on that subject of some of his predecessors, has thus been estimated:

> Works of this kind [*i.e.*, produced by compilation] which appeared after 1800, such

4. Kier, 115.

> as the music-histories of Christian Kalkbrenner (*Histoire de la musique*, Paris: 1802), Griffith Jones (*A History of the Rise and Progress of Music*, London: 1819), Thomas Busby (*A General History of Music*, London: 1819) and Karl Franz Brendel (*Grundzüge der Geschichte der Musik*, Leipzig: 1848, and *Geschichte der Musik in Italien, Deutschland und Frankreich*, Leipzig: 1852) contributed nothing noteworthy to the development of research on the Middle Ages; on the contrary, they bear ample witness — as Kalkbrenner's views on Dunstan, Guido and Johannes de Muris attest — to a definite retrogression in their treatment of medieval music. Kiesewetter, whose History stands as an exception to this, speaks ironically about "popularising" works of this kind.[5]

The supplement of music examples at the end of the *History*, described as "containing the most Ancient Monuments of figured counterpoint," is a smaller selection than that printed with the monograph of 1829, and has no composer later than Josquin. Common to both are Adam de la Halle's *Tant con je vivrai*, Landini's *Non avrà* [*ma'*] *pietà* (both of these are credited to Fétis), an extract from the Kyrie of Okeghem's *Missa cuiusvis toni*, and the Kyrie of Josquin's *Missa Gaudeamus.* In the monograph this last item was attributed to Okeghem and its transcription credited to Stadler. There was no Dufay example

5. Quoted in *ibid.*, 116, from Tibor Kneif, "Die Erforschung mittelalterlicher Musik in der Romantik und ihr geistesgeschichtlichter Hintergrund," *Acta Musicologica* XXXVI/2 (1964), 124, note 3. The translation of both of these extracts is by the writer of this Introduction.

in the monograph, where the first half of the fifteenth century was frankly described as *terra incognita.* The differences between the examples in the German original of the *History*[6] and in Müller's translation may be tabulated thus:

Examples in *Geschichte*	Comments
No. 1	Includes diplomatic copy of the MS, not in Müller; the transcription has "modern" clefs $g^2g^2f^4$, while Müller has $c^1c^1f^4$.
No. 3	= No. 4 in Müller, who gives only the *ripresa* in transcription; the original has the complete item, both in diplomatic copy and transcription.

6. The comparisons have been made with the second edition of the *Geschichte,* printed in 1846. Heinrich Besseler, in *Die Musik in Geschichte und Gegenwart,* s.v., "Dufay," gives music example no. 5 in both editions of the *Geschichte* as the first item in his list of Dufay editions. He does not mention there example 7 a, b, c in the *Geschichte* (= example 5 a, b, c in Müller). In the notes to his edition of *Ce moys de mai (Guillelmi Dufay, Opera Omnia,* VI [Rome: American Institute of Musicology, 1964]), he gives 1846 as the date of Kiesewetter's printing of this item, and his *Schicksale und Beschaffenheit des weltlichen Gesanges* (Leipzig: 1841), No. 16, as the reference. Kurt von Fischer, in his inventory of the Reina manuscript (which was apparently Kiesewetter's source for this piece and also for *Je prens congie*), gives the second edition of the *Geschichte* (1846), pl. XII/XIII as reference ("The Manuscript Paris, Bibl. nat., nouv. acq. frc. 6771," *Musica Disciplina,* XI [1957], 76). However, Charles Van den Borren had earlier pointed out that *Ce moys de mai* appeared in both the *Geschichte* and the *Schicksale* (cf. *Guillaume Dufay* [Brussels: Maurice Lamertin, 1926], 233).

No. 4	= No. 3 in Müller, who gives the text in the transcription — it is not given there in the *Geschichte*. The transcription was by a friend of Kiesewetter, probably Stadler (see below; p. 102).
No. 5	Dufay's *Je prens congie de vous, amours* (no further text in *Geschichte*); not in Müller.
No. 6	Dufay's *Ce moys de mai* (here attributed to Binchois), whose text mentions Dufay and Perrinet; not in Müller.
No. 7 a, b, c	= No. 5 a, b, c in Müller.
No. 8 a, b	= No. 6 a, b in Müller; for the composer Eloy d'Amerval see Gustave Reese, *Music in the Renaissance* (New York: Norton, 1954), 263.
No. 9	= No. 7 in Müller.
No. 10 a	= No. 8 in Müller.
No. 10b	= No. 9 in Müller; the *Geschichte* gave the composer as "Ockeghem vel Ockenheim."

While it is one of the aims of musical historians to distinguish fact from fiction and valid interpretation from misapprehension, the listing of hits and misses is not the main reason for studying the writings of our predecessors. Sympathetic enjoyment of their "boners" is nevertheless a legitimate pastime. Kiesewetter made remarkably few; one, however, is his misreading of the abbreviation for *littera* as *lira* in the Milan manuscript of Franco of Cologne, which made him say (unqueried by Robert Müller), that "the discantus is formed with one or more lyres, or without a lyre" instead of "with one or more texts, or without text." He has an impressive number of "firsts" in the *History*, and even more in his many subsequent writings. The precision of the title of his *History of the Modern Music of Western Europe* is in contrast to many later so-called histories of music which were and are, in fact, histories of European art-music only. Kiesewetter was aware of the problems involved in writing for "musicians, teachers and amateurs" while at the same time avoiding shallow "popularising." His interests in regional research and in lost performance practices were unusual for his time. His musicological pioneering has outstanding value as social history.

Frank Harrison

University of
Amsterdam
September 1972

HISTORY OF THE MODERN MUSIC OF WESTERN EUROPE

HISTORY

OF THE

MODERN MUSIC

OF

WESTERN EUROPE,

FROM THE FIRST CENTURY OF THE CHRISTIAN ERA

TO THE PRESENT DAY,

WITH

EXAMPLES,

AND AN APPENDIX, EXPLANATORY OF THE THEORY OF THE

ANCIENT GREEK MUSIC.

BY

R. G. KIESEWETTER,

IMPERIAL AND ROYAL COUNSELLOR OF STATE AT VIENNA;

TRANSLATED FROM THE ORIGINAL GERMAN, BY

ROBERT MÜLLER.

LONDON:

T. C. NEWBY, PUBLISHER,

72, MORTIMER STREET, CAVENDISH SQUARE.

MDCCCXLVIII.

LONDON:
RICHARDS, PRINTER, 100, ST. MARTIN'S LANE.

TRANSLATOR'S PREFACE.

In presenting to the public an English translation of Kiesewetter's celebrated and valuable treatise, entitled a *History of the Modern Music of Western Europe,* I have been influenced by the desire of furnishing to the English musical student a practical, and, at the same time, a comprehensive as well as a clear view of the slow, precarious, and, not unfrequently, devious steps by which musical art has arrived at its present state of high æsthetical culture.

At the risk of appearing prolix, I may have repeated several things already most probably known to the generality of professional readers, but I considered it requisite to bear in mind that I was addressing those who are but slightly practised, together with those who are well versed, in musical knowledge.

I have no peculiar theoretical dogmas which can be strengthened or inculcated by a dissemination of the work; and I have been farther induced to undertake the translation, from a belief that, in the lucid arrangement of the various epochs into which the author has divided his history, and the correct conclusions he has thence been enabled to deduce, the most satisfactory means were provided for unfolding the elaborate mysteries of musical chronology. I was moreover deeply convinced of the accurate nature and the acuteness of the investigations, and also the careful and extensive research by which the various propositions advanced have been attested and confirmed; this conviction was forced upon me far more by the intrinsic merit of the work itself, than even by the very great popularity it has acquired in Germany, where it is considered as the most superior work ever written on the subject; and particularly since I have myself referred to many of those authorities which the author has cited in proof of his assertions, and am consequently enabled to bear witness to the strict fidelity of the same. Of one thing I feel convinced, that a more correct notion of the history of the art will be obtained from the perusal of this short treatise, in one twentieth part of the time necessary for a complete acquaintance with the ponderous volumes of previous historians, from poring over which the student will probably rise more mystified than enlightened.

In one of his letters to me concerning this history, Kiesewetter indulges in several remarks, which I cannot refrain from introducing as of singular interest on this occasion. He says, "the feebleness of this work I am well aware of, and peculiar circumstances alone induced me to prepare it for publication. It has, however, met with success both in Germany and France. The only merit it possesses consists in the plan; its feebleness is evinced by the superficial method in which the subject matter is worked out; but this may almost be urged as a point in its favour, from the cursory and general view which it gives of the whole progress of the science; because many amateurs or professional musicians would summon courage for the perusal of the present work, few of whom would have the patience to wade through the voluminous histories of Forkel or Burney.

"Without venturing in the most remote degree to compare my insignificant efforts with the solid productions of the ablest writers in this department, I beg merely to remind you that the most diffuse amongst them, such as Matheson, Marpurg, and Rochlitz, in Germany; D'Alembert, Brossard, and others, in France; and even Hawkins and Burney, in England; were, like myself, either amateurs or dilettanti, at all events, more to be regarded as such, than as practical musicians. In fact, my *soi-disant* history, imperfect and superficial as it may be deemed, has the advantage of brevity, in which respect it will suit the convenience of readers in general, and this may be regarded as its principal if not its sole merit, whilst at the same time it constitutes its *foible.*"

I now venture to hope, that having myself derived, not only much gratification, but instruction, from an attentive study of this work in the original, I may have been enabled, by thus presenting it to the world in an English dress, to confer a boon upon a numerous class of my professional brethren; and this hope I may be the more embolden to entertain, from having enjoyed the practical experience of its great value as an introduction to the more elaborate, although scarcely more erudite, publications of others upon the same interesting subject.

ROBERT MÜLLER.

London 1847.

THE

AUTHOR'S DEDICATION

TO THE FOURTH SECTION OF

THE ROYAL BELGIAN INSTITUTE OF SCIENCES, LITERATURE, AND THE FINE ARTS, AT AMSTERDAM.

GENTLEMEN,

THE question which you, who are yourselves so deeply versed in the history of the musical art, lately proposed for a Prize Essay, has given rise to a critical comparison of many facts widely dispersed at the present day over the field of literature; and much that is valuable has recently been brought forward, to elucidate what is historically the most important, but, at the same time, the most obscure period of the art. For this the literary world is indebted to you.

Prompted by the question to which I have alluded, as well as by the applause with which at the same time you greeted my attempt at a reply, I have endeavoured, although in a manner unsatisfactory to myself, to continue my researches, in order, if possible, to throw light on a period still more remote, over which an almost impenetrable veil has hitherto been cast.

It has been my good fortune to become possessed of information and records which illustrate that period; partly extending, and, in many cases, considerably altering the ideas which had previously been entertained of the origin of contrapunctic art; these I have availed myself of in the present work, which represents in outline the entire history of modern Music down to our own times, and in which they form a peculiar and, as I flatter myself, not a useless portion.

Thus far may I venture to assert, that to you, gentlemen, is the present work indebted for its appearance. To you, and to your encouragement, it may be attributed that I undertook it; and I request therefore that you will accept my dedication of the same, as a humble testimony of my great esteem and sincere respect.

R. G. Kiesewetter,
Corresponding Member of the Section.

Vienna, December 1832.

CONTENTS.

APPENDIX OF NOTES.

CORRESPONDENCE WITH THE AUTHOR.

SUPPLEMENT.

The most ancient monuments of Figural Counterpoint.

No. 7.—Kyrie for three voices, ex Missa : *L'homme armé*, composed by Vincentius Faugues, who flourished in the first half of the fifteenth century.

No. 8.—Kyrie for four voices, by Joannes Okeghem ; flor. in the second half of the fifteenth century.

No. 9.—Kyrie and Christe for four voices, ex Missa : *Gaudeamus*, composed by Josquin des Prés ; flor. from about 1480 to 1520.

INTRODUCTION.

ORIGIN OF CHRISTIAN CHURCH MUSIC AND ITS EARLY CHANGES.

PERIOD.—FROM THE FIRST CENTURY OF THE CHRISTIAN ERA UNTIL TOWARDS THE CLOSE OF THE NINTH CENTURY.

It is a preconceived opinion, as widely spread as it is deeply rooted, that modern Music was modelled on that of ancient Greece, of which it is in fact merely a continuation; for we find the several authors who have preceded us, speaking of ancient music having been "revived" in the Middle Ages.

There was a time, indeed, during which the Christian Church Music of Western Europe sought assistance from that of Greece; and for a very long period the ideas of the Greek authors were regarded as the source of all musical theory. But the truth is, that modern music flourished only in proportion as it began to separate and withdraw itself from the system laid down and enforced by the Greeks, and that it reached a considerable degree of perfection only when it succeeded in completely emancipating itself from the last remnant, real or supposed, of the ancient Grecian; with this, moreover, for a considerable length of time it may be said to have scarcely ever possessed more than the common "substratum" (as it were) of tone and sound.*

From the elements of Grecian music, had ancient Hellas even continued to flourish peacefully for a further duration of two thousand years, there never could have arisen a music similar to our own,—an insurmountable obstacle to its growth being presented by the systems to which it was, in the proper sense of the word, strictly confined by the authority of the philosophers, according to usage, and by that also of the civil law: and if the beautiful art of music had been destined ever to unfold itself, before it reached that perfection the germ of which it inwardly contained, it became necessary that in Greece it should die, to be elsewhere born again, a new creature. The ancient Greek music may be described as having died in its infancy, a lovely child indeed, but incapable

* Tone and Sound (Ton und Klang) are not to be taken as synonymous terms: if we accidentally touch a glass or stringed instrument, the common ear only discovers a *sound* in the vibration produced; but the musician recognizes this sound as a certain *tone* or note of the scale.—*Translator.*

of reaching maturity; and so far as regarded mankind, its decay was not a loss to be deplored.*

Modern music,—if at its origin it may so be termed,—had arisen unnoticed in lowly huts and secret caves, even when the approaching downfal of the Greeks was already apparent. It formed itself in the assemblies of the early Christians,—in general a poor, illiterate, and homely people, who had never been initiated into the sublimer mysteries of Grecian music; it was but a very simple, artless song of Nature, free from the trammels of rules; by degrees alone it assumed and retained certain accents or inflections, and acquired at last, through frequent repetition, that settled form among congregations, which was handed down by them from one to another.

But that Grecian, or, as some authors have supposed, Hebrew, melodies, should have found their way into the assemblies of Christians, seems altogether incredible; for had they even been capable of appropriating and retaining Grecian melodies, and of singing these in accordance with their unpractised organs of voice and ear, still their natural horror of everything connected with the heathens, as the most ancient authors have

* All that is required for a knowledge of the theory of ancient Greek music, the reader will find in the Appendix, Note 1.

testified, was too great for the admission among them of such melodies as had been common to the pagan temples or theatres; whilst they evinced an equal anxiety also to separate themselves from the Jews; and their object was, in fact, more especially to found a peculiar art of song, distinct from that of every other religion, in the attainment of which they were most likely to succeed from the mode they had themselves established.

Nevertheless, in whatever way this new art of song among the early Christians may have originated, it is but reasonable to imagine, from its total want of rules, that the regularity and accordance so desirable in the melody, would prove more and more difficult of acquirement as the community increased in numbers ; and at length become impossible.

In the fourth century of the Christian era, when temples, dioceses, and ecclesiastical dignitaries had come into existence, and when men of scientific education had embraced Christianity, a few pious and learned bishops in the East and West undertook to reduce the art of song to some kind of order, and to fix it within certain modulations. This, however, could only be effected by means of a regular scale, and prescribed forms, to indicate the place where, in the progression of the scale, the half-tone requires to be introduced: and, since the want or necessity of a system was now for the first time perceived, nothing was more natural than to seek among the remains of such Greek musical writers as were then known, for the grammar or initiatory system of a language already dead.

There was found undoubtedly by this research a very ingenious, although, at the same time, an extremely complicated theory, by far the greater part of which must have been not only superfluous, but detrimental to the object in view. Their chromatic, and especially their enharmonic genus, with progressions which the most practised ear can scarcely detect, even with the assistance of the monochord,*—progressions, which the

* The monochord, appropriately called Klangmesser (tone measurer) by the Germans, invented by Pythagoras, of a single string, was an instrument furnished with moveable bridges, and contrived for the measuring and adjusting the ratios of musical intervals, by accurate divisions. Arist. Quint. says, that this instrument was recommended by Pythagoras on his death-bed, as the musical investigator, the criterion of truth. It appears to have been in constant use among the ancients, as the only means of forming the ear to the accurate perception, and the voice to the true intonation, of those minute and difficult intervals which were then practised in melody. Guido taught singing by means of the monochord, for the divisions

organ of the voice, notwithstanding the utmost possible culture, could never learn distinctly to articulate,—must have been unceremoniously condemned. Then their semeiography, consisting of 1620 note-characters, it was not likely to have been entered upon. Their fifteen modes, which, according to our ideas, are merely so many transpositions of one and the same minor scale, were altogether superfluous, where the object was to procure only the model or symbol of a single one, the character of which might remain unchangeable by any higher or lower intonation. As to their musical arithmetic (Canonick), it could merely have been of use to the teacher or theorist, and was absolute nonsense in regard to the practical part of music. And their rhythmopeia and melopeia,* the most interesting branch of their whole theory, could no longer be employed with the ancient Greek language, now

of which he gives some plain and easy rules. This instrument had probably a neck and was fretted (like our modern guitar), as bridges, like those on a common monochord, could not, without much practice, have been moved quickly enough. See Burney, vol. i. p. 433, and vol. ii. p. 78.—*Translator.*

* Melopœia, or melopöe (melody and modulation). The composition or arrangement of such sounds as were fit to be sung, in opposition to noise; musical sounds, tones, or notes. —*Translator.*

almost obsolete, and with the prose to which it must have been sung.

On the other hand, there was found a tolerably well regulated scale of the diatonic *genus*, sufficiently easy too of comprehension for a person of moderate musical endowments, and which might have been performed without much difficulty by any one, whose organ of voice was capable of cultivation: there was found, besides, a division (though rather conventional than natural) of the diatonic scale into tetrachords,* which, by continuing to be dovetailed one into the other, formed the scale desired, and a scale indeed of two octaves, wherein each degree, or note, had undoubtedly a very long name, not easily retained in the memory, but at all events properly defined and characteristic. Lastly, there were found certain scales, or series of tones (notes) which were distinguished sometimes as keys (*modi*) so called, and sometimes as an octave species (*species diapason*) of a key; and out of all these methods there were some which could be readily adapted to regulate a melody so simple as that selected for use by the Christian Church.

History does not explain to us in what manner the Church in the East may have arranged its

* See Appendix, page 2,—"Tetrachords."

music during the first centuries of the Christian era; but it informs us, that in the latter part of the fourth century (A.D. 374 to 397), St. Ambrose, bishop of Milan, had introduced a model of church melody, in which he chose four series or successions of tones (notes), and called them simply the first, second, third, and fourth tones, laying completely aside, as inapplicable, the ancient heathen names of Doric, Phrygian, Lydian, Œolic, Ionic, and the like; these successions distinguished themselves only by the position of the half-tones in the degrees of the scale, and are said to have been as follows:

1st Tone.	*d*	*e*	*f*	*g*	*a*	*b*	*c*	*d*		
2nd Tone.	—	*e*	*f*	*g*	*a*	*b*	*c*	*d*	*e*	
3rd Tone.	—		*f*	*g*	*a*	*b*	*c*	*d*	*e*	*f*
4th Tone.	—			*g*	*a*	*b*	*c*	*d*	*e*	*f*	*g*

If these successions of tones may be regarded as borrowed from the theory of the ancient Greeks, still the living breath of ancient Grecian (or Roman-Grecian) music could never have intruded itself among the chants of the Christians; for such music had already ceased to exist, or only survived in remnants, degenerated and fallen into contempt. St. Gregory the Great, who governed the Christian Church from A.D. 591 to 604, devoted particular attention to Church melody, and was in more ways than one its reformer. He collected the existing tunes or chants, improved them, added many new ones, and published an entire collection, with the method of singing them, as fixed precepts for all Christian Churches. His Antiphonary* was chained to the altar of St. Peter's, in order that it might be referred to on all occasions, and be made the means of correcting any changes which might probably occur in the course of succeeding years. He established not only a new system of keys, but in fact a new system of scales, fresh names to the notes, as well as new and simplified characters for writing music. In his scales he retained the four already mentioned of St. Ambrose, adding to them four others, which were produced by transposing those of St. Ambrose a fourth lower; by these means the principal tone, or key-note, as it might be called, which formerly appeared as the first or fundamental note, now appeared in the middle, or more properly as the fourth of the succession, the

* Antiphonarius, or antiphonarium;—the book which contains the antiphons, or anthems. In a more extended sense, the collection of all the music used in the ritual of the Romish Church.—*Translator*.

additional four scales being called the plagal, to distinguish them from the four more ancient, which received the name of authentic. In this manner their order would of course be disarranged. The following are the eight ecclesiastical successions or scales, which still exist as such in the music of the Roman liturgy, and are called Gregorian, after their founder :—

1 Tone.	Auth.	——— *D e f g A b c D*
2 Do.	Plag.	*A b c D e f g A*
3 Do.	Auth.	———— *E f g a B c d E*
4 Do.	Plag.	— *B c d E f g a B*
5 Do.	Auth.	———— *F g a b C d e F*
6 Do.	Plag.	—— *C d e F g a b C*
7 Do.	Auth.	———— *G a b c D e f G*
8 Do.	Plag.	——— *D e f G a b c D*

It will be perceived, at the first glance, that these church scales, or keys, as they were called, differ only from each other in two respects,—first, in the position of the half-notes, or semitones; and again, in the position occupied by the principal note, or more properly the two principal notes of the authentic scale, namely, the fundamental note and its fifth, subsequently called the dominant; but the accordance which prevails between the authentic and the plagal scale allied to it, consists in each being composed of one species of fourths and fifths (the position only of the semitones contained in them being considered); in such a manner, however, that when the authentic has the fifth in the lower, and the fourth in the upper half of its scale, the plagal, on the contrary, contains the fourth in the lower and the fifth in the upper half of its scale.

The manner in which these ecclesiastic scales, in the course of time, (particularly since Glarianus, who flourished in the sixteenth century), received the inappropriate and inapplicable names of Dorian, Phrygian, Lydian, Mixolydian, and so forth, will be explained in another place. St. Gregory little thought that he was laying the foundation for such a sin.

St. Gregory made an important improvement by discarding the thoroughly groundless system of the tetrachord adopted by the ancient Greeks, and by founding in its place that of the octave, the only one which nature indicates, and which the Grecian scholastics indeed also knew, but singularly enough despised: and another improvement no less important, in connexion with his system of the octave, was the introduction of a most simple nomenclature of the seven sounds of the scale, by means of the first seven letters of the Latin alphabet, namely:

		Added by Guido in the 11th century.	Afterwards added by his Pupils.
A B C D E F G	*a b c d e f g*	*aa bb cc dd*	*ee*
1st Octave.	2nd Octave.	3rd Octave.*	

---

* To prevent confusion it may be as well here to remark, that Guido's scale was—

Γ A B C D E F G a b c d e f g

Added by Guido in 11th century. Added afterwards by his Pupils.

But the modern School classes the octaves in the following order:—

C D E F G A B c d e f g a b

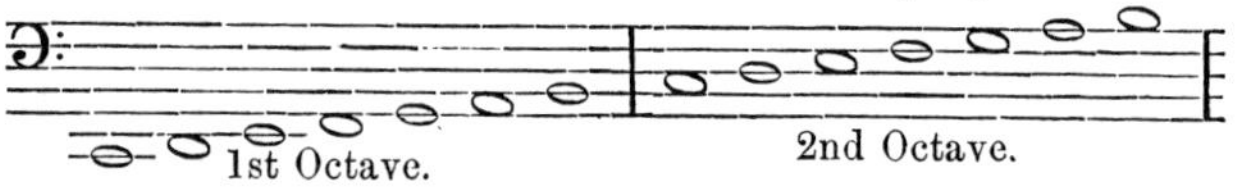

$\bar{c}$ $\bar{d}$ $\bar{e}$ $\bar{f}$ $\bar{g}$ $\bar{a}$ $\bar{b}$ $\bar{\bar{c}}$ $\bar{\bar{d}}$ $\bar{\bar{e}}$ $\bar{\bar{f}}$ $\bar{\bar{g}}$ $\bar{\bar{a}}$ $\bar{\bar{b}}$

The first (Grosse Bassoct, or great octave) is written with capital letters (A); the second (Kleine Bassoct, or small octave) with small letters (*a*); the third (Einmalgestrichene, or single-lined octave) with a single line or stroke above or below small letters ($\bar{a}$ or $\underline{a}$); and the fourth (zweymalgestrichene, or double-lined octave) with two lines or strokes above

These seven letters St. Gregory adopted instead of the incredibly difficult nomenclature of the ancient Greek scales, or in place of those of seventeen or eighteen letters which were employed by Boethius * (a Roman consul, beheaded in 524 at Rome, author of Latin "Commentaries on the Ancient Grecian Musical Theorists"), not with the intention of introducing a

or below small letters ($\bar{\bar{a}}$ $\underline{\underline{a}}$); also with two small letters ($\genfrac{}{}{0pt}{}{a}{a}$ or *a a*.) This system is particularly convenient in works like the present, since without making use of the staff we know that A is the first space in the bass, *a* the fifth line in the bass, $\bar{a}$ the second space in the treble, and $\bar{\bar{a}}$ (or $\underline{\underline{a}}$, or $\overline{\genfrac{}{}{0pt}{}{a}{a}}$, or even a a), the sixth line in the treble.—*Translator.*

* Among the various works which Boethius left behind him, there was unfortunately found a treatise on music, which, as will be seen in the sequel, was the means of retarding the progress of the art for hundreds of years. Burney, in his general *History of Music*, vol. i. p. 487, first edition, says Boethius was born at Rome in 470, and there beheaded in 525. (Vol. ii. p. 29, same edition, the year of his death is stated to have been 526.) On the other hand, Hawkins, in his *History of Music*, vol. i. p. 301, says that Boethius was born at Pavia, the ancient Ticinum of Italy, about the year 476, or somewhat later; and not content with this deviation from Burney's version, he adds, at p. 305 of the same volume, that he was beheaded in prison, on the 10th of the kalends of November in 705, thus assuming that Boethius had lived not less than 229 years, an extent of longevity nowhere recorded of any individual since the days of the patriarchs.—*Translator.*

new nomenclature, but in the text of his book alone, that he might abbreviate his work, and spare the patience of his readers. The idea of St. Gregory was accordingly quite new and totally different.

With regard to the notation of St. Gregory, it was the generally received opinion that he adopted the above seven letters for the purpose of introducing a more simple and comprehensible nomenclature, and they were certainly most suitable for the end in view. I have shown, moreover, in a separate treatise on the notation of St. Gregory's music (inserted in the Leipsig *Musical Journal* for the year 1828, Nos. 25, 26, and 27), that there has never been discovered, previously to the time of St. Gregory, a codex of the Roman liturgy with this lettered notation; that no ancient author whatever mentions a word respecting the introduction of these letters as names for the notes; that, on the contrary, the oldest remnant existing of the musical notation of the Latin Church, at present discovered, is the one preserved at St. Gallen, being an exact, *counterfeit* copy of the Gregorian model chained to the altar of St. Peter's, which one of the Roman choristers, sent by Pope Adrian the First, about the year 780 to Charlemagne, had taken with him; this was marked with the so-called *Neu-*

mata,* styled by the annalists "Nota Romana," and, so far as has yet been discovered, was the only notation introduced into the Roman Church. It was used, with but few alterations, in the books of the liturgy until the fourteenth century, and it may therefore be supposed that St. Gregory had either himself introduced this lettered notation, or must at all events have authorized its adoption.

After the short sketch above given of the character of the ancient Grecian scales, it will scarcely be necessary to adduce further proof that St. Gregory's eight ecclesiastical scales were something entirely different, and were, properly speaking, simply so many octave species of one and the same diatonic, or rather were nothing more than a common diatonic scale. The tunes composed from St. Gregory's scales have, in their original form, a character so truly pious and ecclesiastical, and so little approaching to the much esteemed ancient Grecian music, from which no one could trace them as having been borrowed, that I have never been able to conceive how writers, otherwise very enlightened, could have been so far misled as to maintain

* *Neuma*, a sign or mark; in the Latin of the Middle Ages generally written in the plural, *neumæ*, and sometimes *neumata*.—*Translator*.

that the Gregorian chant presents to the connoisseur a valuable relic of the ancient Grecian melodies and their different keys. (See Rousseau, *Dict. de Mus.:* Article, *Plain Chant;* and Forkel, *Geschichte der Musik*, part 1, page 404.) What though St. Gregory's ecclesiastical scales, considered in place of so many keys, be defective, so far as that in some of them the chief note, or the sub-semitone (sensible note or major seventh of the scale), is wanting, the same being indispensable to us, in order to recognize a scale as a key,—yet, if I explain them properly, these scales possess in themselves something of the character of real and new keys, or have at least the germ of such, inasmuch as in each of them not only a reigning principal note prevails, but the related gradation of tone* also is marked, into which the

* For example: C is related in the first degree with F, G, and A minor, and in the second degree with D minor and E minor, but not with D major, E major, A major, etc. The natural progressions of the melody are, and were at that time, D (with its minor third D-F, not D-F♯), F, G, A, and E minor, rarely B major. Sharps and flats were not introduced, and in the *Cantus firmus* there was at most a ♭ employed, called B rotundum (B quadratum was written by a ♮); and in some keys these were supposed or understood, as in the first, fourth, and fifth. In composition also (Contrapunct, Mensural Music), the artificially-completed scales were first experimented upon towards the end of the sixteenth century, and came into general use only in the seventeenth.—*Translator.*

chant must, or could, have resolved itself in its progress, and which agrees with our dominants and mediants. As therefore, in course of time, there arose in the Church the so-styled counterpoint, or the chant in several parts, which was employed in such a manner that both singers and composers were necessarily constrained to regard the key, as such, by the *subsemitonium modi** it could not fail to be otherwise than that there should arise from the elements of tones I and II our D minor,—from III and IV our A minor (at a later time also E minor),—from V and VI our F major, by lowering the B into B flat (for the sake of avoiding the enharmonic tritonus F to B),—from VII and VIII our G major; nay, further, in consequence of the early introduced transpositions of the Church scales into their fourth or fifth, there would arise our C major, G major, A minor,—and finally, by the invention of other principal notes, namely, by the intonation of every possible degree of the scale, our modern twelve major and twelve minor scales must have been produced.

All this, however, is, and was even in its

* *Subsemitonium modi*, the major seventh of the scale; for example: in the first Gregorian tone, *d e f g a, a g f e d c d.* In order to recognize this as a melody belonging to the key of D, it was necessary to raise *c* to *c* sharp.—*Translator.*

origin, more than the Greeks in their contracted systems * either knew or foresaw. St. Gregory, and the assistants whom he employed in the developement of his new system, must of a certainty have acquired a deeper insight into the character of music than was ever obtained before them; and it redounds to their greatest praise that they did not allow themselves to be drawn into the erroneous methods of their learned predecessor Boethius, which, on their revival in after times, were so long an obstacle to the improvement of our modern music. The system of St. Gregory, by its simplicity, though not so ingenious perhaps in appearance as the theories of the Grecian scholastics, was beyond comparison more reasonable and practically convenient than theirs. His system, which, in continuing a series of seven diatonic degrees, causes a repetition of the first seven notes in a higher position,—namely, the system of the octave—every unprejudiced person must acknowledge to be more satisfactory than that of the old Grecian tetrachord; and likewise that his seven letters are more conformable to the appellation of

* Any interval which had the intermediate notes filled up from one extreme to the other, was called by the Greeks a system. Thus A, *b*, C was a system of a third; A, *b*, *c*, D, system of a fourth, &c.—*Translator.*

the tones, than that extravagantly-composed crowd of words, by which each of the eighteen tones of the Greek scales was characterized, without consideration either of the relationship, or even the identity of the octave. His notation also, the neumata, or *nota Romana*, although before the introduction of subsequently invented lines it was very imperfect, gave nevertheless an indication of the rising or falling of the voice to the mind of the beholder, and was always more reasonable than those multitudes of arbitrary signs which constituted the 1620 straight, tumbling, oblique, mangled, mutilated, or distorted signs of the ancient Grecian semeiography.

The system which St. Gregory left behind him was capable of being cultivated to the highest possible degree; and, under tolerably favourable circumstances, there might have been directly derived from it a perfect music, similar to our modern art. But meanwhile mankind was not destined to be so fortunate; the ignorance of succeeding years caused St. Gregory's good system to fall into oblivion, and even his chants, handed down only traditionally by ear and memory, were in danger of degenerating and being lost. To correct this evil, a few learned and zealous priests took the now orphan Church Music under their protection, and endeavoured to preserve it from total decay, by a foundation, poor perhaps, but scientific. However praiseworthy this endeavour might have been, it is matter of regret that, instead of taking the path easily discoverable and not yet deserted, which St. Gregory had marked out, they again brought forward that fatal Boethius with his Grecian systems; and tried to transfer, however good or bad it might be, the same inapplicable system to the Gregorian Church chants. Some of them endeavoured, moreover, though unsuccessfully, and fortunately without gaining any imitators, to invent quite new and even absurd notations, possessing nothing in common with the excellent Gregorian letters, and without any consideration for the neumata, so hallowed by the Church, and certainly capable of considerable improvement.*

Under the authority of Guido of Arezzo, whom I acquit, however, of all blame himself in this error, there was even introduced at a later period a would-be hexachord, instead of the recently renewed tetrachord of this destitute musical age; and, strangely enough, the ever ready commentators, out of pure respect for Guido, now sought also to show that he had a precedent for its introduction in their Boethius.†

* See Note III.—Hucbaldus, Hermannus Contractus.

† See Note IV.—Hexachord.

But this was not the worst; for the treatises of the Grecian authors, which had been buried for centuries, and considered as lost, were again brought to light, translated, and commented upon. At the period that now dawned of the revival of the arts and sciences in Europe, mankind was certainly much indebted to the Greeks, although believing themselves to be still more indebted to them than was really the fact; and it was a natural consequence of the undue and inordinate predilection and veneration for every thing connected with ancient Greece,—a natural consequence also of the superstitious belief of the effects which its music is said to have produced on the people, that all musical art and science was sought for alone from the same source; and it was perhaps not merely to satisfy their passion for study, but from the sincere wish to be serviceable to mankind, that hundreds of those most zealously attached to learning, and innumerable musicians among their admirers, laboured to revive what they imagined to be the ancient Grecian music, in the theatres even (if possible) as well as in the Christian temples. With the adverse elements, however, of the Christian music, upon which they meant to engraft the other, this aim could not be achieved, and all their labours had no other result than that of retarding for hundreds of years the progress of the new music which in the time of St. Gregory had been so happily introduced.

If the struggles of that age were thus exhausted in creating a kind of music, which was just as little the new as it was the supposed ancient Grecian, it never could have succeeded; for the music of Western Europe, as it may be called, was then struggling most powerfully into notice; and its course deviated totally from the music of all the ancients, as was rendered completely evident, when harmony, or the so-styled counterpoint (*i. e.* the singing of several parts in different intervals at the same time), was introduced into it; although from that time forward the impeding elements of the Grecian theories were felt the most.

That which we call harmony is entirely and alone peculiar to our own modern music (for the words *harmony* and *melody* had nearly the same signification with the Greeks*), and it has become so essential to us, that we, who have from childhood been accustomed to harmony, not only represent to ourselves any kind of music without it as being wretchedly poor, but the very want of it we can scarcely comprehend. And yet harmony, in our own sense of the word, was

* See Note v.—Harmony, Melody.

not known to the ancients, nor, down to the present day, has it been found among those Asiatic nations which have been civilized for thousands of years, though they had a music of their own which they passionately loved, and were in possession also of musical theories very ingenious of their kind.

There is no doubt but that the ancient Greeks knew the symphony or accordance of the tones, but they never could have reached harmony, as we interpret the word, because they threw aside the third and sixth as dissonances; and, in the false arithmetical proportions which their mathematicians had calculated, would never have been able to use them really as consonances. They had therefore at their disposal only the fourth, fifth, and octave, for every case of symphonic use; consequently, since fifths are not cumulative, and do not sound well in consecutive successions, in *motus rectus;* and since the fourth, though recognized by the theory as a consonance, could certainly not be acknowledged by a Grecian ear to be an agreeable euphony,—there remained at last the octave alone, the only one of their consonances, under the name of antiphony, which they could, and did exclusively, employ.

In like manner, no harmony could exist in

our own modern music, were we also obliged to exclude the third and sixth.

With the modern Greeks, among whom we might expect that such a thing as harmony (from the probability of their ancestors having practised it), might have been handed down by tradition in some way or other, however disfigured, there is not the least native trace: they sing and play throughout only in unison, and never accompany the voice otherwise than in unison or octave, even with the harp, or other similar instruments, which are played with both hands.

The use of harmony in our modern European music necessarily introduced into it an essentially different system of keys and scales, and, in the sequel, also a different table for the measure or value of the notes; and in paying a due regard to these new keys and scales, the melody must have gained not only a certain precision, but at the same time a multiplicity of significations, by the harmonious accompaniment, in which the simple song itself must ever have been deficient: instruments, too, the pride and ornament of our modern music, were finally indebted to this perfectly completed harmony, especially in the school of obligato counterpoint, not only for their perfection, but in part also for their origin.

Considered in this point of view, the history

of our modern music, in fact, really commences with that epoch, in which the first traces of experiments in the employment of symphonies (consonances, diaphonies, or polyphonies*) were discovered; on the other hand, the simple Church music of the preceding centuries may be deemed at most as merely its forerunner, and belongs at all events to a distinct period.

Unfortunately, however, the first attempts made to unite consonances were unsuccessful, inasmuch as, more regard being paid by experimenters to the lawgiving Grecian schoolmen than to their own good ears, the fourth, fifth, and octave alone could be understood as consonances, and the third and sixth, condemned by the Grecians as dissonances, were held to be useless. Hundreds of years again flew by, before the right path was discovered; when chords, not taken separately only, but, in connexion with those following, were found to produce an agreeable effect,—when the mixing of real dissonances was ventured upon with success,—when the means were found of soothing the disagreeable emotion created by a dissonance, by its agreeable resolution into the consonance; and, at last, even the more harsh dissonances

* *Diaphonies, polyphonies.*—Union of two or more parts, sounding in different intervals at the same time.—*Translator.*

were made agreeable to the most sensitive ear by preparations on their resolutions. These important improvements being considered, our harmonic music scarcely reaches farther back than the thirteenth century, and is consequently a wonderfully young art.

If, therefore, we now reflect that this absolutely new and formerly unthought-of art, sprang up without a model, of which the sister arts had abundant advantage, in animated nature, as well as in the works handed down from the ancients, such as classics, antiquities, buildings, and monuments,—that under continual and interrupted influences it must have been formed entirely out of its own resources,—we ought, instead of complaining of the apparently slow advancement in its first epochs, to be surprised rather at the rapid progress which it made, when it succeeded in emancipating itself from its Grecianizing masters, and, now conscious of its own strength, began to create works which excited the wonder of contemporaries and the horror of schoolmen, who found themselves soon forced to create new theorems in the productions of their supposed pupils, and endeavoured, as well as these would permit, to insert them in their doctrines, which they still pretended to be Grecian.

The different authors who have hitherto devoted their labours to the history of music, have generally divided it according to historical periods, or to the periods of the reign of native kings ; some also according to countries and provinces, and partly to the so-called schools. I am of opinion, that the art in its own changes ought to form historical periods for itself, which usually differ from those of universal history, and have, in fact, nothing in common with the particular periods of various states: that music, a general blessing to mankind, has no connexion with the political division of kingdoms; and that the division of it into schools of art, particularly at those periods when there can, generally speaking, be no mention made of their existence, would prove, in the history of music, the most useless and deceitful of all; because the boundaries of real or decayed schools, according to time and place, indeed their very existence as schools, would be difficult, if not impossible, to be proved; and because this division but too frequently compels the historian, through the want of complete and authentic information, to assume or supply *data* at the sacrifice of his own conscience, and therefore of truth, in order to force all his materials into one or other of the compartments above-mentioned.

But even the division into certain great periods

of the art does not appear to me a very happy one for its history, as it renders the review of contemporary events, or synchronisms, not only more difficult, but is apt to lead the less experienced or less critical reader easily wrong; when, for example, he finds indicated in one and the same principal section an Okenheim as head of the Netherland, and a Palestrina as head of the Roman school,—two masters who are fully a hundred years distant from each other;* and, if I mistake not, the early development of counterpoint in the Netherlands, and the influence of the Belgian masters in the cultivation of the art among other European nations, are alone to be imputed to this method of discussing musical history, which has so long, nay, even to this day, been overlooked.

* *Okenheim and Palestrina.*—Our author means that, in treating of the one as head of the Netherland, and the other as head of the Roman school, in the same section or chapter, the reader might suppose that these two masters and their schools existed at the same period. This supposition would be quite false, for Palestrina lived a hundred years later than Okenheim, and a hundred years, in the development of an art still young, is a very long time. The Romans appear as contrapunctists about a century later than the Belgians. Okenheim's pupils (second generation) were the first teachers of the Italians. Synchronism is quite as essential in history as matter of fact.—*Translator.*

The system, therefore, which appeared to me the best, was the division of the history of music into epochs, not only as being the best attested, but as the most simple, natural, and authentic. Each of these epochs should be named after one of the most celebrated men of the time,—of him, for instance, who possessed the greatest influence over the taste of his contemporaries in their cultivation of the art, and who, either by his discoveries, by the introduction of new species, or of a new style, or by the signal improvement on the former method of composing, from example or precept, may have demonstrably promoted the art to a higher grade of perfection. The longer or shorter duration of such epochs should scarcely be considered: one epoch may embrace a hundred years; another, after a few decimal terms, may give place to the succeeding; but each must be marked by some one event of importance.

To represent all this, with the immediate and contingent effects which still remain to prove its accuracy: to define the point at which the art flourished generally in each epoch, and simultaneously in different countries in comparison with preceding epochs; and in this manner, with a few but vigorous touches, clearly to show, in a circle of vignettes, as it were, the gradually progressive development of the art of sound to the present day, shall be my endeavour in this essay.

Musical theory, literature, and the history of artists, shall only be taken into consideration, in so cursory an essay as the present will and ought to be, so far as necessity requires them to be noticed in developing the advances of music as an art or science. Those readers who may wish for more information in the above departments of music, may easily obtain it in the manuals and compendiums, already existing, which are dedicated to that purpose, but which could only be given them in the present work at the sacrifice of the evident distinctness of the history of the art. Whatever may, nevertheless, be required concerning the biography of the masters of each epoch, shall have due attention, as also the more celebrated contemporaries of each department, as far at least as may accord with their merits.

My chief intention is,—to furnish to the numerous body of musicians and lovers of music, a work which, without leading them through the misty regions of the defunct music of the ancient nations, or at least that of the ancient Greeks (respecting which last they will find in a supplement all the information most necessary for their previous or subsequent reading), will give them, in one moderately-sized volume, a clear view of the history of their art, which in Burney's large and scarce work, or others in foreign languages, not easy of access, they either forbear to seek, or, owing to the superabundance of the materials, rarely obtain; whilst the same may be observed of Forkel's *History*, which, with the second volume still incomplete, does not reach beyond the year 1500, a circumstance much to be regretted: and this view it would also be difficult to gain from the elegant little works which have appeared, and been translated into various languages, under the high-sounding title of "*History* (Histoire Geschichte) *of Music*." The authors of these last works may be considered answerable for my determination to publish the present essay (originally intended for lectures) with the title of "History," how little soever it may correspond with the pretensions which I have been accustomed to apply to a work so denominated.

Since, however, the contents, as well as the plan of this work, are neither an extract from Burney's or Forkel's histories, nor from any other author that I know of, but the result of manifold studies,—of my own researches and labours at the fountain-head,—my own careful inspection of, and in every case my criticism upon, a vast number of works relating to musical literature (many of them now exceedingly rare),—it may therefore be, and I apprehend it will too often happen, that I do not agree in the views and assertions of the very valuable authors in question, and that I dissent from many generally received opinions and traditions. I can, notwithstanding, most concientiously declare, that I have always kept myself aloof from the vain disease of innovation, as well as from the spirit of contradiction; and that I can answer confidently at least for the accuracy of my statements, though I never, of course, could have dreamed of pronouncing my verdict from such conclusions to be altogether unerring.

CHAPTER I.

EPOCH OF HUCBALD.

TENTH CENTURY.—A.D. 901 TO 1000.

VARIOUS have been the opinions and surmises as to the commencement of Harmony in the early part of the Middle Ages; but from the most authentic source of the history of the art in musical literature, we find, that the first attempt to unite several supposed voices, singing a continuous succession of sounds in different intervals at the same time *(sit venia verbo)*, is to be met with in a treatise bequeathed to posterity by Hucbald.

Hucbald was a very learned monk of St. Amand, in Flanders, and appears also in musical history under the name of Monachus Elnonensis, and who, after a life passed in the active composition of musical theories (according to the views of his time), died at an advanced age in 930.

According to the Grecian system, which he made the ground-work of all his profound treatises, the fourth, fifth, and eighth intervals alone are consonances. He must not only have easily convinced himself of this fact with regard to the two latter (though he seems to have taken the supposition as to the former on credit), but have found, moreover, that being sounded together with a given note they would prove to the ear an agreeable symphony or accordance; and it might thus also have occurred to him to have allowed two or more parts to be sung in progressive consonances, by way of giving variety and strength to the agreeable sensation produced by such a euphony.

He persuaded himself, perhaps, that the Greeks, with their consonances, must have formed symphonies similar to those described; and he probably imagined that by such means he could again revive their music, although he does not express himself in its praise. He called such a union of voices by the old name of *diaphonia* (different voices: *dis-cantus*), or *symphonia* (sounding together, union of voices), or by the entirely new title of *organum*, under which last designation this species of harmony (if it may so be termed) most commonly appears in musical literature.

There are two kinds of the *organum* which Hucbald explains, and for which he gives rules in his treatise: the first consists in the unison of one or more parts, which move with the given principal part *(Cantus firmus)* in fifths, or fifths and octaves; in fourths, or fourths and octaves: these parts Hucbald also doubled in the octave above or below, by which means the organum became a piece of four or five parts, all of which still progressed in similar motion with each other, that is, in a succession of consecutive fourths, fifths, and eighths, such as in our own days is expressly forbidden. "*Videbis nasci*," says the worthy man, "*suavem ex hâc sonorum commixtione concentum.*"

In the second kind of organum, Hucbald introduces between the consonances other intervals which are not consonant, above the principal part; as, the second, and (what by him was considered equally dissonant) the third; sometimes free, sometimes in progression, often in similar and oblique, but rarely in contrary motion; but all employed in such a manner as to be repugnant even to the uncultivated ear, as well as at variance with the rules of musical grammar. This treatment, however, he employs only with two parts, and he remarks that it is not every theme to which it is applicable.

Some examples are here produced from Hucbald's treatise, entitled *Musica Enchiriadis* (see Prince Abbot Gerbert's collection, *Scriptores Eccles. de Mus.* tom. i.), the same being selected from such chapters as treat of "*Diaphonia con-*

sonantia et inconsonantia," and, in fact, a few specimens with rows of syllables between the lines, copied according to his method; but our own A B C is employed instead of the marginal note-characters of his invention. *T* means with him the progression of a whole tone, *tonus;* *S* signifies *semitonium.*

No. 1 is an organum in four parts of the kind first mentioned above, with the employment of the fourth (a similar one with the fifth added to it may easily be conceived). From No. 2 to No. 6 inclusive, are examples of the second kind described, to us in every respect the more remarkable, inasmuch as from these, but never from those of the first kind, a real harmony might in time have developed itself, if the student had not been completely trammelled by prejudice, or if the ear had been consulted instead of the old treatises.

No. I.

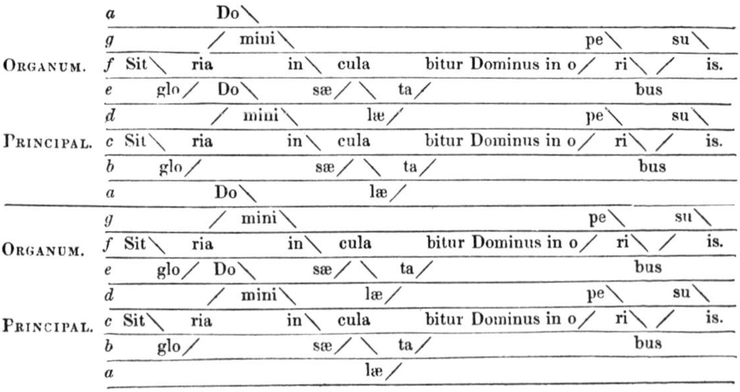

In our notation the above would appear thus:

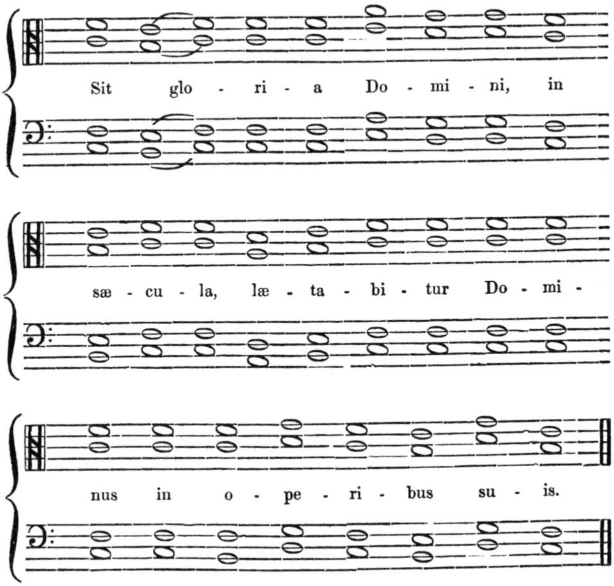

No. II.

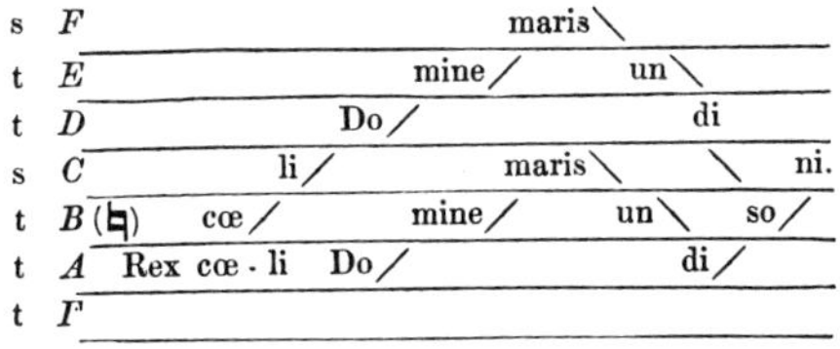

Which set into notes would be as follows:

No. 2.

No. 3.

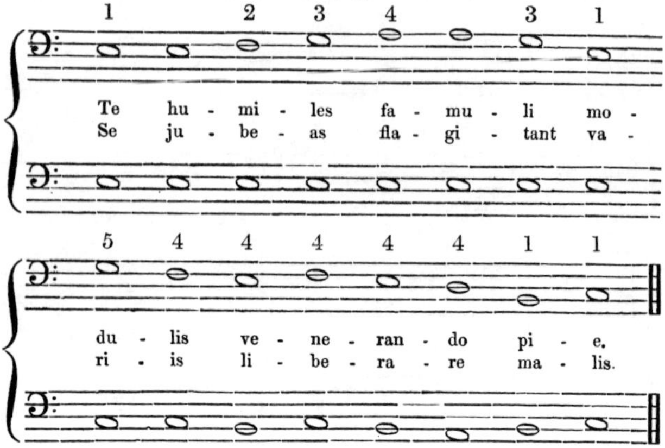
1 2 3 4 3 1
Te hu - mi - les fa - mu - li mo -
Se ju - be - as fla - gi - tant va -
5 4 4 4 4 4 1 1
du - lis ve - ne - ran - do pi - e.
ri - is li - be - ra - re ma - lis.

No. 4.

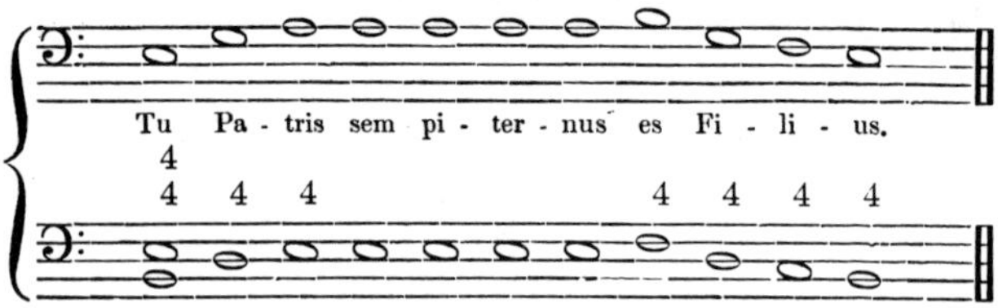
Tu Pa - tris sem pi - ter - nus es Fi - li - us.
4
4 4 4 4 4 4 4

No. 5.

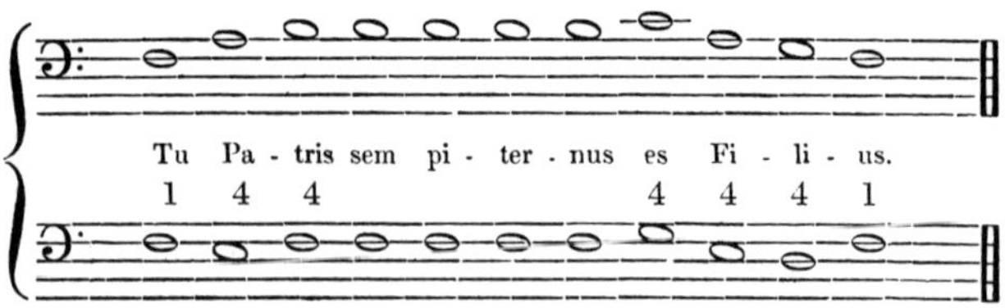
Tu Pa - tris sem pi - ter - nus es Fi - li - us.
1 4 4 4 4 4 1

No. 6.

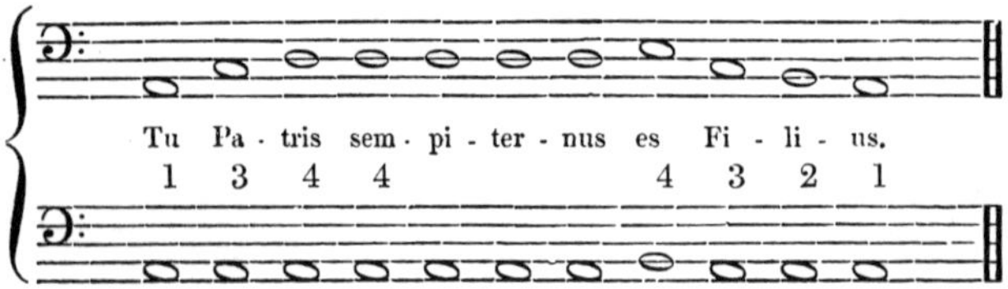
Tu Pa - tris sem - pi - ter - nus es Fi - li - us.
1 3 4 4 4 3 2 1

From these examples it is clear that even in the organum of the second kind, the favourite *diatesseron* (the fourth,—which by itself no human ear of the present day would take for a consonance) plays the prominent part, and that the second and third drop in *only* accidentally, in a manner as meaningless as it is irregular.

It has been inferred from the words "*Nos assuetè organum vocamus*," which appear in Hucbald's treatise, that the employment of voices singing in different parts, which he describes, must have been previously known and in use: but, as we all are aware that authors, particularly of the didactic class, choose always to speak of themselves, like crowned heads, in the plural number; and as none of the older writers, from whom musical treatises have reached us, make the slightest mention of the organum, we should have been justified in rejecting such an inference of its pre-existence, as utterly untenable, were not the same opinion still maintained by writers of eminence, who adduce proofs, whether real or supposed, in support of their assertion.

Not only does that learned and assiduous inquirer, the abbot Gerbert, assure us, in his great historical work, *De Cantu et Musicâ Sacrâ*, that even Pope Vitalian (elected A.D. 655, died

669) had introduced the singing in different parts into the pontifical chapel, but a very clever writer of later date records the same circumstance. It appears, according to the evidence of numerous writers, that, from the time of the pope above-mentioned, singing-boys were maintained in the apostolic chapels, and that, under the name of *pueri symphoniaci*, they lived and were brought up in what was called the *Parvisio (Ord. Rom.* by Mabillon, *Mus. Ital.)*; whilst we have the testimony of Baleus (a compiler of the sixteenth century), that Pope Vitalian had introduced harmony, which from that period was known by the name of *organum*, and the art as *ars organandi*.

Eckehardus of St. Gallen (an annalist of the twelfth century) corroborates this fact *(in vita S. Notkeri Balbuli)*, showing that in the time of Notker (who died in 913), there were certain singers in the pontifical chapel called Vitaliani, who gave out the chant, which the pope, after whom they were named, had introduced, even when the Pontiff himself for the time being was in the full exercise of his functions. It might also be assumed, with some colour of reason, that under the title of *Cantus Romanus* the organum is to be understood as the same which the singers sent by Pope Adrian the First to Charlemagne were intended to teach.

Whatever credit may seem to be deserved by the authors above-mentioned, it still appears to me that the evidence which they have adduced does not warrant the conclusions at which they have arrived. Above all, I should not, from the words *pueri symphoniaci*, be led unhesitatingly to conclude, that they referred to any particular "harmony" or "organum". Such boys might appropriately be called *symphoniaci*, because they merely accompanied with their high voices the melody of the men in the consonance of the octave, and the term *puer symphoniacus* literally signifies nothing more than *puer concinens*, or "accompanying boy," so that it must not be referred to any kind of consonance whatever; for even in simple song a plain melody was often called only *symphonia*, and in this sense the word is used by Guido in contradistinction to *diaphony*. But with respect to the really valuable testimony of Eckehard, it seems by no means proved, in the passage above-cited, that he had in his mind the supposed harmonical song, entitled the organum.

The Vitalian melody, to which Eckehard obviously refers, although he does not describe it, was nothing more, according to all circumstances, than a choral song, or church melody, embellished during performance by the singers. Such probably must have been the style of chant which gave such particular pleasure to Charlemagne, during his visit to Rome (A.D. 776), and which his Frankish singers were commanded to learn, although their voices, as the annalists relate, were harsh and far from pliant, and incapable of being accommodated to the quilisms and semivowels, with other figures and refinements, common to the performance of the Roman singers.

The Antiphonary of St. Gallen, the same which was brought by one of the Roman singers sent by Pope Adrian I to the emperor, and which is still preserved in the library of the monastery of St. Gallen, of which also I have given a descriptive account in the *Leipsic Universal Musical Journal* for 1828 (Nos. 25, 26, 27), shows us beyond doubt, at the end of the verses, many of these same neumata (melisms which were merely vocalised), of considerable length; and above the note characters of the text we find, in minute letters, the manner of performing them carefully noticed, after the methods of the teachers and of the proprietors of the book. The signification of these minute letters (which are by no means tone-characters), S. Notker *(Balbulus)* subsequently explained in his *Epistola ad Lambertum*, receiving in consequence of this explanation a place amongst the musical writers of the Middle Ages. But that the singers of Pope Adrian taught either the organum, or any other kind of song consisting of more parts, the historians, who speak both of their mission and its effects, nowhere inform us.

The prcof cited from Baleus, respecting the early introduction of the organum in the pontifical chapel, loses all its importance, inasmuch as the various interpreters of one and the same passage, or of passages similar in their tenor, differ one with another, and alter according to preconceived opinions what is therein attributed to Vitalian, viz., *organum*, the organ; *organa*, instruments; and *organum*, a song of more parts. Forkel has cleared up these errors with much excellent criticism, although in a different allusion to the subject, being a history of the organ, which may be found at the 356th and following pages of the second part of his *History of Music*.

Some authors feel disposed even to ascribe the introduction of the organ to Pope Vitalian. "Vitalianus," such is the passage quoted by them from Platina in his *Biography of the Roman Pontiffs*, "Cantum ordinavit, adhibitis ad consonantiam, ut quidam volunt, organis." Now, the purport of the passage in Baleus is literally the same, excepting the omission of "ut quidam volunt," a phrase which probably displeased him; he says: "Organa per consonantias humanis vocibus exhibuit." Under such circumstances, therefore, it remains very doubtful as to what was the real meaning ascribed by Baleus himself to the word *organa* (which he might have reverentially copied from some one of the old writers) and whether he did not, perhaps, also intend to signify the organ.

But if there be, or ever had been, any truth in the accounts of the old annalists, considered as the proper source, in reference to Pope Vitalian and his introduction of the *organa*, nothing else than instruments *(organa)* could have been originally meant, according to the old and correct classic signification of the word,—instruments, which, as an accompaniment to the chant, in the most natural and most conceivable consonance (that is, in the unison or the octave), were in constant use from the ancients downwards,—still the organ (called *organum per excellentiam)* could in this instance by no means have been meant, because the first instrument of this kind was sent into the western countries about a hundred years after Pope Vitalian (A. D. 756), as a present from the Greek emperor Constantine Copronymus to King Pepin; and just as little could the organum have been meant (Hucbald's symphony or diaphony), because this derived its technical name, as well as its origin, from the organ, of which it is said to be an imitation.

Independently, however, of these weighty arguments against such a supposition, it appears incredible, that the popes should at any time have taken pleasure in listening to an organum, or harmony, generally speaking, such as was known in the Middle Ages, and even so late as the fourteenth century, or that they should ever have been able to tolerate such a combination. The popes have always been averse from principle to every kind of innovation, as may be proved from one period to another, even to the present day; and so correct have been their views in this particular, that the inventions or improvements which have occurred in music during the progress of centuries, were not permitted by them to be introduced into the churches, until they had arrived at such a degree of perfection and utility, as to be able in reality to contribute to the edification of Christian minds, and to the glory of God in his holy services. Even Hucbald must have renounced the organum, if he could ever have listened to it with his own ears; but the superior of his monastery would most probably have put an immediate stop to its use after trial of the first couplet, since, among the penances and mortifications in the rules of the order, one of a nature so painful to the senses could never have been inflicted.

The different authors who have written on the organum (Forkel among others) are of opinion, that it was originally an imitation of the mixture stop of the organ. The "mixture" (as I ought here to explain for those less conversant with the character of the organ) is an organ stop (register), in the employment of which each key of the finger-board, on being pressed down, had its fifth, and eighth (at the present day also its major third, constituting the major common chord), sounding with it at the same time; a stop which, where it still exists and may be employed, is never used except in conjunction with the other powerful stops, and then the combination produces an extraordinary buzzing, similar to the effect of a thousand bad voices. It is assumed by Sethus Calvisius and Michael Prætorius, authors who flourished at the close of the sixteenth and the beginning of the seventeenth centuries, and to whom Forkel appeals in his *History of Music* (part ii. p. 368), that even in the oldest organs the mixture as associated with $\substack{12\\8\\5}$ was introduced, not as a stop or register, for there was nothing of the kind at that period, but as being invariably united to each tone, and had thus descended to us. Proofs of this, or probable reasons for it, have no more been produced by them than by Forkel. The accuracy of the supposition may well be disputed, because no inducement appears for the oldest organ-builders in the west of Europe to have pressed into their instruments—which, although occasionally very large, were always extremely simple—a note (the fifth), the bad effect of which, in the striking of several consecutive keys, would not only have surprised them, but must have decided them on laying aside so disagreeable and superfluous an excrescence.

The following supposition appears more likely. At a later period, when the application of Mutations (Register) was understood, and when an attempt was made to imitate the organum of the old speculative theorists (arising from an inordinate respect for antiquity, and owing to the authority of Guido having so long been held all-sufficient), it may be imagined that the mixture, in connexion with a powerful mainwork or other strong stops considered useful, or even on account of the monstrous effect thereby accidentally acquired, might have been retained as a welcome discovery, which in course of time was improved (!) by the addition of the major third, in order to make the monstrosity still more apparent. The absolute torture of an isolated mixture-stop, no human being could for a moment have endured without falling into convulsions.

But in what manner, then, the organum may nevertheless have been, and really was, an imitation of the organ, and received its name from that instrument, may thus be explained. The oldest organs, of exceedingly coarse manufacture,—the broad six-inch keys of which, separated from each other by a large space, must have been pressed down with the fists or elbows,—were in truth as little adapted to harmonic performances as to harmonic experiments; these instruments may, notwithstanding, have afforded the first opportunity of representing to our senses in a permanently continuous manner the physical effects of the then admissible consonances, at least in single unisons, by the pressing down and holding out at the same time a second key: moreover, the organ-"thumper" might, whether intentionally or through awkwardness, have hit upon the idea of causing one key to remain sounding, whilst the singers, to whom he had given the note, proceeded with their melody above it, as in the bagpipes; or it might also have happened that, at one time or another, he would accidentally, perhaps, press down the fifth to the fundamental note, and thus have caused an agreeable surprise by its pleasing effect. With this, indeed, there might not as yet have been a proper harmony discovered; but effects would have been perceived calculated to produce in speculative musicians matter for reflection, and for hazarding other systems; the union of different human voices, which now occurred to their thoughts, was an imitation, not altogether happy perhaps, of that which in various instances they had discovered with the organ, and thus their diaphony, or polyphony, received the somewhat appropriate name of organum.

But even if Hucbald, according to these premises, may be said to have received the first idea of his organum from the organ, it may nevertheless be admitted that others also, before or about his time, imbibed the same notion, and that the organum, if not in practice, yet in theory, may have been known at an earlier period among scholastic musicians. It scarcely deserves to be mentioned here,—the question being one concerning the first experiments of harmony,—that some historians (Printz, and afterwards Marpurg, for instance) have ascribed the invention of singing in several parts to St. Dunstan, archbishop of Canterbury (born A. D. 900, died 988); a statement which, as it appears, was originally founded on the simple fact only of this pious dignitary having, according to the legend, zealously promoted Church music; being conversant with the art of building organs and casting bells; and being represented in pictures as playing with both hands on the harp. This opinion, based upon grounds far too weak, has long been abandoned; and the treatise of Hucbald, now that we have become acquainted with it, must of itself establish the priority of his claim to that of St. Dunstan.

I may have discussed, perhaps, too diffusely for the limited plan of my intended work, the "opinions and reports" on the first experiments of harmony in the early part of the Middle Ages. It is the duty, however, of the historian, to verify as far as possible each discovery, important—or regarded as such—either in itself or in its subsequent development, and in the same degree to authenticate its inventor.

If I have been obliged at last, through want of positive information, and consequently by forming a comparison of circumstances, to have recourse also to hypotheses, by which Hucbald's merit, as the inventor, will in some measure be rendered doubtful, I have at the same time been unable to refrain from placing the name of this venerable author at the head of the first epoch; because those who have assigned a much earlier date to the *Ars organandi* have not appeared to me as credible witnesses, and because Hucbald, at any rate, is the author to whom the first description and the first explanatory examples of the diaphony and the organum, so called, must be referred.

CHAPTER II.

EPOCH OF GUIDO.

ELEVENTH CENTURY.—A.D. 1001 TO 1100.

VERY limited indeed must have been the services which a few learned monks rendered to their cloisters, by devoting themselves in various places, either before or about the time of Hucbald, to researches in music, and Church keys or scales, partly by writing treatises, and partly, perhaps, by giving oral instructions; whilst their writings, which could at that period be promulgated solely by the tedious process of transcription, remained in the libraries of their monasteries, or only a copy or two at the most, lay buried, as it were, in a few scattered cells. Such copies, moreover, were rendered far too complicated by scholastic subtlety and Grecian theories, at all times inapplicable to Church music, and could therefore be comprehensible and pleasing to a few select brethren alone. The same may also be presumed of the oral instruction which they bestowed, or were able to bestow, in their cloisters, to a chosen number of their companions. Towards the advancement of Church singing, the only music then deserving of the name, there was nothing in this way to be gained; and as singing in the different churches and choirs not only existed, but would continue to be practised, it may easily be conceived that the chants introduced by Pope Gregory, together with some of his successors in the pontifical chair, and partly also by the founders of religious orders, would have become obsolete, from the total want of a comprehensible theory, as well as from the merely mechanical and meagre instruction at that time given in the schools of the clergy.

The greatest obstacle to the preservation of singing, in the purity of its original precepts, was to be found in the want of a clear and defined notation. The neumata exclusively introduced into the books of the ritual, as explained in another place (see Appendix, No. 2), were, previously to the introduction of the lines, so uncertain, that, as John Cotton wittily describes them (Gerbert, *Scrip. de Mus.* vol. ii. p. 258), the same marks which Master Trudo sung as thirds, were sung as fourths by Master Albinus; and Master Salomò in another place even asserts the fifths to be the notes meant, so that at last there were as many methods of singing as teachers of the art. To remedy this evil, there were new and different tone-characters or methods of notation attempted; although, in truth, only by the schoolmen, of whose inventions the Church took little notice. Hucbald, in like manner, as we have seen above, made use of a series of lines, with the syllables ascending and descending between them; and it was certainly to his invention that we are indebted for variously formed and misformed, curved, straight, or inclined letters of the alphabet (particularly a Latin f) for the whole scale,—a notation, naturally far from being calculated to create a sensation, which appears only to have reached the knowledge of some scholastics, and to have been employed but by a very few of them.

Such was the state of Church music, when, about a century after Hucbald's death (A. D. 1020, or somewhat later), we hear of Guido of Arezzo, a Benedictine monk in the monastery at Pomposa, in the neighbourhood of Ravenna and Ferrara. This venerable man saw more clearly than his predecessors that Church singers were not to be formed after any speculative theory; but that it required for the purpose a most simple and elementary theory, and a reasonably practical method. He was at all events so fortunate as to invent such a method, and his results created some sensation in the neighbouring circles; but at the same time they also occasioned (as it appears from his own writings) the envy of his brethren, who prejudiced the Superior against him, so that he was compelled to fly from his convent, and to wander up and down as a stranger, until Theobald, Bishop of Arezzo, received him under his protection, and enabled him to prosecute his labours in Church music with tolerable success. The reputation of his performances reached the ears of Pope John the Nineteenth (by some called the Twentieth), who governed the holy see from the year 1024 to 1033. This Pontiff invited Guido to Rome, and dismissed him with the most honourable proofs of his satisfaction, after having in one lesson, under his direction, advanced himself so far as to understand, and to sing from the book, a chant previously unknown to him, from the antiphony brought by Guido, and after the manner of notation which he had invented. The singers of those days could scarcely have accomplished the same task in the course of a lifetime.

Guido now returned to his cloister, and was received with joy by the Superior, who had long since regretted his former behaviour towards him. Of the subsequent events of Guido's life nothing certain is known; but the account of the

German annalists, that he went to Bremen, by the invitation of the Archbishop Hermann, and there gave instruction in Church music, is contradicted by his latest biographer, Luigi Angeloni (Paris, 1811), after a discussion on the point which is conducted with much critical acumen.

From the treatises which Guido has left behind him we learn, that, in his instructions, and up to the period when his scholars had properly acquired intonation, he made use of the monochord, known to the ancient Greeks, which had been taught by Boethius, and afterwards by Hucbald, and to which, as Guido says, one tone below, namely Γ (gamma), was added by the moderns.* The scale, which only reached to the single-lined $\bar{a}$, Guido extended to the double-lined $\bar{\bar{d}}$, but it is nowhere clear in what his method of instruction properly consisted. There is some reason to suppose that he taught with successful results, before he stumbled upon the much-prized *ut re mi fa sol la*,† a short men-

* "Γ *a modernis adjunctum*," says Guido,—a mistake on his part however, for the addition is really mentioned by several Grecian authors.—*Translator.*

† Menage, in his *Origine de la Langue françoise*, gives the following derivation of the word *gammut*, and the origin of the *ut re mi fa sol la*. "Guido Aretinus, a Benedictine monk, who had been employed to correct the ecclesiastical chants about the year 1024, composed a scale, conformable to

tion of which he makes in a single passage in one of his later treatises, but without any further explanation, and which he used rather as a means of help for pupils of slow comprehension, and as a kind of example, than for anything else, just as if other syllables might not have

the Greek system, adding to it a few sounds above and below; and discovering afterwards that the first syllable of each hemistich in the hymn to St. John the Baptist, written by Paul the Deacon, who lived about the year 774, formed a regular series of sounds ascending, he placed at the side of each of these syllables one of the first seven letters of the alphabet, A B C D E F G; and because he accompanied the note which he added below the ancient system with the letter *gamma*, the whole scale was called gammut, a name by which it is distinguished to this day." The lowest note of the Greek system was A, called by them *proslambanomenos*, supposed to be the lowest string on the lyre, but which, though the lowest note of all their scales, was never included in the tetrachords. For further information the reader is referred to Burney, vol. ii, p. 85; Gerbert, *Scriptores Eccles. de Mus.* tom. i, p. 45, and the Appendix to the present work. The hymn alluded to is the following:—

Ut queant laxis,
*Re*sonare fibris,
*Mi*ra gestorum,
*Fa*muli tuorum,
*Sol*ve polluti,
*La*bii reatum,
Sancte Johannes!—*Translator.*

been equally well introduced for the same purpose.

Guido himself clings to the system of the octave, even where he speaks only of these six syllables, and we can scarcely suppose that it was his intention to content himself generally with six alone. It is far more probable that the hexachord, explained by the six syllables of his invention (of which there is as little to be found in Guido as there is of the so long-prized harmonic or Guidonian hand), was propagated and extended under Guido's name by his pupils, successors, and commentators, in the first instance; and that subsequently the so-called solmisation, with the chicanery of mutation introduced into it, was originally established in and through the practice which is to be found in the treatises of later authors.*

* Guido taught his pupils to find and name the tones upon the bones of the hand. It was regarded as a wonderful discovery that the Creator should have given to man exactly the same number of members in the hand as there were tones in the scale, according to the system of the great master, viz., nineteen—

from gamma 

to 

The twentieth tone $\bar{\bar{e}}$ was only added at a later period by

Guido's greatest and most important merit consisted in the improvement and appropriate arrangement of notation, which was doubtless the best and most proper method of facilitating the art of singing from the book, and also of making it generally practicable or possible. It has been supposed that Guido was the inventor of the notes; but this opinion, which has prevailed up to the present day, is without foundation; the text of his treatise decidedly proves, that he knew nothing of the system of writing music by means of notes or dots upon or between the lines, but was only acquainted with the neumata and the Gregorian letters, nothing beyond these being mentioned by him in his work. To the latter he was particularly partial, and he declared them to be the best tone-characters; nevertheless he by no means repudiates the neumata, if carefully written and properly applied: to which end he adds two other lines to the two coloured key-lines formerly invented, and then teaches the use, not only of the lines themselves, but of the spaces between them, so that each

Guido's pupils, in order to complete a seventh hexachord, and not being able to find a place for it on the hand, they fixed it over the top of the second finger, whose highest member is called $\bar{\bar{d}}$. See Appendix; *Manus Guidonis*, with a system of the hexachords.—*Translator.*

neuma (sign or mark) receives its due place, which cannot be changed or mistaken, and all ambiguity is removed: thus was there at once prepared the foundation for the subsequent introduction of notes (*i. e.* points or dots) on lines and spaces; the simplest, and consequently the most perfect, system of notation.

The Guidonic method, or that brought to perfection by Guido's pupils under his name, of teaching to sing by means of solmisation (namely, by the use of the six syllables, *ut re mi fa sol la*) and of imparting a knowledge of church-keys by means of the hexachord and the so-called Guidonian hand, was propagated after his death, even during the same century, throughout nearly all the nations and countries of Europe; and it certainly contributed in a special manner to awaken universally the zeal for church music, and for the study of musical theory.

From thenceforth the name of Guido was known wherever civilization extended, and it has enjoyed uninterrupted celebrity to this day. Most authors, those in particular who wrote in the seventeenth century, and especially those of Italy, whilst they appear to be totally ignorant of the works of all his predecessors and contemporaries, have regarded Guido as the restorer of music, whilst many of them even look upon him as the inventor ; and they imagine that to him alone we are indebted for all we know or can perform in reference to the art at the present moment. The following inventions also are expressly ascribed to him: namely, the *gamma*, the *seven letters*, *a b* (or ♮) *c d e f g*, as the name of the notes, the *monochord*, the *explanation of the tropes* or church-keys, the *ut re mi fa sol la*, and consequently the *solmisation*, the *hexachord*, the *harmonic hand*, *notation*, the *clavier*,* and finally the *diaphony* or *organum*, or (as it is erroneously called) the counterpoint.

Mention has already been made of many of the most important of the above inventions, as well as of the ideas which may be entertained of them ; and there now remains chiefly to be examined, what Guido actually accomplished in regard to invention, improvement, or extension both of the knowledge and use of harmony (as it is so termed by us) or counterpoint ; and whether he possesses any advantages over his predecessor Hucbald of the previous century. For this purpose let us refer to such treatises of Guido as are sufficiently known, in Gerbert's

* Clavier, clavicordium, or clavicembalum,— singularly enough called harpsichord by the English,—not to be mistaken for piano-forte, which is an invention of the eighteenth century.—*Translator*.

Script. Eccles. de Mus: and in these we again find precisely the original organum of Hucbald. That with the fifth appears too harsh even to Guido; he wishes to substitute for it his own diaphony, which he thinks more agreeable *(nostra autem mollior)*, and which is again nothing else than that of the fourth; whence it may be presumed, that he did not acquire his knowledge of the organum from Hucbald, with whose treatises he could not have been acquainted, as there is no mention whatever in his own of the Hucbaldic tone-characters. Besides, Guido makes his organum by the doubling of a higher or lower octave, in three or four parts *(Triphonia, Tetraphonia)*, like Hucbald; and the parts in the first species of the organum, moreover, keep with him similar motion, in successive progressions of fourths and fifths, as with Hucbald.

But Guido is equally ignorant of that other species of the organum in two parts, described previously by Hucbald, and to which I might give the name of *organum vagans* (wandering); nor can I find that he was more successful in this respect than his predecessor Hucbald.

I introduce here some examples, certainly the most interesting, of this second species of the organum, from Guido's Micrology, represented with our own notes: in Gerbert's edition (*Script.*

part ii, p. 22, *et seq.*) these are noted with letters in straight lines. There were at that time in the study of church music certain customary formulæ of keys, or *distinctiones*, so styled, which Guido made choice of as a theme: for instance—

No. 1.

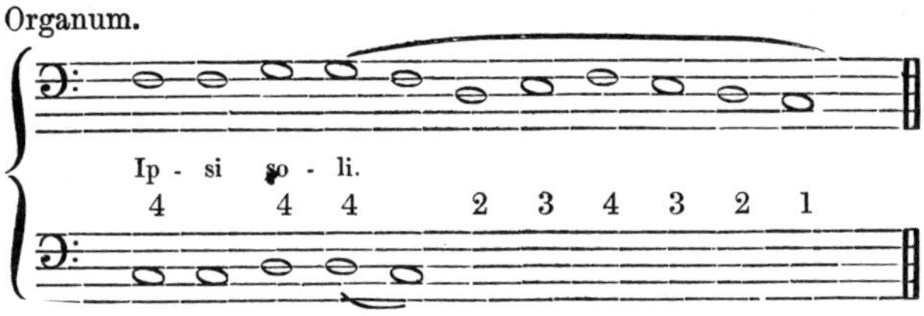

No. 2.

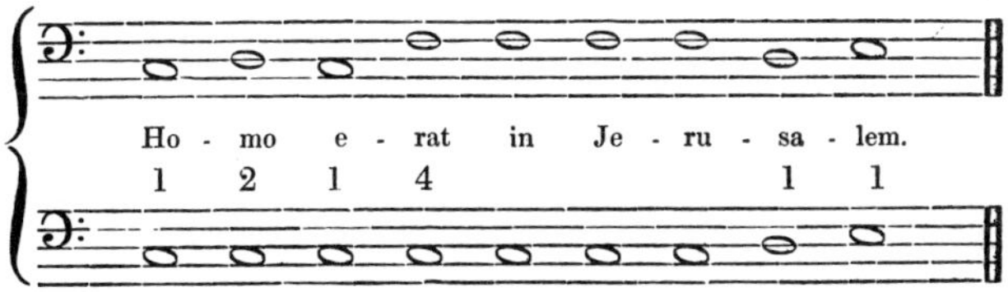

No. 3.

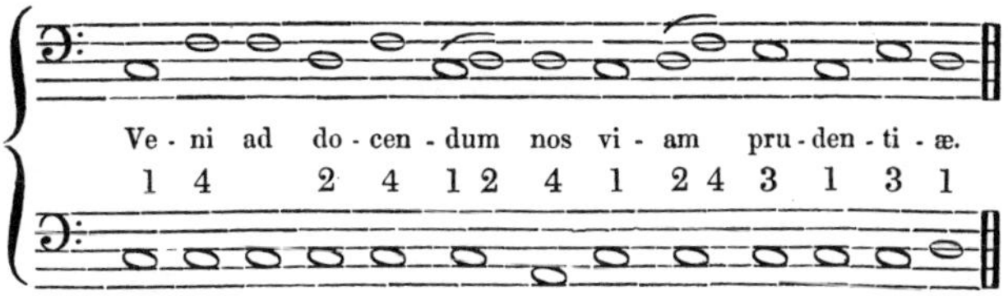

No. 4.

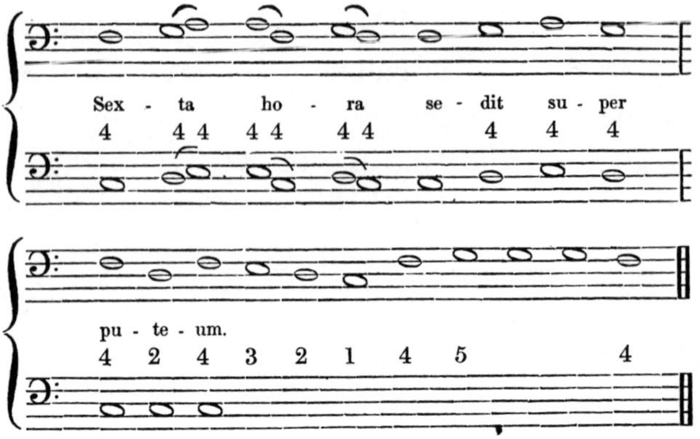
Sex - ta ho - ra se - dit su - per
4 4 4 4 4 4 4 4 4 4
pu - te - um.
4 2 4 3 2 1 4 5 4

No. 5.

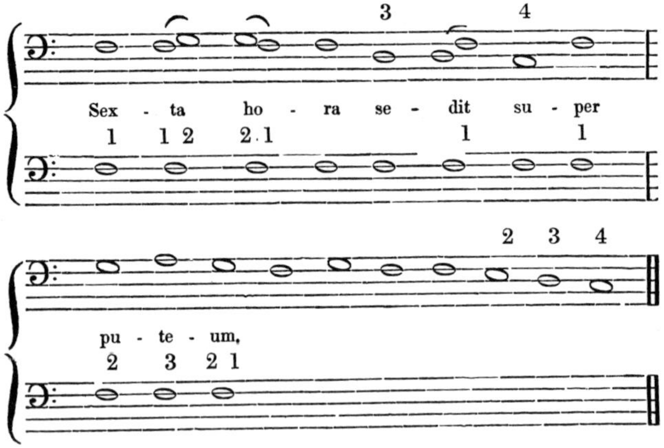
3 4
Sex - ta ho - ra se - dit su - per
1 1 2 2.1 1 1
2 3 4
pu - te - um,
2 3 2 1

No. 6.

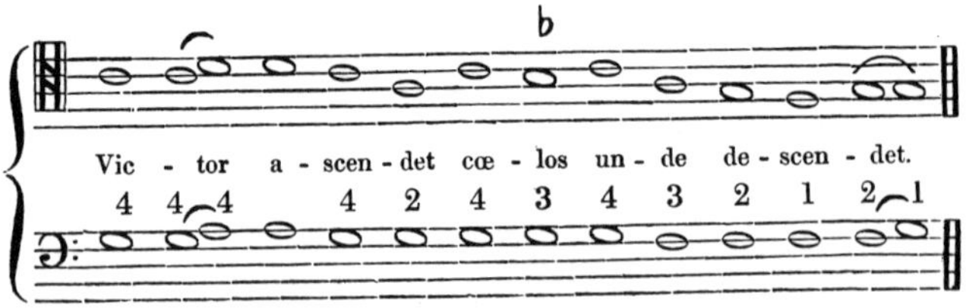
Vic - tor a - scen - det cœ - los un - de de - scen - det.
4 4 4 4 2 4 3 4 3 2 1 2 1

The above examples differed so far only from those of Hucbald, inasmuch as the organum in some places falls below the principal part, as in No. 5; or by the curious melisma (a kind of neuma) above the probably sustained last note of the principal part in Nos. 1, 4 and 5; the conclusion of No. 1, which resembles an organ point, being sufferable by accident alone.

There can be no proof more convincing, if such were required, that Guido did not invent the *clavier* (clavichord, spinet, or clavicymbal) than is afforded by these *distinctiones;* the clavier (or polyplectrum, as it is called by P. Kircher) would have demonstrated to the venerable Guido the monstrosity of such a diaphony, and would have been the means of teaching him different effects, which he never could otherwise have imagined.

The century of Guido, after his death, made not the least advance in this part of musical art (if I may so call it): his pupils, successors, and expounders, left this department quite unnoticed; they had sufficient occupation with the solmisation, the hexachord, and the "hand."

My readers will probably feel inclined to agree, after the proofs here adduced, that neither kind of the organum deserves the name of harmony, and still less that of counterpoint; and that we can with as little justice ascribe the invention of counterpoint to Guido, as to his predecessor Hucbald.

We can most willingly accord every justice to the merits of those worthy men of former days, who passed their lives in laudable endeavours to advance musical art and science; but their experiments to succeed in harmony, or (as they called it) symphony, were falsely conceived, inasmuch as they had not been founded on practice, or by taking the ear as arbitrator and judge, but on previously formed opinions; on the theory, for example, of a music that had long become obsolete, and had never been comprehensible; in which a symphony, in the sense of a successive progression of chords, had at no period existed, and could by no means have arisen.

CHAPTER III.

EPOCH III.
NOT DISTINGUISHED BY THE NAME OF ANY PARTICULAR INDIVIDUAL.

TWELFTH CENTURY.—A.D. 1101 TO 1200.

It may be pronounced a misfortune, when theory takes the precedence of practice, in reference to an art which is merely progressive.

Had the worthy Roman consul Boethius never written his five books *De Musicâ*, and had the musical treatises of the Greeks, at that time considered as lost, never been afterwards brought to light, our European ancestors might notwithstanding have discovered, in a reasonable space of time, the relationship of sounds, and the twelve semitones of the octave, just as the Chinese had thousands of years before discovered their twelve Lü: they might likewise, by some mechanically empirical means, have found out the symphony of sounds, and have left for their more learned descendants the trouble of measuring and reckoning, for the sake of proving the physical and mathematical solution of the problem of that agreeable combination, which their ears, uncultivated at the best, would have experienced in certain successions and unisons of tones. In the course of years, too, the system-makers, theorists, grammarians, and rhetoricians,—indeed even the æsthetic philosophers,—might have obtained ample employment in this respect; and such would have been the natural order of events.

Everything, however, had to be woven into the established Greco-Roman theories, which, with the fullest exertions of the commentators, could never have been made perfectly clear, when transplanted into the entirely new Christian Church music, and this last would not properly flourish in itself, even with all the care bestowed upon it. No wonder, then, that two hundred years had elapsed since the time of Hucbald, without any advancement in the state of the new music, or that the unknown ancient music, of some value also in its kind, should have again been substituted in its place.

Had any one at length hit upon the happy thought of investigating by means of experiments the effect of an harmonic unison of different sounds, using an instrument calculated for the purpose, the organ for example (although from its construction at that time not very applicable), or procuring the assistance of proper associates, he could not have failed to discover effects, totally different from those elucidated by Boethius and his commentators down to the time of Guido; and thenceforth the complexion of music and musical science must in a short time have undergone considerable change.

This appears actually to have been the case about the commencement of, or shortly previous to, the twelfth century. There is every reason, indeed, to ascribe to this very century the most important discoveries, although no mention is made of such in the few treatises that are extant of the writers belonging to this period; nor have either monuments or proofs of what was discovered, much less the names of the discoverers, been as yet made known.

Nevertheless, to this epoch must be ascribed the invention and cultivation of the notes; there must at that time already have appeared some happy experiments in harmony, and even some of a mixed counterpoint; whilst these must have been so far extended as to afford certain rules; and, in order to exhibit distinctly such counterpoint, notes of different value must have been invented and formed.

The most important feature, in respect to the simple note, namely, the writing of tones by means of points or dots (circles or squares) in a system of lines, and how Guido did not even know such a notation, much less that he was, as many believe, the inventor of it—has already been described in its proper place. Manuscripts, reputed to have been written even before the time of Guido, are said to have been found, in which round black points are placed on parallel lines, not in the intermediate spaces, to be used as notation, and in which the latter was also written at the beginning of each line as the key-note or clef, which the point on this line represented. The fact I do not presume to dispute; but I can only regard such a discovery of notation as the ingenious experiment of some clever head, whose invention remained meanwhile long unknown and consequently useless, buried most likely within the walls of a cloister. Guido was certainly unacquainted with such a method of notation; and he speaks solely of the neumata and alphabetical letters, as has already been stated. Moreover, the writers of the eleventh and even of the twelfth century are silent respecting the notes.

Whether the pretended invention of so much earlier a date was anywhere brought to light during the epoch of which we now treat,—whether it may have again sprung up afresh, and in what quarter,—whether the idea of the notes may perhaps have been taken from Guido's neumata, which, although not points, indeed, showed nevertheless the old neumata in a system of four lines,—the two red and yellow ones constituting the C and F clefs, and contributing in all likelihood to the employment of the spaces between them,—all this cannot at the present moment be proved; let it suffice, that there is the greatest amount of probability for placing the introduction of the notes (as circles or squares, points or dots) in the beginning of the twelfth century, together with their adoption by the students of musical science, and the first cultivation of them as tone-writing.*

But what relates in a particular degree to the experiments in harmony, is,—that by means of practical experiments the result must easily have proved the major and minor thirds, major and minor sixths, so much decried by the Greeks as dissonances, by no means to have produced

* If we consider only for a moment the difficulty of fixing on paper the height or depth of a sound, the invention of means by which this could be effected and properly represented without fear of mistake (although to us who have long been familiarized to its use, it may appear simple and even trifling), is nevertheless one of the most ingenious of human contrivances; and it must be admitted to have been of much greater difficulty than the invention of letters themselves, as the representatives of language.—*Translator.*

any disagreeable effect. It is now yet more perceptible that even the major and minor second, the major and minor seventh, and finally the much vilified tritonus (the augmented fourth), if indeed they may not be taken free and separate, are still not only useful in gradual progressions, but even soothe in a very agreeable and surprising manner the bad effect of a continued succession of thirds, fourths, fifths, and octaves. The invention of the syncopations and the dissonances arising from retardation, with their rules, was reserved for a later period.

When there must now have necessarily been two notes, and sometimes three and four against one, in the employment of passing dissonances, there would of equal necessity have arisen that kind of counterpoint which was afterwards called the mixed, in contradiction to the simple, *nota contra notam*, or what more frequently with later theorists has been described as *contrapunctus floridus*.

To develope this kind of counterpoint, or discantus, as it was called in the first periods, the necessity arose of having notes of different value, which probably also at that time received the form in which they appeared at a later date, namely:—

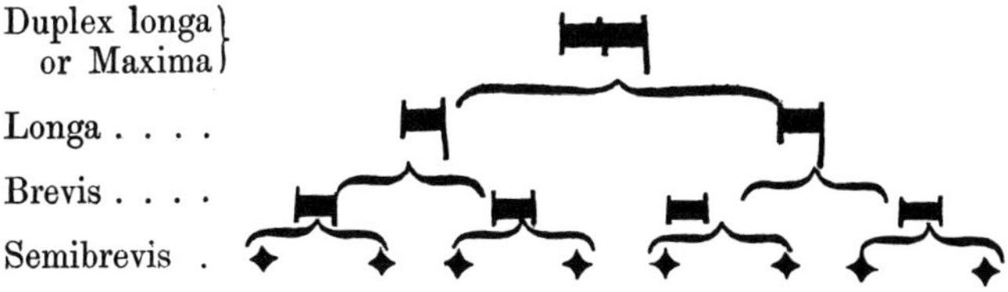

Thus there was a maxima, equal to two longæ, four breves, or eight semibreves. Latterly there was added a minima, sixteen of which were counted to a maxima; and still more recently, in the fourteenth century, the black heads here represented were left without being filled up, 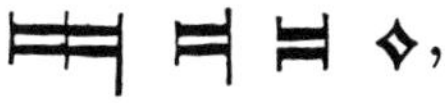, and there were thus obtained a minima , semiminima , fusa , and semifusa .

This is in its character still our present system of notes.

Real bars, or written bar divisions were not then in existence, but only *mensura;* the notes being measured, according to their forms, by constant counting. The brevis, which was called the *tempus*, was at the same time the medium measure.

The *tempus* was either *perfectum* or *imperfectum;* the first being a triple, the other an equal (common) measure; the one agrees with our (obsolete) $\frac{3}{1}$ time, the other with the $\frac{2}{1}$ or double allabreve time; in the *perfectum* the maxima was equal to three longæ, six breves, twelve semibreves, and so on; in the *imperfectum*, the maxima (as in the example above) was equal to two longæ, four breves, eight semibreves, etc.

This is not the place in which to dilate on such a subject in its detail. The theory of measure, or *mensura*, was subsequently one of a very difficult and confused nature, and it became more so through the intricacies occasioned by augmentation, diminution, alteration, sesquialteration, and such like dangerous tasks for practical singers. The introduction of two kinds of notes, white and coloured (blackened), the last of which was the value of one-third less in the perfectum, and one-fourth less in the imperfectum, than the former; then the ligatura (or union of several square notes in one figure) in which each separate note was of a different value, according as it was placed at the beginning, middle, or end, as it ascended or descended, when it had a tail or not, was upwards or downwards, with the tail on the right or left, was white or black, and so on,—undoubtedly occasioned difficulties of no ordinary character.

We ought to congratulate ourselves, that by means of three signs, the bar-stroke |, the slur ⌒, and the point • as a mark of augmentation, by far the greater portion of the mensural theory of those days can be dispensed with, and that the grammar of music, as we now possess it, has been so much simplified.

In examining, nevertheless, the mensural theory of former times, whoever undertakes the trouble of studying it must confess, that resting, as it does, on very accurate propositions, it certainly reflects much credit on its originators and improvers for their acuteness.

I find it requisite here to mention, that this theory was by no means brought to such perfection in the epoch of which I have been treating, as for the sake of connexion I have in this brief and imperfect sketch represented it; but that it became perfect only by degrees, and not wholly so until the fifteenth century.

In conclusion, I beg further to state, that the appellation of *musica mensurabilis*, or measurable singing and figured music (as this kind was called, from the figures employed in it), is to be dated from this epoch, in contradistinction to the *musica plana*, or *cantus planus* of the Roman liturgy, which last, however, long retained its neumata, and only in the fourteenth century adopted generally the note proper, erroneously called the Gregorian note, and occasionally also in barbarous Latin the *nota quadraquarta*.

CHAPTER IV.

EPOCH OF FRANCO.

THE THIRTEENTH CENTURY.—A.D. 1201 TO 1300.

THE thirteenth century may be said to have inherited from that which preceded it the first fruit of a new music, although it was in truth only in the bud, but nevertheless bore within itself the germ of future maturity;—*ex. gr.* notation, measure, and counterpoint, or, as it was then called, *discantus*. The task now belonged to it of nourishing these precious pledges, and bringing them to perfection. Nearly all the teachers in this epoch, who occupied themselves with the improvement and completion of the new theory, appear to have flourished about the same time, or at short intervals only between each other; and this theory, although its development might be owing to their acuteness, was nevertheless deduced beyond doubt from a previous practice, or at least from repeated experiments which had undergone careful consideration.

The oldest teacher of mensural music, who wrote also on the subject, and of whom mention is made in the history of musical literature, was Franco of Cologne. The literati of a subsequent period believed him to be a certain Franco who had already been celebrated in 1046 as a man of distinguished and various accomplishments, particularly in the department of mathematics, and who is described as a scholastic in the cathedral of Lüttich from 1066 to 1088. In the works, however, of the earlier annalists and authors by whom he is first noticed, there is no witness produced, nor are any persons to be found, able to prove that the said Franco, scholastic at Lüttich, either excelled in musical science, or left behind him a work in this branch of knowledge. But it is not to be believed that a man of such profound and well-arranged musical accomplishments, acquainted moreover with correct counterpoint and measure, like Franco of Cologne, could have lived so near the age of Guido, nay, almost indeed contemporary with it, when we consider how totally unknown at that period were the elements of music, and that the science was still in its merest infancy. Besides, the Franco to whom we refer was neither the inventor, nor, by his own account, the very first teacher in mensural music; for, on the contrary, he asserts that in this respect many others, both "ancients and moderns," have given excellent rules, falling nevertheless into mistakes as to various trifling particulars, *accidentibus ipsius scientiæ;* and it seemed necessary for him, therefore, to assist their opinions, in order that no loss might accrue to the "science" from the defect or errors of their teaching.

After such premises, and considering what stages the "science" must have gone through before such an acute observer as Franco of Cologne became capable of representing it in that connected and continuous system in which he certainly did, especially with regard to measure and its signs, the conviction forces itself upon us, despite of all authority, that this worthy man must have lived at considerable distance from the epoch of Guido, and that he could scarcely have flourished earlier than in the first decennial periods of the thirteenth century, at which epoch the earliest treatises on this subject in general appeared; for the authors of these treatises are not so superior in their knowledge to Franco, as would have been the case, if between them and him there had been a space of nearly two hundred years for affording an opportunity of the practice and cultivation of mensural theory and counterpoint.*

We shall here give a brief summary of the most essential portion of Franco's treatise, *Musica et Cantus Mensurabilis*, under which title it is printed in the collection of the Prince Abbot Gerbert (*Scriptores de Musicâ*, tom. iii), in order to afford as much as possible some idea of the condition of music during this epoch.

Mensural music, in opposition to the *musica plana*, is defined by Franco as a measured chant in long or short divisions. (*Musica mensurabilis est cantus longis brevibusque temporibus mensuratus.*)

Mensura is the duration, length, or shortness, of a measured chant (tone?), for in the *musica plana* indeed no such measure is required.

Tempus is a fixed measure, as well of each separate tone, as also of the contrary, namely, of its silence, which is commonly called a rest (Pause).†

* Respecting the age in which Franco lived, the author gives a copious and detailed account in an essay in the *Leipsig Musical Journal* for 1828, Nos. 48, 49, 50, under the title *Franco von Cöln und die ältesten Mensuralisten;* since which period he has not met with any refutation.

† By reference to the original work it would appear, that by mensura, Franco meant the length of notes, and by tempus the time of a melody.—*Translator.*

Franco divides the mensural music into the wholly measured, and the partly measured. In the first he includes the discantus, which in each of its parts is measured by the tempus, *i. e.* according to the determined proportion of time *(in omni parte sui tempore mensuratur)*; in the other he includes the organum, which is measured in each of its parts *(in quâlibet parte sui mensuratur)*; which is perhaps as much as to say, that in each of its parts it gives itself a measure, which with the singers would be only conventional, and not calculated so exactly as the other.

Discantus is a union of different melodies, which agree together in proportion one with another by longæ, breves, and semibreves, and which are distinguished by separate figures in the work. Discantus is of three kinds, viz., a simple continued melody *(simpliciter prolatus);* or it is broken in upon, or interrupted by rests *(truncatus)*, thence called ochetus; or it is bound *(copulatus qui copula nuncupatur)*.

The study of the figures (notes) and of the mensura occupies the greater part of Franco's treatise. The theory of this portion appears, in all that is essential, so thoroughly developed, that, (according to the system at least) there was nothing for his successors to discard, notwithstanding everything might be said to be wanting in it which the necessity of a subsequent and perfect contrapuntic art required. The study of the perfection and imperfection of the notes, and the changes which take place from their position in regard to their local value,—the study of the ligatura, of the notes, apparently a quantity of rules arbitrarily adapted, and throughout merely conventional, although in point of fact the fruit of toilsome and deep-thinking abstraction,—are there to be found the same as for a long time prevailed in the later schools; and less essential modifications were only introduced through time, partly from the employment of so many new facts which had appeared in the practice of counterpoint, and partly from the subsequent introduction in the fourteenth century of the white or unfilled-up notes; besides which, the black (filled-up) were still retained, receiving, however, a changed and diminished value of one-fourth in *tempore imperfecto* (common time), and of one-third in *tempore perfecto* (triple time).

It is not my intention to represent here the very complicated theory of the notation of that period, now long obsolete. Besides, there is nowhere to be found a work from which the amateur of ancient science can obtain any satisfactory view of it, notwithstanding the numerous compendiums to which the literature of the fifteenth and partly also that of the sixteenth century particularly refers. Of this the extracts quoted by Forkel, in his *History of Music*, from the writings of the old theorists, give but a very feeble idea: his work, however, is the best perhaps to which the anxious reader can apply himself on the subject.

Meanwhile insertion may here be given to the Latin hexameters which were introduced into the singing schools, to assist the memory in discerning the value of the notes in the ligatura. They ran thus:—

Prima carens caudâ longa est pendente secunda.
Prima carens caudâ brevis est scandente secunda.
Sit tibi priva brevis lævâ caudata deorsum.
Semibrevis prima est sursum caudata, sequensque.
Quælibet è medio brevis est, at proxima adhærens.
Sursum caudatæ, pro semibrevi reputatur.
Ultima dependens quadrangula sit tibi longa.
Ultima conscendens brevis est quæcunque ligata.

Besides these general rules, there were many circumstances by which the value of the notes was modified, as well with as without the ligatura.

Difficult as it may be to comprehend the mensura, it is still more difficult to obtain a clear perception of the condition of harmony in the age of Franco, in whose work, *Musica et Cantus Mensurabilis*, which has been handed down to us, an explanation is attempted, although one chapter alone is devoted to this subject. Clearness and perspicuity, moreover, are not exactly the qualities for which the musical authors of the Middle Ages have acquired credit; and the printed specimens are so exceedingly faulty, nay even so absolutely defective, in Abbot Gerbert's edition (*Scriptores de Musicâ*, part iii.), Burney likewise in this respect having no better codex before him, that it is impossible to explain the rules from these, or to supply the examples from the rules. However, it may be perceived from the text, that Franco already distinguishes *perfect*, *imperfect*, and *middle* consonances, or, as he calls them, concordances; perfect consonances being with him the unison and the octave; imperfect, the major and minor third; middle ones the fifth and fourth. He distinguishes also the dissonances (or discordances), as perfect and imperfect, the former being the second, the tritonus (augmented fourth) the major and minor seventh; and among the imperfect dissonances he numbers the major and minor sixths, which is somewhat curious, after having accepted as consonances the major and minor thirds.

On the discantus and its different kinds the

following observations may be selected from Franco's treatise.

The discantus is formed with one or more lyres, or without a lyre. This seems as much as to say, that the part which is to be invented (viz. the counterpoint) should be set to the given or arbitrarily composed "tenor," above a prolonged fundamental note like that of a lyre or bagpipe, which with two lyres, had the fifth, and with three lyres, the octave, also, sounding together with it; in this case the "tenor" so called (*i. e.* the thema or *cantus firmus* to which the parts are composed), must have consisted of tones with which those of the lyre accorded. But the discantus without a lyre must have comprised one or more parts placed above or below the "tenor," without any continued chord or fundamental note sounding.

The discantus arranged in this manner was employed,—with a few alterations, to us not very intelligible, as to its treatment,—in motetti, conducti, cantilenæ, and rondelles, and in all sacred and profane music. It may begin with another part in the unison, the octave, the fifth, the fourth, and in the major or minor third. The dissonances must be mixed in appropriate places among the consonances, and in such a manner indeed, that, when the "tenor" ascends, the discantus must fall, and *vice versâ*. In the composition of three parts *(triplum)* care should be taken with regard to the "tenor" and discantus, so that the third part, when it is dissonant with the "tenor," must not at the same time be dissonant with the discantus, and *vice versâ.*

Finally, Franco describes a four and five part discantus; and here again consideration must be given to the parts already existing, so that when the one is in dissonance, the other may be in consonance; nor must the parts always ascend or descend at the same time, but sometimes with the "tenor," and occasionally with the discantus; besides, the value of the notes or rests in all the parts should be well observed, that a greater number of longæ, breves, or semibreves, may not be given to one beyond what it ought to receive in comparison with the rest, and according to calculation, even to the last note, or the *punctus organicus* (organ point), which is not subject to any measure.

These compositions described by Franco must evidently have been quite different to the former organum, or the discantus with lyres: they must, on the contrary, be reckoned equivalent to a real counterpoint, since the parts move in different motions, different consonant and dissonant intervals, according to certain rules: and, as we will pre-suppose, not without regard to their effects on the human ear; while the employment of a mensural theory spun out to such subtleties, with various sorts of figures, may even be looked upon as the origin of a mixed species of counterpoint. It is only to be lamented, that, for the reasons above cited, no example can be given of it.

It is a source of general regret that Franco's treatise, however valuable it may prove in assisting us to form our judgment as to the condition of the theory of his time in respect to mensura, so little enlightens us on the state of the study of harmony at that period. Burney has attempted from its "nine rules"(?) to put together, as a two-part piece, the following harmonies, by way of an example:—

But I cannot in Franco's treatise discover either the presumed nine rules, or any kind of explanation from which such harmonies, even taken singly, can be derived; although Burney also, as already observed, had no better codex; whilst even with him, in the paragraph on the four and five-part discantus, the notes were not placed in the existing lines.

Another very old writer on mensural music, whose studies, though less perfect, agree for the most part with those of Franco, is a certain Beda, of whose residence, age, and condition of life, nothing whatever is accurately known. His treatise, *De Musicâ quadratâ seu mensuratâ*, has, by the error of some literary gleaner, been adopted into the collection of *Beda Venerabilis*, a pious Anglo-Saxon monk, very learned for his time, who died in his cloister, A.D. 735, and amongst whose theological works there was also found a treatise curious on music, so far as in those early days the science was understood. But the treatise above-mentioned of the former Beda, however unlike it is to that of the latter, was nevertheless for a long time regarded by the credulous *literati* as a composition of the Venerable Bede; and as this department of the history of the art has become since that period more elucidated, and the spuriousness of this treatise, as a work of the Venerable Bede, has been placed beyond doubt, the Beda of a later age, even if this be in reality his name, is only known by the appellation of Pseudo-Beda. Forkel is of opinion that he lived after Franco, and this he might the more readily assert, since, in deference to the received authorities, he still places Franco in the eleventh century. This Beda certainly appears superior to Franco in a few trifling points, although greatly beneath him in respect to the general value of his treatise, and he by no means belongs to the fourteenth century, as Forkel assumes to be possible.

It would be inconsistent with the limited plan of this work, to give here any extracts from the treatise of the so-called Pseudo-Beda.

With regard to two other writers on mensural music, Walter Odington, a monk at Evesham, in England, and Hieronymus de Moravia, in France,—the first of whom is placed in the year 1240, and the other in 1260,—although no published treatises of either are extant, and scarcely anything beyond their names and existence is known, it does not appear (according to the index of the chapters, and the fragmentary extracts which have been found), that they possessed any particular information more than Franco, who seems also to have been unknown to them.* Some treatises of still less importance have been discovered in English libraries, and of these a description is given both by Hawkins and Burney. From this we find that the seed of the knowledge of mensural music had taken root at that time, more especially in England and France, and that, however scanty, it was not the less fostered. But in respect to the practical part, there seems to have flourished in the French churches a different and peculiar species of discantus, or *déchant*, as it was there termed; and this was not measured, but was either syllabic, or, by agreement of the singers, a kind of melismatic singing, performed above the sustained notes of a *cantus firmus.* In the first and more simple kind of *déchant*, two voices sang for the most part in unison; in individual instances alone the discanting part separated itself, whilst it descended one degree, as the other ascended, and *vice versâ;* by which means perfectly euphonious thirds might make their appearance. But

* Having been struck with the slight and indifferent notice which the author takes in this passage of an English musical writer so much commended by Burney, the translator wrote to him on the subject, referring him particularly to what had been said by Burney in his work, vol. ii, p. 155, *et seq.* His reply, with Burney's remarks, will be found in the Appendix, Note, *Walter Odington.—Translator.*

the parts flowed again immediately together, and in all cases concluded in unison. In the other kind of *déchant*, the discanting part, according to pleasure, ability, and taste, performed variegated passages, which were called *fleurettes*.

The real theoretical writers have not thought this kind of discantus worthy of a place in their treatises, although such, when cleverly performed, might have produced a tolerably agreeable effect. But as the knowledge of the consonance or dissonance of the intervals was very slight, and by no means general, the ear, nowhere as yet much cultivated, could with difficulty recognize the reference of the given melody to a harmony, either founded upon, or agreeing with it. A purity of taste was not yet generally sought after, and thus it is easy to conceive that the fleurettes in particular must, for the most part, have been bizarres, and very little adapted to the sanctity of the place and the Holy Word.

If, moreover, such a *déchant* (extempore or conventional) had been attempted in several parts and in different intervals, it must have often appeared a very strange uproar, and it is difficult to conceive that such a kind of music could possibly have afforded either edification or pleasure.

A very particular kind of *déchant*, having its

origin likewise in France, was that characterized by the curious appellation of *fauxbourdons.* This was a song of three parts, consisting of a succession of consecutive chords of the $^6_3$, in similar motion above the "tenor" (or *cantus firmus)* as the fundamental part; excepting that, at the end, the highest part passed into the octave instead of the sixth, so that the end concluded with $^8_3$; for example:—

	$\bar{c}$	$\bar{d}$	$\bar{c}$	*b*	$\bar{c}$	*b*	$\bar{c}$	*b*	*a*	♯*g*	*a*
	g	*a*	*g*	*f*	*g*	*f*	*g*	*f*	*e*	*d*	*c*
Tenor	*e*	*f*	*e*	*d*	*e*	*d*	*e*	*d*	*c*	*B*	*A*

The performance of these fauxbourdons presupposed at all events the singers to be well practised, and could have been heard therefore only in a few places in any degree of perfection. It is probable also that this kind of harmony appeared at a somewhat later period, when the senses of hearing and taste had already arrived at greater perfection, and when singers had made every kind of experiment, in order to risk such a succession of $^6_3$ chords, which even the theory would not for a long time suffer itself to accept. This kind of fauxbourdon is the same which the singers of the popes (as we shall afterwards learn) brought from Avignon to Rome, towards the end of the fourteenth century, where they long maintained their place, even after the introduction of the figured counterpoint, and are said to be still in use for certain occasions in their original form.

When in the fourteenth, or more probably in the fifteenth century, there arose for real musical composition the technical term counterpoint (*contrapunctus*, from *punctum contra punctum*, point against point, or written notes placed one against the other), in place of the originally universal and indistinct appellation *discantus*, this last name was then given to the extempore singing of several voices, for which the theorists subsequently invented the peculiar name of *sortisatio*, in opposition to that of *contrapunctus*.

Many examples of a regularly written discantus, notwithstanding it was in general only performed extempore even by uninstructed singers, or such as had not been scientifically brought up, if regarded merely as studies, must have appeared in the epoch of Franco, although they have long been lost in the stream of time; and it appears to have been by the veriest accident that the only one which has been preserved, and which M. Fétis has communicated in a manner most accurately deciphered, in the first part of his *Revue Musicale*, is an old French chanson for three voices, the supposed production of a singer and poet, by name Adam de la Hale, called also Le Boiteux d'Arras, who was in the service of the Comte de Provence. It may be placed about the year 1280, if indeed a dilettante of the discantus of the following age may not perhaps have experimentalised on the melody left by De la Hale, as on a "tenor" or *cantus firmus;* since the very pretty songs, in similar notation, produced also by M. Fétis, and which Adam de la Hale has left behind him in his pastorals, are not counterpointed; and the codex, in which M. Fétis discovered the above chanson, may be assigned to the fourteenth century.

To consecutive fifths and octaves the author has not the least antipathy; this must be excused in him, because theory had not at that time, to our own knowledge, proclaimed its prohibition against the progressions of two perfect consonances in similar motion; but the composition could have met with little success, even allowing for the time at which it appeared, nor could it have afforded much delight to those who heard it. This chanson occupies so little space, that I cannot forbear laying it before the reader, who will find it at the end of this work, among the Musical Examples, No. 1.

CHAPTER V.

EPOCH OF MARCHETTUS AND DE MURIS.

A.D. 1300 TO 1380.

In the first decennial periods of the fourteenth century we find two teachers, who not only brought to considerable perfection the theory of mensura, but also in an especial degree advanced that of harmony, as it is called; they originated rules, which, although wanting that complete form reserved for a later period, were nevertheless so constituted, that our ideas of pure chords and pure harmonic progressions might have been deduced from them.

The name of Marchettus of Padua, known as it was to the musical *literati* of a more advanced age, appeared to have fallen, during the course of time, into oblivion, although the seed sown by this meritorious teacher must have long continued to gain strength in Italy, among the schools at least, if not perhaps in the practical department of art. We have to thank the Prince Abbot Gerbert of St. Blaise,—to whose manifold services ancient musical literature is much indebted,—for the publication of two treatises by Marchettus, exceedingly profound for the time at which they were produced: viz., *Lucidarium in arte Musicæ planæ*, and *Pomerium in arte Musicæ mensuratæ;* the latter of which was finished about the year 1309, as may be inferred from its dedication to King Robert of Sicily, whilst the former was certainly written in the previous century. These are printed in the third part of the *Scriptores de Musicâ*, etc.

The other teacher above alluded to was Johannes de Muris, a highly accomplished French ecclesiastic and doctor of the Sorbonne in Paris, whose name is about as well known and familiar to all intelligent lovers of music as that of his predecessor Guido; although it appears that he was less indebted for this reputation to his services in musical theory, than to the long cherished errors, through which even the invention of the notes and of mensural music was ascribed to him. Two of his treatises, and these it may be presumed were the best, *Summa Magistri de Muris*, and *Tractatus de Musicâ* (entitled likewise *Musica Speculativa*, as also *Theoretica*) were printed in like manner by the Prince Abbot

Gerbert, in the third part of the *Scriptores de Musicâ*, and their date may be fixed about the year 1323.

To enumerate the rules which these authors have given for the discantus or the polyphonia, would be to overstep the boundary prescribed by the plan of the present work; moreover, they would scarcely come up to the expectations of the reader, especially if he neglected at the same time to bear in mind, that each addition of a rule, by which the pureness of harmony in any one point was secured for later times, however insignificant and insufficient it may now appear to us, was of consequence at that period, and deserves, accordingly, our best acknowledgments.

There is, besides, a fault attached not only to these old authors, but to all the books of study throughout the following centuries, the authors of which immediately made a rule for every new phenomenon; for they were not yet so far advanced as to be able to add together the isolated cases, and thus lead back the theory to a few universally valid principles. It is further to be regretted, that the composers and theorists of this period, and those who came afterwards in direct succession, trusting to their erudition, considered their works or examples perfect as soon as the mere labour of writing had been completed; and, as if they toiled only to please the eye, they disdained to sit down in the stillness of their study, and try the effects of such works upon their senses by means of the spinet (should it have then existed), the psalterium, or any other suitable instrument, whereby many a false relationship *(mi contra fa)* of the harmonic progressions would have become manifest, but which otherwise continued to be unnoticed by them when represented only on their parchments.

Above all, we find in the work of Marchettus, as well as in that of De Muris, the very important rule laid down, that "two perfect consonances (unison, fifth, and octave) must not follow each other in similar motion." These teachers knew also the nature of the dissonances, and the necessity of resolving them into the nearest consonances; but they knew them only as passing dissonances, for, in regard to the prepared or retarded dissonance, nothing appears in the writings of either.

A few examples from Marchettus may here find a place; they are what the author has given in the different explanations of tone-relationship, and which he has accompanied with only one added underpart:—

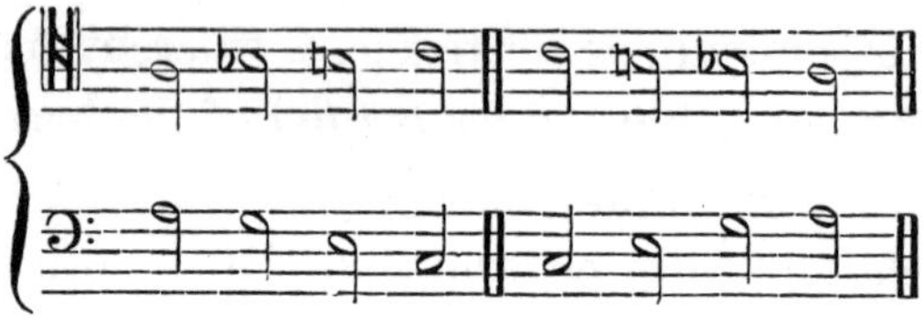

To these may be added the following examples, extracted by Forkel from the rules of De Muris, in illustration of which he has appended them; they are only indeed in two parts, but are as pure as can be desired even at the present day, although the rules themselves are generally partial; and, since they apply merely to the cases indicated, they must not be regarded as wholly and universally valid, nor can they in any degree be deemed sufficient towards the necessities of a comprehensive theory:—

The history of musical art and literature mentions other theorists after Marchettus and De Muris, who have doubtless made valuable contributions to the science in their treatises, such as Prosdocimus de Beldomandis, the elucidator of De Muris; Philippus de Vitriaco (of Vitry), who is regarded as the inventor of many innovations; Philippus de Caserta, Anselmus Parmensis, and a few more, whose writings are to be found in the Italian libraries, and are mentioned by the *literati*, but have never been published. Musical studies, however, both general and special, were at this time only propagated and extended by verbal instruction, through which means indeed the science was promoted, but owing to which, many differences also in the use and meaning of terms were at the same time promulgated, whose adjustment and connexion occasioned endless trouble to the teachers and writers of a later period, stirring up frequent disputes among them.

Very few productions have reached us of a written discantus belonging to the epoch of which we now treat (A.D. 1300 to 1380); and these, without boasting much excellence, have probably been preserved by mere accident; being considered unworthy of notice, as better compositions in the course of time appeared: a great number probably still lie buried in old libraries, to be some day brought to light, especially in the Netherlands, where, early in the fourteenth century, the study of composition was cultivated with good results.

Kalkbrenner (the elder) has communicated the fragment of a *Gloria* for four voices, in his work entitled *Histoire de la Musique ;* Paris, 1802. It is taken from the codex of a poem by Guillaume de Machaud discovered in the Royal Library at Paris, and the author is said to have once been *valet de chambre* to King Philip, who reigned from 1285 to 1314, and afterwards secretary to John of Luxembourg, King of Bohemia, who ascended the throne in 1312 and reigned thirty-five years. The first deciphering of this fragment I have communicated in my treatise *Die Tabulaturen der älteren Praktiker*, etc., in the Leipsig *Musical Journal* for 1831, No. 25; and I have inserted it here among the Musical Examples, No. 2, at the end of the volume. This fragment, in the original, as I beg particularly to point out to the observation of the reader, is still noted with black figures. I have always regarded it as the work of a presuming dilettante, who, being an adept at versification, and having a superficial degree of knowledge in regard to most things, was bold enough to try his skill in a musical composition. But we are told by M. Castil Blaze (*Chapelle Musique du Roi de France;* Paris, 1832; page 42), that this mass was performed at the coronation of Charles the Fifth of France (1364) by the choir of the chapel royal. Such was the state of music in the country where forty years previously a Johannes de Muris had been a teacher.

The Italian canzone for three voices (see No. 4 of Musical Examples) M. Fétis communicated in his *Revue Musicale.* He found it in a MS. which contained a considerable number of similar compositions by about a dozen Florentines, whose names, excepting that of the author of the canzone in question, Francesco Landino, have long since perished. It is chiefly characterized by the immoderate use of a kind of syncopation (showing no knowledge, however, of the origin of a prepared dissonance by a retardation), in which successions of fifths and octaves are avoided; but this, indeed, is all that can be recorded in its praise. The author is supposed to have lived in Florence about the year 1360, and was for his time a very distinguished performer on the organ. In admitting this, we must not forget, that at the period in question, the organ was an instrument no more adapted to the practice of counterpoint, than the pedal keys of a modern organ would be, if they were played upon by the hands instead of the feet.

Incomparably more worthy of consideration than the attempts above cited, is the old French chanson for three voices, of an unknown author, which the Prince Abbot Gerbert has communicated to us in his large historical work, *De Cantu et Musicâ Sacrâ*, part ii, plate 19, which is a *fac simile* of the separate parts, as he found them upon the parchment cover of an old book. This remarkable piece of antiquity remained unnoticed for fifty-eight years; at least I am not aware that any one has tried to decipher it. Not long since a friend very well skilled in musical palæography sent me its decipherment in score. It will be found among the Musical Examples, No. 3, and in juxtaposition with it also the *fac simile* from the work of Gerbert, the sight and comparison of which will doubtless prove most interesting to the observer.

This chanson is *in tempore perfecto*, composed, according to all rules, with a mixed counterpoint, and being noted moreover with many subtleties of a perfect mensural theory. It is as pure in its harmony as can reasonably be expected from a composition of that early period; the dissonances appear only as passing ones; anything similar to a prepared dissonance or syncopation is only to be found in the concluding cadence: ${}^{7}_{3}\ {}^{6}_{-}\ {}^{8}_{5}$.

The great antiquity of this chanson is evident by the example which appears in it of an ochetus (*hocetus*, *hocquet*, similar to sobbing, certain strongly-accented notes, separated from those which precede and follow by rests or suspires), a figure which has not been mentioned by the theorists since the time of Franco and pseudo-Beda, and which does not appear at all in the works of the oldest (Belgian) contrapunctists: it is, in further respects, an evidence of the employment of notes wholly black, the oldest Belgians* now known having even at that time

* In the present work the word Belgian is understood to mean, a native of any of those Provinces at that time belonging to the Netherlands.—*Translator*.

made use of the white ; and, lastly, a particular circumstance is worthy of remark: namely, that the chanson, or melody, is in the upper or highest part, by which again it is also distinguished from similar pieces of the oldest Belgians. This chanson, therefore, which is curious again on account of the very ancient language of the text, might have been the production of a Frenchman, who had been very early instructed in a good school, probably under De Muris. The connoisseurs of French palæology might possibly arrive at some conclusion as to its age from the language of the text. At all events, amongst the whole number of works belonging to an early age which have been hitherto discovered, it is by far the most interesting.

CHAPTER VI.

EPOCH OF DUFAY.

A.D. 1380 TO 1450.

THE progress of music from the time of Franco, and again from that of Marchettus and De Muris, in the course of the described period of another hundred and fifty years, must appear to us anything but satisfactory, since those teachers had not only already introduced some order into the *mensura*, but had also left behind them very good, if not sufficient, rules for harmony, or (as they termed it) *discantus*. They had therefore prepared the means by which the art was very shortly to be further promoted, and to attain considerable perfection; and that such was not the consequence, can only be explained by considering that it was customary from the earliest periods to regard music more as a subject of erudition and science, than as an art, and that it was thus accordingly treated.

Ancient Grecian doctrines, Christian church-keys, and modern *ut re mi fa sol la*, jumbled in strange brotherhood together, formed the basis of all previous theories; but, according to these methods, instruction in the commencement was entirely speculative, being concealed, moreover, in a cloud of things, words, and ideas, whose reference to music is positively beyond discovery. Were we to instruct our musical students in conformity to the doctrines of the treatises of those early days, and even of those published so late as the seventeenth century, they would remain in doubt whether the object of their study were really music at all.

That music is an æsthetic art, the essential aim of which is to please and to affect, had been made clear at that time neither to teacher nor pupil, both of whom in their theories believed themselves to be possessed of its sum and substance. But the theory, or (as we might rather say) the grammar of music, could not flourish so long as there was no perception that theory must be united with practice, to which it should give precedence, according it even a reasonable freedom and self-activity; nay, in fine, also condescending to be instructed by it.

Under these circumstances, then, the study of music was naturally reserved only for a few;

and it may well be conceived, that, as an art, there would be much difficulty, during this early period, in obtaining for it a general hearing and circulation in the world, whilst at the most there could be produced only an extempore discantus, the excellence of which would depend on the degree of knowledge and taste, and still more on the common capabilities, of the singers who composed the choir; thus, owing to these obstacles, the study would make but little progress.

The mode of singing in several parts was not at that period, nor until one much more recent, received into the church in Italy; and even if, as Abbot Baini, in his *History of Palestrina*, supposes, "certain simple harmonies" may have been used in the pontifical chapel (though we should require perhaps more proof for the truth of this than the assertion of a Baleus), still the chapel in question must have formed an exception to all others, or enjoyed a prerogative, which other churches would have found it difficult to procure, owing to the extremely limited number of educated singers. But until harmony could be practised with considerable purity, the proper and accurate sense of the inhabitants of that district must have preserved them from the introduction of a bad discantus, such as the French probably was, or of a bizarre counterpoint, like that of the

Florentines. From the organ, according to its structure in those days, the people could not possibly have imbibed their taste for harmony, such instruments being as little adapted to the study as to the practice of harmony, whilst the duty of the organist was merely to give out the key-note, or at the most to keep it sounding; and if at any time he took sufficient courage to "thump" something like an accompaniment, it could have been nothing more than a second consonant interval, and employed in isolated places alone, the theory, as well as the practice, having then and long afterwards no defined idea of a bass *(basis)*

There is no ground for supposing that it was otherwise or better in Spain or England, although there was already a professorship of music appointed in the university of Salamanca, by King Alphonso of Castile, who reigned from 1252 to 1284; and another in Oxford, by King Alfred, so early as 886(!) when he laid the foundation of that seat of learning. In Germany there is nothing to be found relating to harmony until late even in the fifteenth century: the national melodies, which had early introduction into the Church throughout many dioceses of the German provinces and in Bohemia, were only in the unison throughout, like the Roman choral. Such a discantus or biscantus as that of which Abbot Gerbert has given us some written examples from the library of a cloister, could only have been tried in the chapel, and by brethren alike deficient in ear and taste. Of institutions in Germany for the study of music, or where discantus or figurate music may have been taught, we have no intimation; and several of the German teachers and writers,—the above-mentioned Hieronymus de Moravia for instance, in Franco's epoch, a certain Johannes de Erfordia in the fourteenth, and a Johannes Goodendag even in the fifteenth century,—the latter of whom became preceptor to the celebrated Franchinus Gafurius (supposing him to have been a German),—must first have acquired their knowledge in foreign cloisters, where they are known to have passed their lives.

In France alone have we conclusive information of the use of song in several parts in the churches. The *déchant* was there cultivated with a fondness amounting to frenzy in all the larger towns; and in all the principal churches singing-men and singing-boys were kept under the direction of a *maître*. Of the nature of these *chapelles* or *maitrises*, so called, and the manner of singing employed in them, some idea may be formed by regarding the condition of the "art" in the Chapel Royal *(Chapelle Musique du Roi)* from which we are entitled to draw an inference as to what prevailed in the provinces.

According to the data now presented on the condition of music in France, even towards the end of the fourteenth century, it is to be hoped there can no longer exist any doubt, that the belief in the pretended early and very ancient French school of counterpoint, of which the musical historians have everywhere spoken even to the present day, and which, in their opinion, must have preceded that of the Netherland school, is founded in error, to be explained only, or perhaps excused, by the obscurity in which hitherto the long period from Guido to Ockenheim (1450) was veiled, and by the total want of any monuments of the time prior to Ockenheim.

Now, however, the scene gradually brightens, the clouds roll away, and we are enabled at the present day to obtain a tolerably clear insight into a province of the history of art, which to the literary world, until very lately, had remained a *terra incognita*, the nearest boundaries of which no one possessed the courage to define. At the same time that the *déchant* still existed in France, and when even a Machaud was there esteemed a composer, we shall see how the musical art was practised in the neighbouring Netherlands.

The valuable school of Joannes de Muris was quickly lost again in France in the *déchant* of the *maitrises*,—possibly, indeed, passed over by them without notice. Fortunately, however, on the other hand, the practice of his theorems (or those of another unknown but equally good teacher) was begun successfully in the Netherland provinces at an early period of the fourteenth century, if not sooner; and, as the inhabitants of these provinces were living in a certain degree of comfort by means of their manufactures, commerce, and shipping, which were prosperous even at that early period, particularly in the well-regulated municipal and privileged towns, they were naturally more capable of fostering "the beautiful art which enlivens life," than could then have been the case in the French provinces, which were continually distracted by civil and foreign wars, by the most uncivilized feudal system, and by deplorably bad government. That counterpoint was practised and improved in the Netherlands, and likewise at the same time, though with less favourable results, in Florence,—first in domestic circles with favorite songs, and afterwards introduced at different courts for the entertainment of the great, before it found its way into the churches,—is perfectly clear. This opinion the Abbot Baini has also expressed, and all that has been hitherto discovered distinctly proves the truth of this supposition.

In France it could not thus have happened; Perrault, a French writer, declares, in the preface to his translation of Vitruvius, that about the same period in France, owing to wars and tournaments, there was no possibility of acquiring a taste for the fine arts; and another author, who certainly found it important to cause the evidences of the musical art in his native country to be esteemed as the most ancient,—Laborde, in his *Essai sur la Musique ancienne et moderne*,—goes so far as to assert, that it was scarcely known whether music of any kind whatsoever had existed in France, before the reign of Francis the First (1515).

This last assertion is but little exaggerated, and requires only to be modified by mentioning, that (as we shall afterwards learn) Louis XI, who reigned from 1461 to 1483, had already engaged in his service an Ockenheim and a Josquin des Prés; and that Mouton, a pupil of the latter, was the head of the Chapel Royal under Louis XII, from 1498 to 1515. Thus even at that time had commenced in France the practice of engaging contrapunctists and teachers of counterpoint from the Netherlands, and of sending young Frenchmen occasionally to study in the school of the Netherlands, such for instance as Certon, Clement Jannequin, Moulu, Maillart, Burgogne, Claudin (Sermisy, not le Jeune), and many others.

We will not, however, anticipate history, but pursue the order of the epoch commenced in this chapter.

According to the testimony afforded in the valuable work on Palestrina by the Abbé Baini, already so frequently mentioned, and who at this time was the worthy superintendent of the Pontifical chapel, it appears that some natives of the Netherlands, about seventy years before the age of Ockenheim, brought to Rome the first masses written with counterpoint. We learn also from the same source that the members of those choirs, which were procured and maintained by the popes at Avignon, during their temporary residence there (1305–1377), and whom Gregory XI took back with him, and united to the ancient choir still remaining at the Vatican, when, in 1377, the seat of pontifical government was again transferred to Rome; had as yet no written counterpoint, but only brought with them the extempore discantus and the fauxbourdons used by them in France.

In the year 1380, by means of existing account books, Baini finds inscribed by name among the singers of the Pontifical chapel, as a tenor, Gulielmus Dufay, afterwards so celebrated, and at that time the oldest real contrapunctist and composer belonging to the establishment, and, generally speaking, the earliest contrapunctist of the same period, whose name the better musical historians have brought forward, though without describing accurately the time at which he lived, his origin, or condition of life, much less producing specimens of his art or even referring to such. This is the identical Dufay, to whose practice, a hundred years later, the most famous theoretical writers, such as Franchinus, Gafurius, Petrus Aaron, Joannes Spatarus, and Adam de Fulda, have often and willingly appealed, as to a valid authority.

Dufay lived as a member of the Pontifical chapel, highly respected, until 1432, and its archives are enriched by the rare possession of some masses of this great master, as well as of several others whose names have acquired celebrity, and who were contemporary with Dufay; among these may be mentioned Elay, Brasart, Faugues, Binchois, etc. For the information that Dufay was born at Chymay in Hainault, and was not (as Tinctoris has asserted in his *Proportionate Mus.* MS. 1476) a Frenchman, we have to thank M. Fétis, who proves the fact by a reference to the source from which he gained it, in his valuable memoir affixed to the *Prize Essay*, on the influence exerted by musical teachers of the Netherlands on the improvement of musical art.* There can be no doubt, according to our present knowledge of the state of the art at that period, that the other contrapunctists above mentioned belonged also to the Netherlands.

I have been fortunate enough to gain possession of a few very important fragments of single parts in facsimile from the works of these remarkable authors, particularly from those of Dufay, which I have succeeded in deciphering and putting into score. After the perusal of such works, it can no longer be questioned, that even before the age of Dufay, at the time when counterpoint was either never practised at all in other countries, or introduced only in very feeble and rude experiments, the Netherlands must have been the nursery of a very advanced state of art.

Above all, it is a remarkable circumstance, that with Dufay, as well as with the oldest contrapunctists hitherto known, the white (unfilled

* For this essay M. Fétis obtained the second or silver medal of the Royal Institution of Amsterdam; the author of the present treatise having received the first or golden medal in the same competition.—*Translator*.

up) notes first made their appearance, by the introduction of which the figurate and mensural music received its completion: this circumstance alone would undoubtedly place the early existence of a peculiar school in the Netherlands, as De Muris (1323) was only at present acquainted with the black characters, of which Machaud also made use in France about the year 1367.

The works of Dufay, generally speaking, manifest, in every respect, a perfectly finished or cultivated art, and exhibit even many of those contrivances of counterpoint, the invention of which has hitherto been ascribed to Ockenheim, who lived considerably after Dufay, or at least the invention has been dated from the age in which Ockenheim flourished.

However faulty may have been the opinions of those writers who, like Vincenzo Galilei *(Dialogo della Musica antica e moderna;* Florence, 1602), or previously to him Glareanus (in his celebrated *Dodecachordon*, Basle, 1547), have awarded the origin of counterpoint, in the extended sense of composition in several parts, to the age of Ockenheim, or even of Josquin; not less erroneous, on the other hand, were those of the celebrated teacher, Tinctoris, who ascribes the origin of "this new art" to the English, whose chief in this respect was Dunstable.

This Dunstable, of whose musical talents even his countryman Burney (author of the valuable general *History of Music*) could find no specimens, he being unable to produce anything to his credit, may, notwithstanding, have been a clever person, and by far the most accomplished contrapunctist among his brother artists in England; the more likely so, indeed, as Franchinus Gafurius, in some part of his writings, refers to a "tenor" of this name: yet, if Dunstable did live even at the same time with Dufay, he must have been considerably his junior; since the latter, after an honourable career of fifty-two years passed in the Pontifical chapel, died in 1432, at a very advanced age; whilst the year of Dunstable's death was 1458. And, finally, we have merely to bestow a cursory glance on the works of Dufay to confirm us in our conviction that he was not himself the inventor even of his own art.*

* Tinctoris, so generally endowed with high accomplishments and deserts, has given us, in the extracts of his manuscripts, more than one proof of the slender information he possessed respecting the history of the art and artists, whilst he bestows very faulty intelligence regarding men who lived just prior to, or during his own time; not his countrymen, indeed, as Brabanters, but such nevertheless as being natives of the Netherlands.

In my treatise, *Die Verdienste der Niederlander um die Tonkunst* (Amsterdam, 1828),* having been restricted to the data which the literature at that time existing could supply me with, and being compelled to follow the best previous historians, I have commenced the great musical period of the art of the Belgians with Ockenheim, who distinguished himself about the middle of the fifteenth century. Now that I have the works of Dufay and some of his contemporaries before me, I must refer the period of the Belgians—or, what is one and the same thing in those early days, the era of methodical counterpoint—to a much more remote time, and even fix it two ages prior to that of Ockenheim; namely, the one before Dufay, which begins with the fourteenth century, if not earlier, and reaches to the year 1380, when Dufay first appeared. I come afterwards to the epoch of Dufay himself, which (although his decease took place in 1432) I place immediately next to that of Ockenheim, about 1450.

And if, in the treatise above-named, I derived the Belgian school from Ockenheim, I must now, without regard to the anterior school of the

* The prize essay to which reference has already been made.—*Translator.*

fourteenth century, from which Dufay and the other first-rate master emanated, acknowledge the existence of *two* Netherland schools,—the ancient and the modern. The former might well be termed that of Dufay; not as if Dufay were its originator and first teacher, but because he has been known to us as the oldest and most celebrated master of that school, in the style of which, also, throughout a long period, all the Netherland musicians composed. In this elder or first Netherland school, I do not admit those composers alone of the first decennial periods of the fifteenth century, for instance, Brasart, Eloy, Egidius Binchois, Vincentius Faugues, but several also of those who partly reach even beyond the epoch of Ockenheim; such as Carontis, Regis, and Busnoys, with Hobrecht, and many others, who afterwards went over to the new (modern) school.

In concluding the short history here given of the epoch of Dufay, I will only briefly advert to the characteristic appearances of those examples which I have before me.

Their harmony is thoroughly pure, and even their intended effects on the hearer have met with more careful consideration than can always be attributed to the thousand artists of the succeeding epoch. If these compositions be deemed such as a piano without black keys would represent, and not as diatonic stereotypes, but as adding to them at striking passages the augmenting or diminishing ♯ or ♭ which belongs to the original key, or to that formed by the modulation introduced, and which must have been supplied by singers—(who still sang for human, and, indeed, for cultivated ears, again demanding at each modulation, even if only in other higher positions, the diatonic scale)—they may obtain listeners at the present day not only without giving offence, but even communicating pleasure. The dissonances appear partly as passing ones, and then always in such a manner, that the consonant interval falls on the accented, and the dissonant one on the unaccented part of the bar, that which the schools of the present day call the "regular passing notes"; but there appear also dissonant chords as retardations of a consonant chord,—for example, $^{4}_{2}$, $^{5}_{4}$, $^{6}_{5}$, $^{7}_{3}$;* which were indeed properly

* To those unacquainted with thorough-bass *(basso continuo)* I subjoin the notes which these figures represent.—*Translator*.

prepared and resolved, and as regularly as the musical grammar of the present day can desire. The forms of the cadence are the same which are found in later days everywhere; in the conclusions on the *quinta toni* with $^{5}_{4}$, or on the *secunda* with $^{7}_{3}\,^{6}_{-}$. A curious *nota combiata* is to be found in the cadences of the part which conducts the melody, inasmuch as before it steps out of the leading-note *(septima toni)* into the tonic, it touches first the *sexta toni*, which is quite strange to the harmony; for example:—

Instead of $\bar{c}$	*b*	| $\bar{c}$		$\bar{c}$	*b*	*a*	| $\bar{c}$
			thus				
d	—	| *c*		*d*	—	—	| *c*

This figure remained also with later composers, and was in use until an advanced period of the sixteenth century, but after that time it became obsolete.

The counterpoint is for the most part placed above a "tenor", choral, or a secular tune, although occasionally also of a more free inven-

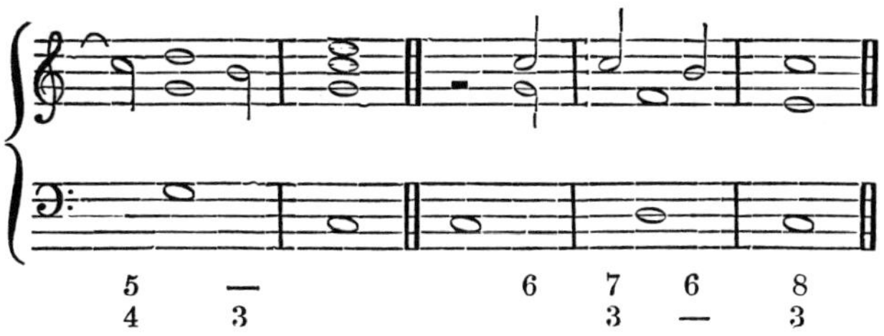

tion. There appears already in the works of Dufay a "tenor" with augmentation, under the formula of later use, *Crescit in duplo;* and there are also found, although not often, short canons *all'ottava;* one likewise *in arsi* and *in thesi;* in another place, moreover, a canon "*Ad medias referas pausas linquendo priores,*" in which, to speak the truth, I could never discover the pretended indication of art. With Eloy, too, there is a short piece as "tenor," which, measured in sixteen different ways (namely, with changes of the mensural signs on the margin), fills up the whole mass, and bears the inscription, "*Canon pro totâ Missa; non faciens pausas super signis capiens has; tempora tria primæ semper benè pausa, sex decies currens cunctaque signa videns.*" In the same author we also find a tenor with *signo contra signum.*

The properly figured style, such as was latterly universal, I could not meet with in the examples which I received. The compositions are mostly in four parts, seldom in three or five; a *duo* appears in a few places: in the notation, all the subtleties of the mensural-theory are employed; and it was from the works of these authors that the celebrated theorists, towards the end of the fifteenth century, extracted their rules; such as Tinctoris, Gafurius, Aaron, and others.

I cannot resist the pleasure I feel in being able to give a few select examples from the works of these old contrapunctists, none of which have hitherto been produced. A facsimile of the parts accompany some of them for the sake of comparison.

The reader is referred to Musical Examples in the Appendix, No. 5, *a b c*, by Dufay; No. 6, *a b*, by Eloy; and No. 7, by Faugues.

CHAPTER VII.

EPOCH OF OCKENHEIM.

1450 TO 1480.

In proportion as a greater degree of expertness was acquired in counterpoint through constant practice, in musical compositions, the students of music became ambitious to surpass their predecessors in this branch of the science; and as these composed their counterpoint for the most part above a chosen "tenor," and only occasionally tried an imitation in the free style, or restricted themselves to a diminution or augmentation of the "tenor", which had already assumed a tolerably ingenious character, so did their successors now endeavour to make themselves prominent and distinguished by the invention of new contrivances, showing that they were capable also of producing a pure counterpoint under any kind of restriction, however arbitrarily (obbligo) imposed.

The greatest master of his day in the above style,—which, in contradistinction to the simple, might be termed in an extended sense the ingenious, or artificial,—was considered to be the highly celebrated Johannes Ockegheim, more usually called Ockenheim, who, not only from his excellent compositions, but from his having been the teacher of the most distinguished men of his own as well as the following epoch, has always very justly been regarded as the head of the Netherland school, or, according to our present ideas, as the chief of the new or second school of the same country. The remaining composers of the old Netherland school, contemporary with him, adapted this fresh style with success, and united themselves with the new, the common characteristics of which are to be found in the works of nearly all the Belgians of this period.

Of the parentage and education of this great master, and of his circumstances in early life, nothing is known; of his Belgian origin, however, there has never been a doubt; and from documents which have lately been brought to light, it appears that he was born in Hainault (probably at Bavay), between the years 1420 and 1430. Where, or by whom he was instructed, is not shown; but no want of good teachers was felt even at that time in the Netherlands, since many of those enumerated in the former epoch must have flourished during the youth of Ockenheim. As early as the year 1455 Josquin was in the same school. In 1476 we find that Ockenheim was at Tours, as treasurer* in the abbey of St. Martin. Louis XI, who sometimes held his court in the vicinity of this town (Plessis les Tours) had engaged him in order to organize the choir of the chapel.

According to the recently discovered proofs here mentioned, Ockenheim was still living at Tours in 1512, and must therefore have reached a mature old age. The following year may be regarded as that of his death.

Ockenheim, owing to the extensive reputation which he enjoyed, must doubtless have formed, in the course of his long life, a large number of pupils, although no more than eight can be brought forward, whose names are contained in two funeral dirges *(nænia)* written and set to music on the occasion of his death, and who have in a peculiar manner preserved the brilliant fame of their "good teacher and father", and his school, by their own works in the epoch which immediately follows. These were Josquin des Prés, Anto-

* *Thesaurarius* is the word in the original text. This office was probably similar to the one held by the Chancellors of English dioceses.—*Translator.*

nius Brumel, Alexander Agricola, Gaspard, Loyset Compère (surnamed also Piéton), Pierre de la Rue (called often simply Pierchon, or Pierçon, and by the Italians Pierazzon), Prioris (probably one and the same with Philippus de Primis); and lastly Verbonnet, whose other, and more probably correct name, is unknown.

As contemporary also with Ockenheim must be mentioned Jacob Hobrecht, a much esteemed master, and several others, who, although existing at the concluding period of the former epoch, still lived in the beginning of this, and flourished at the same time with Ockenheim, amongst whom were Caron (or Carontis), Johannes Regis (Le Roy), and Busnoys; and then, possibly, several of those whose counterpoint to the favourite chansons universally current, is published in the first edition of Petrucci, particularly in the collection of songs for the year 1503 (see *Verdienste der Niederlander um die Tonkunst*, p. 93), and whose names are not even known, much less their proper age or general circumstances.

In the epoch of Ockenheim no contrapunctist can be named as belonging to France, Spain, Germany, or Italy.

It was in England alone that a native school had sprung up (possibly since the time of Dunstable) different from that of the Netherlands, the pupils of which flourished in the reign of Edward the Fourth (1461-1483); of their works, however, even Burney could find but few examples, which he declares to be very coarse, and far beneath those of the Belgian school of the same period.*

By the new Netherland school is meant, the works of Ockenheim, his contemporaries, and their pupils, who appear and are celebrated in the epoch immediately following; and who distinguished themselves, in comparison with those of the elder school, by a greater facility in the treatment of counterpoint, and greater fertility of invention, as their compositions may no longer be regarded in the light of mere premeditated submissions to the contrapunctic operation, but are for the most part indicative of thought, and are sketched out with manifest design; they are further distinguished by many ingenious contrivances of an obligato counterpoint, at that time but just discovered, such as augmentation, diminution, reversion, imitation; together with canons and fugues of the most manifold description, which are frequently concealed, and notified to the singer in very curious devices, or a kind

* Burney has also (doubtless from the above circumstances), quite against his usual custom, given us no examples from the works of these his countrymen.

of enigma; as, for instance, *Clama ne cesses; Otia dant vitia; Dii faciant sine me non moriar ego; Omnia si perdas, famam servare memento, qua semel amissa postea nullus eris;* and such like; which may be seen in Forkel's *History of Music*, part ii, p. 538;—contrivances which may truly be said to degenerate into great abuses, and wherein each master tried to outdo the other.

In justice to the laborious efforts of so many meritorious persons, who have on this account been censured far too severely by the writers of modern times, I consider it my duty to remind the reader that canons and enigmas were by no means the only things they composed, as we are bound to believe, if they are to be judged according to the compendiums, abridgments, and even the great and learned treatises of succeeding theorists and didactic writers, especially those of Germany, who set out from the first with the intention of collecting and promulgating, as examples from the works of those masters, only such greatly admired contrivances and unseasonable jocularities. Thus it occurs that we have hitherto known the "incomparable Ockenheim," as the Abb. Baini calls him, only from a canon, difficult to be sung, under the title of *Fugo trium vocum in Epidiatesseron*, and from that comical *Missa ad omnem tonum*, in which there are no clefs written before any of the parts, examples which are received by the very learned Glareanus in his *Dodecachordon;* and who could tell us nothing more of this great master than that he found a pleasure "in deducing many parts from one," or that he had even arranged a piece of prattle, a "*garritum quendam triginta sex vocum*"; which he, however, the informant, had never seen. Under this title of *garritus* we are, nevertheless, not to understand Motetts in thirty-six different parts, but a circular canon, similar to those which were produced in later days, for as many or more voices, by the lovers of this species of composition.

It is certainly true, as may be perceived, that very few compositions of these masters were preserved in any country. Petrucci has published nothing of this celebrated Ockenheim beyond a few songs, and not many proprietors of libraries can congratulate themselves on possessing any of his works. I shall add to the Musical Examples at the close of the treatise, under No. 8, *a b c d*, first,—some fragments of his previously mentioned contrivances, which have been elsewhere printed; and next,—some pieces also belonging, in their way, to the free style of composition, extracted from his *Missa Gaudeamus*, being deciphered and put into score; and which appear for the first time in this volume. These examples will suffice to prove his merits, and even his great superiority over his celebrated predecessor Dufay.

To this epoch may with justice be ascribed the real foundation of that fame which the composers of the Netherlands enjoyed throughout the whole civilized world in the epochs that immediately follow; and although Dufay and his contemporaries may have appeared illustrious as predecessors, there are, notwithstanding, good grounds for dating the bright period of the Netherland musicians from Ockenheim, through whose pupils the art has been transplanted into all countries, and who, as can be proved by genealogy, must be regarded as the founder of all schools, from his own to the present age.

Before we take our leave of this remarkable epoch, in order to proceed to that of the great pupils of the school of Ockenheim, let us take a retrospective glance at the condition of an instrument, which, how much soever it may be indebted to counterpoint for its development and perfection, has, on the other hand, subsequently repaid in a most ample degree the obligation incurred. The organ (for to it alone can be referred what we have to remark) must even in the time of Dufay, and still more especially in the course of the fifteenth century, have received very considerable improvements as to its structure and mechanism, but particularly in the arrangement of the manuals, or interior works connected with the keys; upon the utility of which for harmonic performances could solely and of necessity depend the origin of real artists and virtuosi, in the proper sense of the word, capable of doing justice to this instrument of instruments, emphatically named the organum. The history of the art has preserved to us the names of two remarkable men amongst the contemporaries of Ockenheim, who were brilliant in this department,—ANTONIA SQUARCIALUPO, called also ANTONIO DAGLI ORGANI, of Florence, and BERNHARD, of Venice, commonly called *The German*. Authors relate wonderful things respecting the performances of these artists; and although a portion of the enthusiasm may be attributed to the influence of novelty, still it is allowable for us to believe that they accomplished something in their way of an extraordinary nature. Antonio was even so clever in music, that he gave public lectures at Florence; and for these musical services his grateful fellow-citizens honoured his memory with a monument, which still exists. But our countryman Bernhard was not contented with the manuals hitherto known; he seized upon the bold idea of tuning them an octave higher, and of accompanying the song of the voices, thus embellished, with a doubled bass: and when in 1470 he invented the pedal, he formed his instrument into a gigantic machine, producing a discovery more calculated to immortalize his name than even his performances, splendid as they may have been, and in which he was, certainly, inferior to no musician of his age, as is evident from the improvements he made on his instrument.

CHAPTER VIII.

EPOCH OF JOSQUIN.

1480 TO 1520.

OUR æsthetic philosophers, whilst they include the fine arts altogether as one fine art, take a pleasure in representing to themselves that the histories of these several arts are united by the closest ties; that they had, so to speak, always flourished in unison about the same time, because the very circumstances which produced and fostered any one of them, had also been serviceable in promoting the rest.

Whatsoever attraction and accuracy this representation may boast, according to the latter supposition, it can only be applied to music with some limitations. Although music was that art in the family circle which first revived in the early period of the middle ages, and is therefore entitled to be considered as the eldest of the sisterhood, it could at no period ever make the same advance as the others, for reasons which we have elsewhere mentioned (*Introduction*, p. 25); and it first reached the greatest perfection, that we can suppose, at a period which is not exactly acknowledged to be that of the golden age, in respect to poetry, painting, architecture, etc. But true it is that each period which was favourable on the whole to civilization, to science, and the fine arts in general, could not fail to exercise a happy influence on musical science and musical art.

From the time of the revival of the sciences in the fourteenth century, music also as one of the number was more encouraged than it had been; and its influence was particularly manifest, when, towards the end of the fifteenth century, the effects of printing (an invention assigned to the year 1440) began to make themselves powerfully prominent. Choirs of music were instituted in Italy and other countries towards the close of the fifteenth century; Ferdinand I of Naples, founded one about the year 1470, and three highly accomplished Belgians (Joannes Tinctoris, Gulielmus Guarnerii, and Bernardus Hycaert) were contemporary as public teachers in that monarch's capital. Somewhat later, Duke Sforza opened one at Milan, at the head of which was the highly celebrated Franchinus Gafurius, himself a pupil of the German or Belgian Goodendag.

These meritorious teachers developed to great perfection not only the theory of the *Mensura*, but also that of counterpoint, which they extracted, to the best of their ability, from the practical works of contemporary Belgians, and partly from those of earlier writers of the same country. After these quickly followed Petrus Ramis de Pareja of Toleda, one of the pupils of Johann of Mons; Johannes Spaturus of Bologna, and Petrus Aaron of Venice.

Thus the musical art seemed allied to the fate of the other fine arts. The compositions of a Dufay, together with those of his contemporaries and brother artists, and even of Ockenheim, appear only to have been particularly sought after in the Pontifical Chapel, notwithstanding that the reputation of these men had become tolerably well established over the whole of Italy: but as soon as the great painters and sculptors of the fifteenth century shone forth, and a fondness had been widely cherished for the plastic arts, princes and nobles felt the desire also to listen to music. Chapelles (choirs) were founded at the different courts, and Belgian musicians were sent for, the most munificent and alluring offers being made to procure them. Josquin came to the Pontifical Chapel during the popedom of Sixtus IV (1471 to 1484); two Belgians, Habrecht and Heinrich

Isaac (the German Arrigo Tedesco), dwelt about the same time in Florence; but these, as well as Josquin, returned after a short residence to their native place. The important moment for Italy had not yet arrived.

It was first in the splendid age of a Julius the Second, and his successor Leo the Tenth (1513-1521), that the Belgians were invited in great numbers to Italy; and then commenced properly the flourishing period of Belgian musicians, who, not only in Italy, but in Spain, Germany, and France, composed, taught, and directed the choirs. The invention of movable note-types, for the printing of music, by Ottavio Petrucci, of Fossembrone, in the Papal States, had an important effect at this period, and contributed much forthwith to extend the taste for music and musical science. This ingenious and enterprising printer commenced his labours in the year 1502, and brought them at Venice, *cum privilegio Signoriæ*, to great perfection. He departed, however, in 1513 to his native town of Fossembrone, where he still continued his occupations in printing, with a privilege from Pope Leo the Tenth, that extended over the whole of Christendom for twenty years. A considerable number of musical works were issued from his establishment up to 1520, in which year, as we learn from the list of his editions known to the public, his privilege expired with his life.

Petrucci printed, almost exclusively, the works of the Netherland masters, then living or recently deceased, and latterly confined himself in general to their compositions. I have given a catalogue of all his editions, now become very scarce and but little known, in an appendix to my treatise, so often mentioned, *die Verdienste der Niederländer, &c.* under the title, *die Incunabeln des Notendruckes*, where notice is also taken of the printing-offices which were established in the different cities of Italy, France, Germany, and the Netherlands, from the year 1520 until about the middle of that century.

If we take into consideration the trouble, with which the works of the great masters were in those days procured, and the expense at which they must have been transcribed (all music, especially choral, being written, or rather painted, with quadrangular notes of nearly two inches in height, and in books of a tremendous size, in conformity with the desks on which they were laid), and if we reflect how much more prolific, and therefore less expensive, was the new method, at this time introduced, than the wood cuts used in many places about the year 1500, occasionally with some degree of perfection and even of elegance, and which lasted as long as the exclusive privilege of the printers,—it may well be conceived that the new note-printing must have been as advantageous to the musical art, as the book-printing of an earlier invention had been to the revival of science half a century before.

After these general, and in some degree special, considerations of the causes which led to the rapid progress of the musical harmonic art, and its theory, in the age of which I am treating, let us now take a cursory glance at the distinguished characters of the eighth epoch, or that of Josquin, and compare the relative condition of music at this period in the several countries of Europe.

Foremost among the men by whom this epoch was enlightened, stands Ockenheim's worthiest pupil, the much celebrated JOSQUIN DES PRÉS (*Jodocus Pratensis*, or, *a Prato*), who was born, according to some authorities, at Cambray, although others mention Condé as the place of his nativity, whilst the supposition of those who affirm that he came from Prato, a town of Tuscany, and endeavour in this way to stamp him as an Italian, scarcely deserves notice, much less the task of any serious refutation. The year of his birth is not given; it merely appears that he left St. Quentin, where he was engaged as a singing boy, and went, after the breaking of his voice in 1455, to pursue his studies under the personal superintendence of Ockenheim.*

During the papal sway of Sixtus the Fourth (1471-1484) we find Josquin in the Pontifical Chapel, as cantore, where he was greatly respected; but he returned soon afterwards to his native country, and resided several years at Cambray. In 1498 he arrived at the court of Louis the Twelfth, and here also he only remained for a short time, going next, as it is conjectured, to Brussels, where he was eventually director of the Court Chapel, to the emperor Maximilian the First, and where he closed his active life about the year 1515.

Josquin deserves to be classed, beyond doubt, among the greatest musical geniuses of any period. He has been reproached (and, to say the truth, not without reason) for having practised musical tricks and contrivances to an inor-

* Concerning the birth-place of Josquin, the author has produced clear evidence in a late treatise (*Leip. Allgem. Mus. Zeitung*, 1835), that *Josquin des Prés was born at St. Quentin*, where he received his first musical instruction. The oldest and most authentic record, to which the assertions of late French writers must give place, is a collection of compositions in a codex, at St. Gallen, from the year 1530, wherein it says: *Jodocus Pratensis, vulgo Josquin du Pres, Belga Veromandus omnium princeps.* St. Quentin was the capital of the then so called *Vermandois.*

dinate degree, and with having exercised by his example in this respect a prejudicial influence on the art. This was, however, the failing of the age in which he lived: it is certain that each of his pieces, in the most laboured as well as in the most unpretending species of composition, is distinguished from every one of the innumerable works of his brother artists and imitators, by some decided trait of genius.

Josquin himself had many pupils, whose names appear as follows:—the Frenchmen Certon, Clement Jannequin, Maillart, Bourgogne, Moulu and Claudin Sermisy (not Le Jeune), who brought the art to France; among the Belgians, Mouton (director of the chapel to Louis the Twelfth and Francis the First); Adrien Petit, named also Coclicus, who afterwards taught and wrote in Germany; Arcadelt, Jacquet von Berchem, called in Italy, Jachet de Mantua, Gombert (afterwards director of the chapel to the emperor Charles the Fifth), the German Heinrich Isaac, (Arrigo Tedesco, director of the chapel to the emperor Maximilian the First), and many others.

At the same time with Josquin there flourished likewise other masters of the school of Ockenheim; particularly Pierre de la Rue, already mentioned, who was often erroneously taken for the Spaniard De Ruimonte, his junior by a century;

Agricola, Compère, Brumel, and Gaspard; not to enumerate several others, whose works appear in the editions of Petrucci, and are noticed in my treatise on the Musicians of the Netherlands.

During the epoch of Josquin, however, other nations had already began gradually to dispute with the Belgians, not indeed their precedency, but their former monopoly in music. There sprung up in Germany, in the last decennial periods of the fifteenth century, some keen contrapunctists; as such we may name, Adam de Fulda, a writer also on music; Stephen Mahu, Hermann Finck, and probably many others.

In France, those whom we have mentioned as pupils of Josquin, distinguished themselves during the latter half of this epoch, at which time also the Frenchman, Eleazar Genet, called *Il Carpentrasso*, (from his native town of Carpentras), was highly esteemed in the Pontifical chapel, and was even honoured with the dignity of a bishop by his great patron Leo the Tenth.

The Spaniards, too, were much liked in the Pontifical chapel as singers, and many of them became eminent as composers in the following epoch; in the present, however, there is no Spaniard deserving of notice as such.

England appears to have produced little of importance in this epoch.

The Italians, up to this period, had willingly supplied themselves and felt satisfied with the music which the ultramontanes gave them ready formed. Petrucci, with the exception of some trifles, of a certain Tromboncinus (1502), had only printed from Italian works as late as 1509, some very insignificant, and, in fact, bad samples of songs, which he calls *Frottole*, or ballads. The first Italian, worthy of the name of contrapunctist in this epoch, was *Costanzo Festa*, a singer in the Pontifical chapel, who is first noticed by Petrucci in 1514, and of whose works there were afterwards several prepared by him for the press. Ab. Baini regards him as the precursor of Palestrina; indeed, his contrapunctic works, (such as have become known) though distinguished neither by boldness nor energy, possess considerable gracefulness in the motives; a *Te Deum* in that simple style, of which Palestrina is reckoned the founder, if not to be compared with similar works of Palestrina and the subsequent Romans, is nevertheless performed once every year on a particular occasion in the Pontifical chapel.

In general it may be affirmed of the epoch of Josquin, that in it the contrapunctic art was most developed, and could scarcely have been carried farther. On the contrary, it belonged to the succeeding period to lead it back again within reasonable limits, and to regulate the forms of the more useful species of the obligato, or artfully completed counterpoint.

With regard to the organ, it is well known that, in the course of the fifteenth century, many new instruments were built and erected in the principal towns and cathedrals, nor can it be doubted but that the invention of many additional stops and other improvements in the mechanism may be ascribed to this period; still, in the representations of the organs of that time, we miss the pedal, which Bernhard the German had previously invented at Venice in 1470. However, it is not therefore less to be credited that the organists, who had at least a proper key-board for the fingers, already of considerable extension, would now be well skilled and practised in the science of counterpoint, having an instrument affording every means for its cultivation, and that in this respect they must have made no unimportant progress. One of the most celebrated is named Paul Hoffenheimer of Vienna, organist to Maximilian the First.

My honoured readers, and particularly those who are professors and amateurs of noble instruments, have, ere this, doubtless felt a desire to learn something of the condition of instrumental music at that early period; but hitherto there was little, if anything, to be told concerning it. During the periods, of which we have previously treated, there never existed the smallest idea of a proper, artistical, and substantial instrumental music: for strengthening or supporting the chorus, i. e. the singers, cornetti (in German, *Zinken)*, trombones, and perhaps trumpets, were mostly employed, all of which moved in unison with the voices.

The violin, viol, or violon, which had its origin in France from the old rebec, was, like the vielle—called by us the lyre or Bettlerleier—resigned to the hands of village fiddlers or itinerant musicians, being just as little in esteem as the performers, and at most only called for at a dance.

The instruments which obtained use in Germany about 1500, are described and represented in wood cuts, by Ottomanus Luscinius, in his *Masurgia* (Strasburg, 1536), and by Wirdung in his *Musika getutscht* (Basle, 1511). The violin is found among them, almost similar to that of modern times; flutes, or more properly fifes, of various dimensions, and with different names, even to the bass fife called Pommer or

Bombard; the square flute, shawms, trumpets, and trombones; the tromba marina, cythers and lutes, claviers and organs, with perfectly regulated key-boards. But still the instrumentalists, with the exception of the organists, were totally separated from the real or proper (scientifically educated) musicians, i. e. from the singers, (for the music masters were singers); and they formed a peculiar sect, under the name of town-fifers, music-fifers, or warders. They had also their own peculiar method of notation for the instruments, namely, the so-styled German *Tabulatura*, a notation which was formed of the old Gregorian or Guidonic letters. The lute-players, and cytherists, were also excluded from the rank of "musicians", and formed a separate class of themselves, with a very quaint and remarkable method of notation.* The harp was scarcely known at this time by musicians, probably because it wanted all the sub-semitones of the related keys. The clavier, or harpsichord, was merely for domestic use, and appropriated particularly for study. The organ we have already described.

Now, although these instruments had assumed as yet no importance in the musical world, there

* See my treatise already mentioned, *Die Tabulaturen der älteren Praktiker*.

nevertheless appeared from time to time certain persons who might be styled *virtuosi* in their way, and who were distinguished and rewarded, according to their merits, by different princes: to give, for instance, a striking example, such was Conrad Paulmann, of Nürnberg, a man blind from his birth, who is said to have excelled on all instruments, and is considered to have been the inventor of the lute-tabulatura. He died at Munich in 1473, after having formed many pupils.*

It has, moreover, been noticed by many writers,—and their observations are evidently confirmed by a perusal of the compositions of that early period, which contain a great extension of the parts, and frequent change of key,—that counterpoint, particularly such as was set to familiar songs, was performed by instruments of one kind or another, whatever may have been their nature or construction.

* For an interesting biography of Conrad Paulmann, see Gerber's *New Lexicon*.

CHAPTER IX.

EPOCH OF HADRIAN WILLAERT.

1520 TO 1560.

AMONGST the Belgians, who were partly invited and came partly of their own accord to seek their fortune about this time in Italy, was Adrian Willaert, himself a pupil of Mouton, and therefore in the second degree from the school of Josquin.* When still a young man, of about twenty-six years of age, after having become known as a composer, and having acquired some reputation in his own country, Willaert went first to Rome in or near the year 1518. One of his subsequent pupils, the celebrated Zarlino, relates the circumstance of Willaert having laid claim to the authorship of a favourite *Motette*, which had previously been considered, in the Pontifical Chapel, as the composition of Josquin; and that so great was the veneration and prejudice of the singers in favour of Josquin, who formerly be-

* According to some accounts a Pupil of Josquin.

longed to their body, that the *Motette* in question was from that moment entirely put aside. This was perhaps one of the reasons why Willaert met with no success at Rome, where the Pontifical Chapel set the fashion, and was probably the sole institution on which a musician could depend. He proceeded, therefore, to Venice, where he quickly found protection and employment.

In 1527, Willaert succeeded to the situation of maestro in the church of St. Mark, an office which had always been considered one of great dignity. He was the founder of the distinguished and afterwards renowned Venetian school; and it might be sufficient for his reputation here to state, that Cipriano de Rore, one of his countrymen, whom the enthusiastic regard of the Italians called *Il divino,*—Zarlino, the greatest theorist of the age, and even the reformer of theory,—Costanzo Porta, one of the greatest masters in the art of counterpoint,—and many other eminent composers, men of science, and writers (to say nothing of Alfonso della Viola, Nicolo Vicentino and others) were Willaert's pupils; and the pupils of these again established themselves in numerous towns of Upper Italy, where they composed and taught; by these means greatly extending the art and science of music.

Willaert was the first, as far as we know, who produced compositions for a greater number of voices than had previously appeared, namely, for six or seven; not in Canon, *plures ex una*, as was formerly the case; but, according to the testimony of Zarlino, he was also the inventor of compositions for two and three choruses, a species which was deservedly much liked and generally adopted, not only on account of the greater facility which it afforded to the singers in their performance of grand compositions without the aid of instruments, but also for the changes and union of the choruses and the superb effects thus occasioned, particularly in the larger churches of Italy, where there was always a sufficient number of voices for this purpose. The inventor of this species of composition had even from the beginning attached to it the normal law, invariably to be observed, that, in the union of the choruses, each one was compelled to contain separately within itself a regular and perfect harmony.

Willaert ended his industrious and praiseworthy career in 1563. His celebrated pupil, Cipriano de Rore, immediately succeeded him in the office of maestro at St. Mark's, and he was in turn succeeded two years afterwards by Zarlino.

Many other Belgians flourished during the epoch of Willaert, in the larger towns, principal churches, and courts of Italy: of these we need here only name some of the most remarkable: Arcadelt and Ghiselino d'Ankerts, both of them singers in the Pontifical Chapel; Jachet de Mantua, more properly Jacob von Berkhem, near Antwerp; and Claudius Goudimel of Burgundy, who opened a school in Rome about 1540, from which emanated (according to Baini's testimony) an Animuccio, a Giovanni Maria Nanini, and afterwards even the great Palestrina himself, with several more. The Belgians, moreover, enjoyed in this epoch, if not the monopoly, at least the supremacy, as regarded music, in Italy.

In the country of the Netherlands itself, as well as in Spain and Germany, Belgian musicians, in almost incredible numbers, industriously pursued their profession; their names and occasionally their productions are noticed in the author's treatise "*die Verdienste der Niederländer*," and in this place there is only occasion to mention, Clemens non Papa, Gombert, Crecquillon, Vaet, Maessens, all at the Imperial Court; Lupus, Manchicourt, Richefort, Cornelius Canis, Nicholaus Poyen, &c. &c.

Several Frenchmen were likewise much esteemed at this time in Italy, in the Pontifical Chapel; such as Carpentras, before mentioned, and Leonardo Barré of Limoges; besides the pupils of Josquin already spoken of, who still even belonged to this epoch, and many of whose works were published in Italy. About this time there sprung up in France also a multitude of composers, whose chansons, motettes, and even masses, were extensively circulated by means of the printing establishments of Paris and Lyons, opened in 1530, which produced specimens of printing as prolific as they were beautiful.

Among the Spaniards may be here named Morales, one of the most excellent musicians of his time; and Escobedo, particularly distinguished for his erudition; each was a member of the Pontifical Chapel; Vaqueras, and Guerrero, who was Maître de Chapelle in Madrid to Charles the Fifth.

England's most distinguished contrapunctists appear for the first time, in the epoch which immediately follows; but in the present one we find mention made of a crowned head, Henry VIII,—a Hymn of whose composition, quite free from grammatical errors (*Te lucis anteterminum*, probably with English words) is said to be still used in English Cathedrals. Many other names, such as those of Fairfax, Cornish, Tudor, Banister, &c., have been preserved by the historians of the country, which nevertheless, strictly speaking, did not attain extraordinary celebrity.

The Germans reckoned in this epoch no inconsiderable number of musicians, who composed and taught, more especially in the boundaries of the empire, at the Courts, Free Cities, and Monasteries; and who published their works in Augsburg, Nürnburg, Leipsic, and Wittemburg; such were Benedictus Ducis of Ulm, much esteemed in all quarters; Sixtus Dieterich; Adam Renner; Hulderick Brätel; Thomas Stolzer; Martin Agricola, who was also a writer; Johannes Stahl, and not a few others, who appear in the throng of this period. Their works are by no means inferior, on the average, to those of their foreign contemporaries; and it can only be imputed to the prejudice continually entertained in favour of the Belgians, that German musicians were not heard of in Italy: that no examples of their works are to be found among the publications which issued from the printing establishments of that country; and that even several of the great German Courts preferred, in those days and long afterwards, in an especial degree, the musicians of the Netherlands.

It might be deemed invidious to bring forward in a prominent manner the name of one person in preference to another, among so great a number of these active German composers; still I cannot refrain from a particular mention of two men of acknowledged merit,—Johann Walter, the singing master and maestro di capella to the electoral prince of Saxony, and Ludwig Senfl, pupil of the famous Heinrich Isaac, and maestro di capella to the duke Louis of Bavaria.

At the beginning of this epoch Italy possessed only Costanzo Festa, who already has been honourably noticed as having belonged to the former epoch, or that of Josquin. He died in 1545. Even Baini mentions but one master of any reputation, who existed at Rome about 1540, of the name of Dominico Ferabosco, and a young man not yet arrived at mature age, Gio. Bettini, of Brescia, to whom, however, may be added a few from upper Italy,—for instance, Girolamo Parabosco, Claudio Veggio, Michele Novarese, Vincenzo Ruffo, P. Maria Riccio of Padua, Paolo Jacopo Palazzo, Perison (Cambio) of whose talents Ant. Franc. Doni, in his (otherwise perfectly worthless) *Dialogo della Mus.* 1544, has communicated some respectable specimens; these were all, generally speaking, merely beginners, springing from the Venetian school, but some of them, at a later period, obtained considerable celebrity.

Willaert's most distinguished pupil, Giuseppe Zarlino, formerly mentioned, is regarded as having been in this epoch a most classical theorist and scientific writer. Another scarcely less celebrated in the same age is Henricus Lorritus, commonly called Glareanus, from his native town of Glarus, of whose Dodecachordon we have already been called upon to pronounce an opinion. In this work which appeared at Basle in 1547, the author teaches twelve church scales, which he wished to be regarded as ancient, instead of the eight which existed up to his time, current only in the schools; and from these he appears, being a zealous Hellenist, to have wished a revival of the ancient Greek scales, although their names are only given in an arbitrary manner. The above scales, or rather their nomenclature, became afterwards very popular, but were the source of many errors, inasmuch as they caused those of Glareanus to be regarded as the ancient Greek scales; in fact, they are nothing more than a continuation of the old Ambrosian, for, as these included merely the scales of D E F G, Glareanus completed the cycle by adding the scale of A with that of C, omitting the B, whose fifth G would have been a false one.

In the above scales or keys, which are distinguished by the nomenclature of Glareanus, the chorals (psalm tunes) which were adapted by learned German composers to Luther's metrical text, are for the most part composed; although some of these scales, which contain within themselves false relationship, are never employed, or at, least, not in their purity (if I may so express myself); and have at all events been obliged to undergo necessary modifications in their contrapunctic treatment, in the same way as the Ambrosian and Gregorian scales were modified long before them. The knowledge of them is only necessary, perhaps, in our own days for the organist, and has merely an historical merit, in so far as it leads to an acquaintance with the different authors, many of whom still attach to them a certain degree of importance. Those who may require more accurate information on the subject of them, will find all they can wish for in any musical lexicon.

If we examine the effects of this epoch, embracing a space of about forty years, we shall find that music had experienced indeed no essential reform, but that the composers had reached a certain degree of dexterity quite uncommon with their predecessors,—that the parts move with more certainty, and even partake of something graceful,—that the immoderate tricks of art, such as canons and enigmas, gradually went out of fashion,—that a great portion of the subtleties of the old mensural theory by degrees was laid aside as superfluous,—that the ligatures, with a few exceptions, disappeared,—and that the reading and deciphering of the compositions of this epoch into modern notation and score, now no longer present any serious difficulty.

One innovation of this epoch was the introduction of madrigals about the year 1540. The madrigal is a short poem, which has for its subject either love, or the scenes of pastoral life, and concludes with some witty or intellectual idea; in which respect it resembles an epigram, which it generally somewhat exceeds in length. The composition of madrigals first afforded to composers the opportunity, and inculcated indeed the necessity, of inventing a motive or melody which should be characteristic of the sense implied in the words, and to which no attention had hitherto been paid in the composition of masses, motetts, and such like productions.

The madrigal was composed for three, four, or five voices; sometimes, but very rarely, for six or seven,—with a tolerably free counterpoint; and it was not until a far more advanced period that artificial counterpoint was employed in the madrigal beyond what had been previously attempted in this kind of composition. The introduction of the madrigal style, as chamber music, was the most important step towards a refinement of the taste, not of the composer alone, but also of the musical public. In this species of composition, which had its origin in the Venetian school, the Belgians located in

Italy particularly distinguished themselves; and subsequently the Italians, who began at that time to flourish, acquired in it some notoriety. The predilection for the madrigal, and the demand for compositions of this kind, if we may judge from the number produced, must have been unbounded. Madrigals, or effusions of art in a similar style, under the name of ricercari, fantasias, or toccate, were also composed for instruments, or performed upon the organ.

With the madrigal there appeared about the same time another, but less dignified species of chamber music for several voices,—songs, which imitated the tone of the people in their poetry, and which were set to music with a still simpler counterpoint; these were called *Canzoni villanesche*, or *Villanelle alla Napolitana*, and were peculiar to upper Italy alone.

The printing establishments, especially that of Gardani at Venice, were unwearied in producing the works of composers living in Italy, whether natives or foreigners; the art of singing from the book was now more and more extensively cultivated, from the esteem in which practical music was held as a social talent; and it would be difficult to point out in succeeding years any other period at which music had taken a flight comparatively so vigorous and universal.

CHAPTER X.

EPOCH OF PALESTRINA.

1560 to 1600.

From what has been already stated, we have been led to perceive that many composers of no ordinary talent had before this time attained a degree of eminence; and that their works, notwithstanding many defects or errors of the school which still prevailed, had elevated the minds of their contemporaries in the temples, and delighted them in the circles of social life, prior to the appearance of the justly celebrated Palestrina, who became famous by his musical compositions about the middle of the sixteenth century. He had published, in 1554, a volume of masses, his first work, which gained him the esteem of all learned men and the favour of Pope Julius the Third; his epoch may, however, with more propriety be dated from 1560, or even a few years later, when some of his other compositions were performed by the singers in the Pontifical Chapel, and so delighted Pope Pius the Fourth and the Cardinals, by their sublime simplicity and force, that they laid the foundation of his subsequent reputation.

Giovanni Pierluigi da Palestrina, more commonly known simply as Palestrina or Prænestinus, was born not far from Rome, in the small town of Palestrina, the ancient Præneste, in 1524, according to Baini's account.

In 1540 (consequently at the age of sixteen) he was sent by his parents to Rome, that he might study and cultivate the much esteemed and profitable art of music, for which he evinced a peculiar predilection, and where all who pursued the science, foreigners in particular, more especially Spaniards, Frenchmen, and Belgians, were greatly respected. Among the latter, at that time, was Claudius Goudimel (of whom we have spoken in the former epoch), who superintended a school in Rome from which emanated many a famous pupil. This excellent composer, who afterwards established himself in Lyons, where he was put to death as a Huguenot in 1572, had the honour (as Baini has proved by documents, in reply to the doubts entertained by Burney and others) of being the teacher of the illustrious Palestrina.

In 1551, Palestrina was appointed *magister puerorum*, and afterwards *magister capellæ*, in the chapel founded by Pope Julius the Second, and called, after him, the Julian Chapel, in the Basilica of the Vatican of St. Peter. In 1554, as we have already observed, he published his first work, which gained him the patronage of Pope Julius the Third; and in 1555 he obtained a situation amongst the singers of the Pontifical chapel, on his acceptance of which he resigned the situation of *Magister capellæ* above mentioned. His patron died a few months afterwards; and the countenance of Pope Marcellus the Second, the successor of Julius in the Holy See, could have been of no great service to him, though he was formerly prepossessed in his favour, as this Pontiff ceased to exist after a brief sovereignty of only twenty-one days. The successor of Marcellus, Pope Paul the Fourth, having discovered that some of the singers in the Pontifical Chapel were not in holy orders, and were besides actually married, raised objections to this state of things, and Palestrina, who had not the plea of celibacy to advance, was discharged in the course of the same year in which he had been appointed, receiving only a meagre pension; and he would have been reduced with his family to penury, had not the vacant situation in St. Giovanni di Laterano been soon afterwards offered to him. This office, though but a poor one, he thankfully accepted, and continued in the faithful discharge of its duties for six years, until he received in 1561 a somewhat more lucrative situation in St. Maria Maggiore. Though none of his works during this period were printed, he was by no means inactive; and among the compositions which he wrote for his church was one called the *Improperia*, which was performed for the first time on Good Friday 1560, and created such a universal sensation, that Pius the Fourth begged to have a copy of it. From that time until the present day, the *Improperia* has been performed every year on Good Friday, and it may be found in the collection of music selected for the Holy Week, in the Pontifical Chapel. It was published in 1772 by Burney in London; and afterwards by Kühnel at Leipsic. To the same Pontiff Palestrina presented, in 1562, a six part mass, upon *ut re mi fa sol la*, the *Crucifixus* of which particularly delighted both his holiness and the cardinals.

At the Council of Trent, which, after an adjournment of nearly ten years, met again about this period (1562), the purification of church music was deemed essential, and underwent discussion. The fathers strongly objected to the mixture of profane and frivolous strains with sacred music; for the abuse still existed of having masses composed on the airs of profane and frequently even frivolous songs. It must be admitted that such a compound was in every respect highly indecorous; but the objection, in fact, applied only to the name; for the song, as a *Tenore* or *Cantus firmus*, could in no degree be recognized by the listener, owing to the counterpoint of the other parts, and the ecclesiastical text which accompanied it. But the greatest fault concerned the style of composition itself; because, as the complaint purported, the holy text was quite incomprehensible through the contrapunctic contortions in the canons and fugues. Figural music was on the point of being excluded from the church; the defence set up by some of the legates, however, *Non impedias Musicam*, and a representation made by the emperor Ferdinand the First, through his ambassador, soothed the angry disposition of the fathers; and it was resolved, that the regulations for any improvement that might be considered necessary, should be left, wholly and solely, to the determination of the council.

In 1565 the pope nominated a commission, comprising eight cardinals, who were to take charge of this matter; and to this council were added eight members of the chapel. It was specially urged by the above conclave, that masses or motetts on profane melodies should be no longer performed, even when the same were united to sacred words or christian sentiments. The demand of the cardinals, that the sacred words of the text should be uninterrupted and distinct, met with great opposition, the singers representing that the required intelligibility could not always be obtained; that the essence of harmonic music consisted in imitation and fugues, the withdrawal of which would be tantamount to its annihilation; and, moreover, that in long pieces this demand could not possibly be fulfilled. It was ultimately decided, that experiment should be made of some subject in a grand yet simple style; and, owing to the favourable impression that still remained on the minds of the cardinals regarding the *Improperia*, and *Missa ut re mi fa sol la* (particularly the *Crucifixus* of the same), Palestrina was employed to solve this problem; whereupon he composed three masses, each for six voices, in the spirit of the appointed theme. On the performance of these works, the difficulty was declared to have been obviated; the third composition in particular carried away the palm; and an opportunity was embraced for introducing it at the first ensuing festival, in the Pontifical Chapel, when it gave universal delight, the Pope and cardinals, together with many other competent judges, being present.

These are the masses which, with a few others, Palestrina dedicated in one volume to Philip the Second of Spain, in 1567, under the title of *Missa Papæ Marcelli*, which name he bestowed upon them in gratitude to the memory of his great benefactor, Pope Marcellus the Second. The tradition hitherto common respecting the origin of these celebrated masses,—that Pope Marcellus had determined, in 1555, to banish music from the church, —that Animuccia had persuaded his holiness to postpone the issue of the Bull until he could hear a mass written in the true ecclesiastical style of the young composer Palestrina,—that the latter, by his six part masses, had not only succeeded in reconciling the Pontiff to music in general, but even induced him to become its patron, —and that these masses had consequently received the name of *Missa Papæ Marcelli*,—is now proved to have been without foundation, from the excellent historical and critical researches of Baini; although it is no less true that it was the compositions of Palestrina which convinced the council assembled for the reform of church music, that the judicious and tasteful employment of the harmonic contrapunctic art was fully adapted to elevate the mind of the hearer, and to assist devotion; and that by these means he succeeded in establishing for it a lasting place in the ritual of the church.

The Pope honoured Palestrina with a testimony of his satisfaction by naming him as composer to the Pontifical Chapel (not as *Magister capellæ*, for this post could only be invested in the person of a church dignitary); and his income derived some augmentation from the appointment.

In 1571, on the death of Animuccia, one of the pupils of Goudimel, Palestrina succeeded him as master of the chapel in the Vatican of St. Peter, the same office which in a former year (1555) he had resigned so greatly to his disadvantage.

About this time Giovanni Maria Nanini and Palestrina, who had long been friends, and originally fellow-students under Goudimel, opened the celebrated school in Rome, which gave birth to many an eminent composer. This school was afterwards continued by Bernardino Nanini, the nephew and pupil of the former; and the beneficial influence which it exercised in all quarters was no where more conspicuous than in the Pontifical Chapel.

Palestrina ended his active and useful life in 1594; and his son undertook after his death to publish a considerable number of his works, most of which have appeared in various collections. These are reckoned generally as—twelve books of masses for four, five, and six voices (Ab. Baini is in possession of a thirteenth and fourteenth book in MS.); one volume of masses for eight voices; two volumes of motetts for four, and five volumes of the same for five voices; one volume of offertories (sixty-eight pieces); two volumes of litanies, besides many single compositions of this kind which appear in different collections (Ab. Baini possessing three volumes of still unpublished motetts, and a third volume of litanies); one volume of hymns for all the holy-days of the year; one volume containing the *Magnificat* for five and six voices, and another for eight; one volume of lamentations (two or three volumes unpublished in the possession of Ab. Baini);* two volumes of madrigals for four voices; two volumes (sacred), for five voices, independently of some madrigals dispersed among other collections.

Palestrina's works were, like all other musical productions at that time, printed only in separate parts, most of which have since been put into score by his admirers; and not only does every collector of ancient and classic music pride himself in possessing Palestrina in this form, but wheresoever vocal societies have been established, his music and its effects are no longer unknown.

* Since published by Alfieri.—*Translator.*

Authors appear never to be wearied in expressing their admiration and praise of Palestrina; and it is difficult to resist the temptation to quote in this place a number of excellent passages from the most approved *literati* and writers. In the meritorious Ab. Baini, Palestrina has found a most faithful biographer, from whose great work an appropriate extract has been communicated by Winterfeld, in a short treatise published at Breslau in 1832, which is so far excellent as it relates to the life of Palestrina, without any reference to the treasures revealed in the Abbé's work concerning the history of the art or its literature; but a better conception or estimate of the spirit of Palestrina has rarely ever been made than in a small pamphlet published at Heidelberg in 1825 (second edition 1826), under the title of *Ueber die Reinheit der Tonkunst.*

The striking style of Palestrina has been appropriately described by a modern German writer (*Darstellungen aus der Geschichte der Musik von C. Chr. F. Krause*, Göttingen, 1827) in the following manner: "With respect to the peculiar style of Palestrina, it is characterized by an elevated and severe grandeur, similar to that which a century later was introduced by Leonardo Leo into the style of church music, and which was distinguished by beautiful and substantial melody freely united with harmony. In Palestrina's works we find the chord successions are for the most part pure, and but little prepared or accommodated, and seldom tempered by chromatic tones; rapid progressions to distant keys, whose fundamental notes lie in the diatonic scale; a sparing, but at the same time forcible, use of the chords of the seventh and ninth; and generally a rare but consequently more effective employment of the chromatic.* In my opinion this style possesses an imperishable worth, as one perfect of its kind, and founded on an intimate knowledge of the human mind and feelings. The predilection for it therefore can never decay; the most intelligent connoisseurs of both ancient and modern music are at the same time the greatest venerators of the style of Palestrina, and as the simple song of the Choral by the pupils of the Thomas school at Leipsic drew tears from a Mozart, no lover of art, with feeling in his soul, will ever be able to subdue his emotions at the tones of Palestrina."

We should form but an imperfect idea of this master, were we to conclude that all his works are composed in the same simple style as the *Missa*

* Notes which were raised or lowered chromatically by a ♯ or ♭, in contradistinction to the *c d e f g a b*, which alone were regarded as natural.—*Translator*.

Papæ Marcelli, by means of which the fathers of the church were reconciled to figural music; the biographer of Palestrina himself remarks, that he never wrote a second work in the same style—*Non seppe ricalcar le proprie sue orme.* In his best works he finds it difficult to conceal his education in the school of the Netherlands, how much soever he may have elevated its style by his own originality. In him, or more properly speaking in his works, every gradation of the contrapunctic art may be found, from the simplest species, which consists of a mere succession of chords, or note against note,—through the *stile familiare*, as it is called,—up to the most complicated canons, as learned as even a Belgian could have conceived them. Of the *stile familiare* one example Josquin had already left behind him in his masses; and early specimens of it are here and there to be found among the Italians, as in Costanzo Festa; in the contemporary Belgian composers of madrigals, such as Cyprian de Rore, Arcadelt, &c.; and even among the Germans of a much earlier age, of whom Stephen Mahu (in the *Lamentations*) may be cited as an instance. Still, in the fetters, with which Palestrina apparently restricted himself, he moves with a freedom and grace that never allow the restraint to be perceived; the fire of his genius, as may be gathered from Burney, glows throughout, in spite of the cramping bonds of the *Cantus firmus*, of the canons, fugues, and their inversions, which caused all other composers, except himself, to appear cold and inanimate.

As examples of Palestrina's simplest compositions we may cite his *Improperia*, and in some measure also the vesper-psalms, the litanies, and lamentations. Of the more erudite and artistic works, among many others may be noticed his canonic mass, called *Ad fugam;* the concluding strophes of his inimitable hymns, in which the *Cantus firmus* is conducted generally with two voices, in the strictest canon, whilst the remaining parts imitate the single members of the phrase most independently one with another; or that offertory, *Tribularer si nescirem*, in which a middle part ascends with a short theme (Pes) interrupted by rests, five times a degree higher, and then in like manner gradually descends, and is repeated in the same order in the second part, whilst the remaining parts perform among themselves various fugued pieces. Even the *Missa Papæ Marcelli* presents throughout imitation among the parts, of which the spiritual commissioners, not having been initiated into the mysteries of the art, had certainly no suspicion.

Baini explains and describes no less than ten different styles, which he assures us he has discovered in the works of Palestrina. Baini's reviewer (Winterfeld) disputes these different styles, and will admit only one as belonging to Palestrina, in which respect, according to the definition which he gives of this term, he is perfectly right; but this is a mere contest about words. If Baini had written his work on Palestrina in German, he would probably have used the expression so technical with us, "Schreibart," or "Setzart";* and the strictest æsthetical critic would have raised as little objection to the idea as to the expression, although according to Sulzer *(Theori der schönen Wissenschaften)*, and Koch *(Musical Lexicon)* even the term "style" may be very properly defended in the sense attached to it by Baini. We must, however, admit that Baini does not furnish the reader with a plain understanding of the difference in these ten styles, notwithstanding all the sumptuousness of language employed in his explanation; he ought to have annexed a characteristic example of. each of them; or he should at all events have referred the possessors of musical libraries to such an example. And

* Writing, or setting music to words—composition.—*Translator.*

yet, all the connoisseurs of the musical productions of the period, the works of Palestrina more especially, will certainly feel as little doubt that he adopted many different styles of composition, as they will entertain the conviction that he is known by one wholly peculiar to himself, which in every instance is easy to be recognized.

Among the fellow-citizens and contemporaries of Palestrina in Rome, who particularly distinguished themselves in the church style of music, were Animuccia, who died 1571, both his predecessor and successor in the office of music director at the Vatican, himself also a pupil of Goudimel; Giovanni Maria Nanini, to whom we have already accorded our meed of praise; and after him Tomaso Lodovico da Vittoria, a Spaniard by birth, but educated at Rome. The two last were singers (members) in the Pontifical Chapel, where their works are still held in estimation, and where certain of their motetts are performed at the present day on particular festivals.

Those who became most eminent in the latter years of this brilliant epoch at Rome, were Felice Anerio; Dragoni (a pupil of Palestrina); Ruggiero Giovanelli; Bernardino Nanini, and Ingegneri; the two last belonging to the new Roman school: and in the department of the madrigal, Luca Marenzio *(Il cigno più soave dell' Italia)* may be named as having been particularly celebrated.

Meanwhile the pupils of the Venetian school had established themselves in all the larger cities of upper Italy, and propagated their science and art. Their school by degrees became blended with that of Rome; maintaining, however, continually even to later times, its peculiar character; making itself remarkable by a propensity to follow a more artificial kind of composition, approaching to that which was, rather improperly, called the chromatic; and by its gradual desertion of the old scales (keys).

Among the most distinguished masters of upper Italy may be specially enumerated, Andreas Gabrieli, and somewhat later his nephew Giovanni Gabrieli, each successively organists of the cathedral of St. Mark; Baltassare Donati, *Magister capellæ* in the same place of worship; Gastoldi at Milan; Claudio Merulo and Pietro Ponzio at Parma; Andrea Rota at Bologna; Orazio Vecchi at Modena; Alessandro Strigio and Marco Gagliano at Florence, &c.

Naples was not at this time celebrated for composers of any great merit, neither can a native school in any respect be assigned to it at the period in question: a learned *dilettante*,

Gesualdo Principe di Venosa supplied the public in these days with a large number of madrigals, which were much liked at the time, frequently sung, and said to have been highly commended. Examples of these have been produced in modern times by Hawkins and Burney, and have even been quoted by Padre Martini as models of the madrigal style; but this praise would, perhaps, have been applied to them solely with regard to form and manner, since it never could have been an enviable pleasure to listen to them; and it is impossible that the splendid melody of the more recent Neapolitan school could ever have emanated from them, as it has somewhere been asserted.

The Belgians had even in the epoch of Palestrina, if I may be pardoned the expression, a *hand* in the *game;* although their influence in foreign countries was visibly on the decline, owing to the strenuous opposition already given by able composers of other nations. The Netherland school, however, had produced one master among many others who was of the same age and contemporary with Palestrina, and who contended with him for the palm of reputation. This was Orlandus de Lassus of Mons, who, after having visited various foreign parts in his youth, held the office of *Magister capellæ* in one of the principal churches at Rome; then filled a similar office for several years at Antwerp; and was finally invited to the court of Munich, in which city, after a long and successful career, he closed a laborious and profitable life, highly respected and loaded with honours, in the same year (1594) which witnessed the death of Palestrina. This illustrious man at once enlightened and ended the great period of the Belgian masters, which for two hundred years had given to the world a vast number of excellent composers, among whom many arrived at no inconsiderable distinction. Music, which had been transplanted by them into Italy, now flourished in that country as a native art; and in like manner as the Netherlands had acted in former years, so now did Italy despatch her sons into all lands where music was cultivated, until they attained that supremacy throughout Europe which they have upheld to our own times, and which at the present day yields only to the German school in the department of instrumental music, brought of late to so much perfection. With the decreasing demands for Belgian musicians and composers, there was naturally a diminution of encouragement for natives in the mother-country to devote themselves to an art which no longer, as formerly, promised them fame and fortune in a foreign land. This circumstance, together with the religious disturbances and the oppressions which about this time harassed those once flourishing and contented provinces, led to the downfall of their schools of art; and from this prostration they were less able to raise themselves again, since the sense and taste displayed in the epoch which immediately followed, inclined towards the newly invented dramatic music, and the styles in affinity with it, which at the period could not be cultivated in the Netherlands, from the want of theatres, the rarity of opportunities as well as of models, and even from the deficiency of public opinion in its favour.

Musical literature in France during this epoch has displayed no small number of titles and names; but these have not reached any celebrity beyond the precincts of their own country; and we have just reason, I think, to draw the conclusion, that the art must there have made a retrograde movement. Claude Goudimel of Burgundy, and Claude le Jeune of Valenciennes, who were domiciled about the end of this epoch at the French court, each being from the Netherland school, can form no exception to this remark.

The school that still existed at this time in

England had a Tallis and his pupil Bird, both organists to Queen Elizabeth, whose works may indeed be placed in juxta-position with those of the best of their contemporaries. Towards the end of this epoch, and partly in the beginning of the following, there flourished in the same country Dr. Bull, and a multitude of popular madrigal writers, whose very pleasing works have now become known in Germany by means of a new edition lately published in London, in which among other names we find those of Bateson, Bennet, Dowland, Gibbon, Morley (a writer also on theory), Ward, Wilby, Weelkes, and many others, the memory of which has been revived by Hawkins and Burney.

In Germany both composition and printing were assiduously cultivated throughout this epoch. At the imperial court, we find two able masters, Jakob Gallus and Hans Leo von Hasler, the latter a pupil of the Venetian Giovanni Gabrieli; and towards the end of this period the following masters also distinguished themselves: Hieronymus Prætorius in Hamburgh, who had himself visited Rome, where he was much esteemed for his compositions; Jakob Mayland; Gregor Aichinger, and others.

In the review of the same epoch and of the productions belonging to it, we find, what could not well be otherwise, a considerable progress not only with regard to purity and richness of harmony, but also in respect to invention, and to melody both expressive and agreeable; the modulation of the harmony in particular being more varied and decided than in former epochs; although the composers, except in rare cases, still limited themselves to the keys of the diatonic scale and their natural common chords, not easily permitting themselves to modulate into the (then called) *Cantus durus*, i. e. keys with one or more sharps. Even at this time, however, many composers had made experiments; and Cyprian de Rore published a whole volume of madrigals entitled *Chromatic*, which are so far-fetched, both as to harmony and melody, that, as we may well imagine, they found no particular favour, and met with few imitators. Still it is not improbable that in the course of time they may have given to the reflecting artist, as well as to the theorist, an impulse towards research, and the gradual knowledge of the relationship of keys, together with the means of modulating into new ones, a method never in former days attempted. This source of information might probably have been sooner attained, had not Palestrina's example too splendidly proved what a great variety of most charming modulations might be gained in the diatonic scale without such an innovation; and had not the school asserted with the most constant pertinacity the exclusive value of the old keys, and defended itself against those innovators with two flats or two sharps more than the normal key.

One thing we must not allow to pass unnoticed, namely, that the composers of that time, the Italians of the new school as well as the Belgians, firmly believed themselves to have completely satisfied the demands which were exacted respecting the purity of the harmony, when in the movements of the several parts against each other there appeared no kind of error. The relationship of the chords in their succession seems to have been no object of their particular care; but we should be doing them injustice were we to complain of their disregard of rules which did not then exist; although, precisely on account of this deficiency, their works cannot be recommended as free from objection in respect to harmony, or as models for imitation; neither should they be performed before a modern public without previous examination and selection (in some cases, also, not without the addition of the fundamental and necessary sharps, flats, or naturals required in the modulations); nor should access be permitted in general to the study of them, except to pupils as well versed in the knowledge of our rules as of those belonging to the old scales (keys). It is, however, perfectly true that the circumstance above quoted, together with that of clinging to the old conventional keys, gave in a direct manner the necessary impulse to these exceedingly heterogeneous, and often incredibly effective modulations, which we admire in the works of the time as of a character exclusively their own, and now incapable of imitation.

One practice peculiar to this epoch, in common with those which preceded it, since the time of Dufay, consisted in an avoidance of the thirds in the concluding chords, where the established rule demanded what was called a "perfect" consonance. Composers who have written in the *stile da capella*, or the so-called style of Palestrina, down almost to our own day, have affectedly imitated this caprice, which was at best merely a remnant of the Grecian theory not yet rejected by the schools, where the rank of a consonance was denied to the third, and which therefore the theory of the middle ages scarcely dared to adopt, or only adopted with timidity and by no means as absolute.

CHAPTER XI.

EPOCH OF MONTIVERDE.

1600 TO 1640.

A VERY remarkable epoch now opens upon us;—remarkable, not as if music had now undergone an immediate and important revolution, or even a considerable reform, nor as if this epoch had been in any particular manner distinguished for having given birth to works eclipsing all which had previously appeared; although many very able composers flourished in the course of it, such as Agostini, Catalani, Cifra, Croce, the two Mazzochi, Giacobbi, Montiverde, and even Allegri (author of the much prized *Miserere* of the Pontifical Chapel); in Germany also an Erbach, Michael Prætorius, and many others; but because in this epoch there sprang up a new kind of composition, signalized at first, indeed, only by feeble efforts, from the cultivation of which, however, music shortly received an essentially different bias; and because a path was now prepared for arriving at the highest perfection of the art of sound.

About the commencement of the seventeenth century there appeared, almost at the same time, three different styles;—the dramatic, which was the origin of what is termed the opera; the monody, or melody for one voice with harmonic instrumental accompaniments; and church concerts, a species of composition, in which, whilst one, two, three or more voices performed the *Cantilena*, an accompanying instrument (generally the organ) was required to complete the harmony.

In the former dramatic representations accompanied by music, which had taken place in various towns of Italy and Germany, the dialogue was declaimed, and choruses in the style of the motett or madrigal were sung either in front of or behind the stage, at the conclusion of the acts or some of the scenes. A work so composed is no more deserving of the name of opera than the attempt would be which Orazio Vecchi made at Modena, in 1597, with his *Anfiparnaso*, a production wherein choruses, after the fashion of five-part madrigals, were sung behind the wings, after a succession of burlesque scenes had been enacted on the stage by the *dramatis personæ;* and it can just as little be pronounced a work of dramatic musical art, as it can be looked upon in the light of the beginning of the *Arioso* style, or even of the *Opera Buffa*.

Real musicians knew and practised nothing but their counterpoint; as to songs or melodies for one, two, or three voices, with an accompaniment, according to our modern interpretation of the word, they had not even been thought of: but in the class of real musicians there can, of course, be no intention of including ballad singers, terpsichorean and holiday fiddlers, itinerant pipers, cythera-beaters, nor (with deference be it spoken) even the *dilettanti*.

The first idea of monody had its origin at Florence, in an assembly of artists and literati, accustomed to meet at the house of the noble Giovanni Bardi, Conte di Vernio, where they amused themselves generally with subjects of art, and discussed the possibility of bringing such to perfection. Vincenzo Galilei, a good performer on the lute, and a clever musician as well as an esteemed writer (the father of Galileo Galilei, afterwards so pre-eminently distinguished as a mathematician and astronomer), was encouraged by these discussions to attempt, in the first instance, the performance of some fragments or passages from the works of popular poets, which he set to music for his own voice, and accompanied on his favourite instrument. This undertaking was received with great applause; and, so far as we know, it was the first experiment in monody. The inclination and feeling, however, of this very learned body tended strongly to the revival of that dramatic music which is said to have been used in representing the ancient Greek tragedies, and to have produced such wonderful effects; but this object could alone be accomplished, as was most justly observed, by the discovery of a style of composition which should occupy a place between real song and mere declamation, and which would totally differ from the one previously in use.

Among the musicians who at this time visited the house of Count Vernio, were Jacopo Peri, and Giulio Caccini, a Roman, who had established himself at Florence, and was distinguished as a singer and teacher. Another Roman, Emilio del Cavaliere, was also connected with the society, and various circumstances render it probable that he even remained for a season at Florence, taking part in the discussions of this flourishing private academy.

Emilio del Cavaliere, whom we find at Rome in 1590, may probably during his stay at Florence have seized upon the idea with the execution of which he employed himself on his return to the holy city. He gave at Rome, with wonderful success, in several private circles, some pastoral poems: namely, *Il Satiro*, *La Desperazione di Fileno*, and *Il Giuoco della Cieca*, in 1590; whilst Peri, about seven years afterwards, performed his pastoral poem of *Dafne*, in Florence.

Subsequently to these preparatory experiments others were undertaken on a more extended scale; and there were performed almost simultaneously in 1600, a grand oratorio at Rome, entitled *L'anima e corpo*, composed by Emilio, and a drama at Florence, under the title of *Euridice*, the work of the celebrated poet Rinuccini, set to music by Peri and Caccini, the latter composition being produced on the occasion of a particular solemnity. Peri and Caccini each thoroughly completed his share of this production; and the *Euridice* appeared twice during the same year. It was printed first with the music of the one composer, and then with that of the other, both being published at the same time with the oratorio above mentioned. The earlier experiments, however, in 1590, to which we have alluded, have not been handed down to us, either in print or manuscript.

In 1600, moreover, the *Arianna* of Rinuccini, with music by Peri, and *Il Rapimento di Cefalo* of Chiabrera, with music by Caccini, were produced successfully at Florence; and the same *Arianna*, with music by Claudio Montiverde, at the court of Mantua, where the *Orfeo* of Rinuccini, set to music also by Montiverde, was likewise performed in 1607.

The path was now opened; and though for some time longer the public was contented with the already existing operas, still Montiverde, *Magister capellæ* at St. Mark's, wrote three more in Venice between this period and the year 1642. At Bologna there is said to have been performed, in 1610, a work called *Andromeda*, by Giacobbi; and it is reported also, that, in conjunction with Gagliano the Florentine, and Quagliati the Roman, the same composer produced in 1616 another opera named *Euridice;* but of this there is no trace extant even at Bologna.

Little can be said in praise of the above dramatic compositions. The recitative, accompanied by a *Basso continuo*, is quite as pitiful as it is stiff and void of all expression; and was still inconceivably distant from the recitative we find in Scarlatti some forty years later.

The intermediate choruses, which are extant, prove the originators of the dramatic style neither to have been great contrapunctists, nor possessed of an inventive genius. There is nowhere the least semblance of an aria, nor anything whatever deserving to be called a dramatic melody. What we know of the dramatic works of Montiverde is not calculated to raise them much higher in our estimation than those of his predecessors; although he is otherwise regarded as an able contrapunctist in the church style, and has proved himself a spirited composer by his very valuable madrigals.

Thus insignificant at first was the grain of mustard-seed, which at a later period took such deep root, and grew to that gigantic tree, whose branches overspread and shaded the entire field.

From the year 1637 until nearly the end of that epoch of which we are now treating, several composers of operas appeared at Venice; but as they arrived at distinction in the following period, we will advert to them hereafter.

The experiments made by Caccini in monody (in his *Nuove Musiche*, 1601) are unfortunately not much better than his *Stile rappresentativo;* and I am at a loss to conceive how these could have derived any great assistance from the new method he at that time adopted in singing, according to the description given of it by Michael Prætorius in the *Syntagma.*

Church concerts, the constitution of which we have already defined, were an invention of Lodovico Viadana, and by his own account they were first attempted in 1596 or 1597, his leaning towards them being first excited "by observing the frequent and evident deficiency in the number of singers, who wearied themselves unsuccessfully in endeavouring to execute, in twos or threes, a composition of many parts"; and again, "by the wish to create compositions for different voices, well adapted to their several capacities, and in the execution of which they might acquit themselves with credit." For the performance of these pieces, to complete or fill up the harmony, the organ was necessarily in requisition. The organists were perfectly equal to the task, as the organ service was always and in every place performed by the best qualified members of the chapel, who were fully as conversant with playing "accompaniments" regularly, that is purely, on a keyed instrument from an unfigured part, as from a figured bass; since they had been accustomed to put these together for their own use from single parts, and to figure and play them as a *Basso continuo;* a practice very general long before the year 1600, and which was adopted as the means of assisting the memory, as well as a most useful method of indicating those successions of harmony which the composition demanded. After the introduction of the monody and the concerted style, it may readily be imagined that more attention and ability were required for accompanying with due taste than on former occasions, when a chorus only required accompaniment, which from being perfect in itself could go correctly, even without the organist's assistance.

Thus the rules of accompaniment and of thorough bass, with figures, had their origin as a peculiar study, the cultivation of which at a subsequent period afforded no slight assistance towards establishing a clear knowledge of harmony in itself, and without regard to counterpoint.

It has very erroneously been conjectured, even to the present day, that Lodovico Viadana enjoyed the merit of having invented thorough bass and its figuring, the practice of both of which had existed long before his time; and he taught them, moreover, just as little as he invented them, although the contrary has been falsely inferred from the celebrated preface to his *Concerti* (see *Die Tabulatur der ält. Praktiker*, art. 4.)

But, nevertheless, in the *Concerti* of Viadana, particularly in those of one and two parts, a real melody is for the first time to be perceived. This is not asserted as if among the old composers,—particularly in Palestrina, and also in the composers of madrigals,—patches of melody were not here and there to be discovered; but with these they have the appearance of being rather a subject for contrapunctic action, or as a melody which has to thank the counterpoint or the chord-succession for its casual existence. Viadana's melodies, as may be observed in their separation from the accompaniment, are invented really as melodies; they flow with facility, are easy to sing, and their expression is tolerably appropriate. The accompaniment, to say the truth, is not exquisite in its harmony, neither does it evince any depth of thought; and the entire work, therefore, is not to be placed among the classical productions of the former period. But Viadana deserves, at all events, the honour of having invented, or at any rate he has the merit of being the first who successfully cultivated, the performance of a melodious style. Caccini cannot dispute this honour with him by his *Nuove Musiche*, even if this work had been of an earlier date, which it is not. Those writers, moreover, who regard Orazio Vecchi as the Coryphœus of the melodic style, and even designate him as the predecessor of Emilio del Cavaliere, Peri, and Caccini, in the dramatic style, have certainly not seen his *Anfiparnaso*, on which alone this opinion must be grounded.

They knew, besides, that this *Commedia armonica*, which was performed in 1597 at the court of Modena, and printed the same year at Venice, consists only of a succession of five-part madrigals, in which there is to be perceived just as little of a dramatic style (*recitative* or *arioso*) as of any other kind of the melodic.

Musical instruments must have undergone considerable improvement about this period; for they were honoured by having parts assigned to them in the performance of the oldest operas. In Emilio's oratorio, the orchestra, according to the preface, consisted of a *lira doppia* (probably a *viola da gamba*), a *clavicembalo*, a *chitarrone*, two flutes, or *tibie all' antica.* Montiverde's orchestra was more numerous; it comprised two *gravicembani*, two *contrabassi da viola*, ten *viole da brazzo*, one *arpa doppia*, two *violini piccioli alla Francese*, two *chitarroni*, two *organi di legno*, three *bassi da gamba*, four *tromboni*, one *regal*, two *cornetti*, one *flautino alla vigesima seconda* (third octave, a kind of flageolet), and one *clarino*, with three *trombe sordine:* the overture, entitled *Toccata*, had to be performed with all the instruments three times before the rising of the curtain: it consisted of a kind of *Intrada*, which never modulates from the key of C; in other respects there was nothing in the whole opera appropriated to the instruments, which could only have performed a few intermediate pieces and dances, and probably supported the singers in the chorus, but only in the unison. Instrumental music had not at that time made any further advancement.

Italy at this period, 1630, could boast of the highly celebrated organ-player Frescobaldi, to whom many German organists made voluntary visits, or were officially sent, in order to study the organ-fugue under his direction. He was the teacher of Froberger, afterwards distinguished as an organist at the imperial court. From this time, may be said to have commenced gradually the cultivation of that species of counterpoint called the "double," and the fugue; although at a later period it received its more perfect consummation as to form and rules.

In Church music,—if we except the introduction of Church-concerts, which were of somewhat early adoption,—no other changes had occurred worthy of remark; neither can I find that any very meritorious composition made its appearance. Nevertheless, the composers of this epoch began to lay aside the old keys in compositions which had not been necessarily founded on the *Cantus firmus* of the Roman Church, and even to set whole pieces in feigned (transposed) scales.

They began by degrees to perceive, with regard to harmony, that there were in fact no other keys or scales than those, which were afterwards called *modus major*, and *modus minor;* and which agreed with those once known, since the time of Glarean, as the Ionian and Æolian.

Madrigals, and such like compositions, for several voices, were still the sole and favorite amusement of private circles, and were printed in thousands.

Montiverde—in other respects as strictly a contrapunctist as any one—began to use in his madrigals, and no less in his dramatic productions, new combinations in chords never before attempted; and more particularly unfamiliar dissonances without preparation. He was, on this account, violently attacked by his learned brother artists; and not without reason, since, according to our modern, and doubtless more free ideas, very many of these combinations cannot be justified. It did not precisely appear that he created any reform by this proceeding; but it may have been, that he thus gave the first impulse to researches and experiments, by which a more unrestricted use of many a dissonance formerly avoided, without preparation, or as *nota cambiata*, was afterwards established both in practice and in theory.

I have entitled the epoch, the history of which I now conclude, that of Montiverde, because he was, in every respect, the most remarkable character belonging to it, and because he accomplished more than any other composer in the several departments of the new opera and the madrigal.

CHAPTER XII.

EPOCH OF CARISSIMI.

1640 TO 1680.

IT may readily be imagined that, from the novelty of its appearance, even whilst yet in its infancy, the musical drama must have produced a very extraordinary effect, by its union with the other sister arts, music, poetry, and acting, to which dancing was sometimes added,—as had already been the case in the scenic representations of the first oratorio, *L'Anima e Corpo.* There were no means now of satisfying the desire to enjoy this new spectacle, which affected so many senses, as well as the mind itself, at the same time; and when it became accessible to a greater number of auditors,—for at first it was only provided for a limited assemblage, at the expense of courts, republics, or some rich and eminent families, on the celebration of particular festivities; when, in fact, the representation of operas became an object of profitable undertaking, and either private persons, or the citizens of rich towns, built opera-houses in which the opulent class could procure this pleasure at a moderate cost, which formerly was of rare occurrence, and reserved only for those who abounded in wealth,—the demand for it increased, as may be well supposed, to an immoderate extent. Operatic performances succeeded first at Venice, where, from 1637 to 1700, there were uninterrupted representations ; and during this period of sixty-four years, there were no fewer than three hundred and fifty-seven operas produced, in seven theatres, the composition of about forty musical writers.*

Among the numerous composers of operas at the beginning of this period, Francesco Cavalli, *Magister capellæ* at St. Mark's, and Marco Antonio Cesti, were especially esteemed. The latter was a pupil of Giacomo Carissimi, *Magister capellæ* in the church of S. Apollinare at Rome, after whom we have named the present epoch. Cesti wrote and produced several operas at the court of the emperor Leopold the First,—himself a lover of the art, in which he was also tolerably proficient. Carissimi, although he wrote no

* A complete catalogue of the operas which were represented at Venice from 1637 to 1730 may be found in *Marpurg's Historico-Critical Contributions*, vol. 2.

operas, so far as we know, contributed nevertheless greatly towards the cultivation of the form to be used in operatic music; and is considered as the inventor, or at all events as a great improver, of the chamber cantata,—a species of composition to which dramatic recitative, and dramatic melody, are indigenous, as in the opera ; and differ but little in their form, whether written for the chamber or the stage, to which they could readily have been transferred, if we may judge from the models we find in his cantatas. The merit is generally ascribed to him of having been the first who improved the recitative; of having brought dramatic melody to a considerable degree of perfection ; as likewise the first, who, in his cantatas, employed instruments in a concerted manner, especially for ritornelles and intermediate pieces.

Such then was the form in which we find the operas of Cavalli and Cesti in 1640. The recitative begins to approach the natural accents of declamation, and allows itself some modulations in the accompanying harmony; the aria, if indeed it were deserving of the name, was still far removed, as to its form, from that of a later time, and often differed but little from the recitative ; nevertheless it contained even then some truly expressive and agreeable cantilenas ; and there frequently appear embellishments somewhat after the manner of the *Aria di bravura* of later invention. The accompaniment consisted in a mere unfigured *basso continuo.* What we call the *ritornelle* was performed by the violins at the conclusion of the aria, or in the intermediate pieces. Choruses were of rare occurrence, and only at the termination of the acts.

The period immediately following,—during which Rovetta, Ziani the elder, and Legrenzi, successively filling the post of *magister capellæ* at St. Mark's, appear, among several others, to have been held in great esteem,—not only brought the recitative gradually to perfection, but gave also a more definite form to the aria, which, as an independent piece, was now easily distinguished from the recitative, and often consisted of two verses to the same melody, between which there was played a ritornelle.*

Such was the construction of the opera, and also of the sacred drama (*azione sacra*, or oratorio): compositions which in this shape may even now delight an audience, if we can dispense with the form and luxuriousness of the opera of our own day, and if the singers, particularly in

* Or symphony, as it is generally termed in England.—*Trans.*

the arioso pieces, restrict themselves to an appropriate and simple delivery.

The cantata (chamber cantate) advanced at about an equal pace with the opera; it became a favourite among private circles, and gradually began to encroach upon the madrigal. The less noble kind, such as the villanelle, villote, ballate, etc., had in the meantime wholly disappeared.

In Church music the public taste inclined to the *stile concertante*, which now divided the supremacy with the *stile da Capella*, frequently called also the *stile alla Palestrina*, to the use of which was added about this time the accompaniment of bow-instruments, more particularly introduced into the Church during the intermediate pieces of the composition, where *cornetti* and trombones had alone been formerly allowed, in order to strengthen the choir.

The motettes and concerti of Carissimi were very highly esteemed, and are still even anxiously sought after by the collectors of old and what is styled classic music.

Notwithstanding the introduction of the new, and what may be almost termed more splendid, kind of music, the Church style was always ostensibly separated from secular compositions, and maintained its superior dignity. Learned counterpoint was especially cultivated in the steadily flourishing school of the Venetians, even in their churches, and it was everywhere practised with success by the organists.

The simply grand church style, commonly called that of Palestrina, continued to flourish in the principal churches of Italy, especially in the pontifical chapel, which has always adhered to it, and which still excludes every instrument, not even excepting the organ. Century after century some one or other of its members has been continually distinguished in the church style of composition. But in this epoch and style, the palm belongs without question to Orazio Benevoli, *magister capellæ* at St. Peter's, in the Vatican, about the year 1660; and his compositions for three or more choirs, particularly in the learned fugue pieces, will continue to excite the admiration of all posterity. With him, however, Carissimi, the teacher of a Cesti, and subsequently of Bassani and Alessandro Scarlatti, could alone dispute the credit of being the " man of this epoch"; that Carissimi, who, whether as inventor, or at least, as the great rectifier of the new species, had made himself notoriously eminent, and who, even in his life-time, had enjoyed such a reputation as has rarely been accorded in the first instance to any great genius, until after the grave has closed over his ashes.

Of the Frenchmen who belonged to this epoch there is not much to be recorded. Musical history, however, mentions a great number of them; but they had long retrograded from the old school of higher counterpoint, without evincing any emulation of the Italians in regard to that of recent invention.

The English celebrate at this time their Henry Purcell, who was not only a composer of the first order for the church, but also for the theatre.

The Germans, in the course of time, even amidst the storms of a war that seemed of endless duration, and that left only desolation and a wilderness in its track, did not suffer the ancient art to decay. Counterpoint and organ playing were assiduously cherished; and even the concerted church style had penetrated into their country, where it was cultivated with some degree of success. The events of this period and of many succeeding years were, of course, unfavourable in Germany to the progressive advancement of the dramatic style; nevertheless it is said that Schütz, called also Sagittarius, who was *magister capellæ* to the Electoral Prince of Saxony, composed a German opera at Dresden, about the year 1628, the *libretto* of which was the *Daphne* of the Florentine Rinuccini, of 1597, translated by Opitz; but of this no specimens have hitherto transpired.

For instrumental music little or nothing had anywhere been done; still it was in this epoch that musicians began to direct their attention to accompanying instruments and the improvement of them, more especially to that of bow instruments, the tuning and construction of which were at that time duly regulated. At Cremona, Brescia, and Inspruck, instruments of this description were produced of so superior a quality, as to preclude the possibility of making any alteration in their form or disposition with advantage. The violins, in particular, made at the above places during that period, are even at the present day more valued, appreciated, and sought for, than those of any other place or time.

Towards the end of this epoch, music, generally speaking, had made considerable progress, particularly in the new species of composition, the opera, and chamber cantatas, concerted motettes or sacred cantatas, as well as in the employment of the bow instruments now adapted for the accompaniment of vocal pieces.

The praises lavished on Carissimi by his contemporaries were inexhaustible, and they seemed to consider, that through his means an approach had been made to the golden age of the art of sound. But if indeed Carissimi, who was unquestionably a splendid composer, may be admitted to have created his own style, and to have reared some distinguished pupils, there still appears no sufficient reason to consider his productions as the beginning of a new Roman school, particularly as in that capital the grand style of the old school continued to maintain its supremacy, whilst that of Carissimi was comparatively but little cultivated there. If, as Paccini alone tells us, Carissimi had really been a native of Padua, he must nevertheless have been regarded as a pupil of the Venetian school, the stamp of which is more conspicuous in his motettes than that of the Roman. Ferrari, at Venice, one of the oldest opera composers, had at least commenced about the same time with Carissimi (1640) to labour in the department of the cantata; the Venetians soon adopted universally the forms of Carissimi's compositions, and the genius which glowed in his works alone distinguished them from those of all his Venetian contemporaries.

CHAPTER XIII.

EPOCH OF SCARLATTI.

1680 TO 1725.

THE extraordinary reputation which the name of Carissimi had every where obtained, attracted to this composer, in his old age, at Rome, a young Neapolitan (according to some authorities a Sicilian), who burned with intense desire to render himself perfect as a composer, under the guidance of so distinguished a master. By his wonderful performance on the harp (perhaps in English, *harpsichord*, and in German, *clavier*), this young person had succeeded in ingratiating himself with Carissimi, who treated him with paternal affection, and initiated him into all the mysteries of his art. The name of this talented youth was Alessandro Scarlatti, born about the year 1650; an individual who was destined to assist the art in a still more elevated flight, and by his exertions to prepare it for its future exalted condition.

After having taken leave of his master, Scarlatti travelled through Italy, seeing and hearing the great masters and their works in the theatres of Bologna, Florence, and Venice ; and studying the characteristic spirit of the Venetian school. He next went to Munich and Vienna, where his first operas and church compositions were received with great favour. He composed afterwards, in Rome, several excellent operas ; and was finally invited to Naples, where he received the appointment of chief master in the chapel royal; and devoted himself, during the remainder of his life, to the composition of works for the church and theatre, as well as to the instruction of juvenile composers. In 1725 he closed his long and useful life, in high reputation, and crowned with honours, at the advanced age of seventy-five years.

Alessandro Scarlatti was indisputably one of the greatest masters who have appeared in any age ; equally eminent in the art of the higher department of counterpoint, and in dramatic recitation; nor less so in the invention of melodies of a character noble, grand, and strikingly expressive, and in a free and judicious style of instrumental accompaniment. Fully acknowledged as the reformer of each of these kinds of music, it may well be said of him,—that he was a century in advance of his time; that he powerfully influenced the taste of his contemporaries; and that, by kindling in his brother artists a spirit of emulation, he prepared the way to that eminence which the art of sound attained in the period immediately following; and which was greatly promoted by the pupils of his own formation in the Neapolitan school, the dawning of whose glory he survived to witness.

Scarlatti may be regarded as the link which united the new (modern) music to that of ancient times; as the harbinger of that period which is called by some writers—"the *beautiful* period of Italian music," in contradistinction to "the *grand* period," by which name the epoch extending from Palestrina to the advent of the Neapolitan school has generally been charactized.

Scarlatti has brought the recitative to the highest possible state of perfection: his cantatas are reckoned models of expression, as studies for composers; and not only was he considered the inventor of the accompanied, or *obligato* recitative, but even the form of the aria (with two parts, and the *Da capo*) is likewise ascribed to him; and he is also believed to have been the first who composed overtures to his operas, since, prior to his time, it had been customary to perform one and the same overture, by the well-known Lully, of Paris, as a prelude to every opera, no matter by what composer it might have been produced. (See *Rousseau, Dict. de Mus., Art. Ouverture*.)*

In Scarlatti's time, however, there were also excellent composers of various countries, among whom those of the Venetian school particularly distinguished themselves, about the year 1700, and even at a later period. To name one, for instance, who, in the sublimest counterpoint, as well as in the concerted or solemn church-style, in the sacred drama also, no less than in the madrigal, was never surpassed,—we have only to refer to Antonio Lotti, *Magister capellæ* in the church of St. Mark, at Venice, a pupil of Legrenzi, under whose direction, along with Francesco Gasparini (afterwards established at Rome), he studied counterpoint in 1684; and he may indeed be classed with the boldest, and at

* This supposition I must now contradict, having since discovered in the Court Library of Vienna a great number of dramatic compositions from the period prior to Scarlatti, which, like the operas of Scarlatti, contain a completely original introduction of proportionable length, from which the name of overture cannot be withheld. The aria with the *da capo* is likewise found to have existed before Scarlatti. Unfortunately, in the history of the opera, the long period from Cesti and Cavalli to the time of Scarlatti is still in darkness. —*Note, by the Author, to the second edition.*

the same time, the most grammatical, harmonists of any age. Besides him, there were also deserving of notice, Joseph Fux, the celebrated *Magister capellæ* to the Emperor Charles VI, who created masterpieces of art, both in the sacred and dramatic style;—Francesco Conti, at the imperial court of Vienna, who, by original and daring invention, successfully risked many innovations, deserving to be called the Mozart of his time; and whose *Don Quixote* (1719) contains such a rich fund of wit and humour as to be scarcely unworthy of the original conception of the Spanish author;—Benedetto Marcello, a patrician of Venice, who (excepting in the opera department, to which his muse never inclined) has left behind him masterly pieces in all styles, and whose celebrated fifty Psalms of David have been reprinted in countless editions, having already outlived many valuable works of the same period, and being likely still to outlive as many more;—Ant. Caldara, *(sub-magister capellæ* at the court of the Emperor Charles IV), whose works the connoisseur cannot look at in the score, without admiring the sprightliness, scientific texture, and richness of invention which they contain; nor can he listen to their performance without being affected by the grace displayed in them, and pleased with the striking effects produced in the treatment of his subjects. To the above may be added Paolo Colonna, at that time in Bologna, much celebrated as a composer and teacher of the higher department of counterpoint, and as being the founder of the school of Bologna, which rose afterwards into such great esteem.

During this epoch, much admiration was excited in France by the operas (tragedies and ballets) of the singularly famous Giovanni Battista Lully, who was "Intendant" of music to Louis the Fourteenth; indeed, for more than thirty years, even to the time of Rameau, the French would listen to nothing but the music of the "divine Baptiste," as they called him. It is truc, that the union of dances and choruses with the action, was an advantage which the Italian opera in those days did not possess; the dialogue, however, was more like psalmody than recitation, interrupted only here and there by short, and by no means developed *arioso* ideas, or by brief ritornelles; and it is difficult to conceive how the lively French native could have taken any pleasure in the drawling and psalm-like music of Lully's productions.

In Germany, the operatic style (German opera) took root and flourished with difficulty, although the history of the art relates, that towards the end of the seventeenth century, and at the beginning of the following one, Reinhard Keyser, of Hamburgh, wrote an incredible number of German operas (116 it is said) for his native town, and partly for the court of Brunswick, which unfortunately have not acquired the publicity they deserved. Hasse is said to have spoken of them invariably with the greatest respect; and he declared Keyser and Scarlatti to be the best composers of the age. In Munich and Vienna, only the *Italian* opera and *Italian* oratorio were esteemed, several pieces of which kind were written by Joh. Jos. Fux, the celebrated author of the *Gradus ad Parnassum*, and *magister capellæ* at the imperial court.

At the beginning of this epoch, instrumental music was scarcely known, even by name, in Italy; but the French court, from the time of Louis the Thirteenth, had kept in pay *vingt-quatre violons du roy* (violins and violas of different dimensions), for which Henry le Jeune and Boesset wrote a sort of chamber music; and an example of this has been given by P. Mersenne, in his work entitled "*Harmonie Universelle;*" although it can merely represent chamber music in its infancy amongst a people but little devoted to the art. Lully's compositions for the royal chamber may have been somewhat superior; his overtures, in comparison with his songs, are tolerably interesting, and occasionally remind one of the style of Handel, by the accented *(punctirten)* notes, in the pathetic parts. But of the contrapunctic art he appears indeed to have brought with him but a slender portion from Italy.

Notwithstanding this, it may be asserted that the first real elevation of instrumental art proceeded from Italy, through Corelli, Geminiani, and Vivaldi, who became eminent, towards the end of the seventeenth and the beginning of the next century, for their violin solos, trios, quartettes, and "concerti grossi": their skill, however, was more prized, and their productions were more sought after and rewarded in foreign countries (England and Germany), where they constituted for a long time the chief delight of the musical dilettanti.

There was no want of good organists at any period, either in Italy or Germany; these continued to maintain their established reputation; and to them are we principally indebted for the support of the fugued style, which prevailed in Church music, and on which the industry of the composers of all schools, even at the period of which we are now treating, was constantly and successfully employed. During this epoch, also, the theory of every kind of *obli-*

gato counterpoint was first clearly developed, and the form of the real fugue established by Berardi, Buononcini the elder, and Fux.

One department of musical practice alone remains to be noticed, of which no mention has been hitherto made, and which, to a certain extent, was first developed and advanced to a considerable degree of perfection in this epoch,—namely, the art of singing. It may easily be conceived that, in the earlier time of counterpoint, that is from Dufay to Montiverde, when singing was merely practised in the choruses, the talent of greatest, and perhaps only value in the vocalists of the chapel, consisted in the perfection of their theoretical knowledge, and in the facility with which they could read music at sight; and whoever among them might be possessed at the same time of an agreeable voice, was only esteemed more valuable in proportion. Boys, whose fitness for singing the *soprano* or *alto* is limited to a period of a few years, could never become useful for chapel singing, according to the state of practical music in those days; and females were never employed in such a serious office, Church etiquette forbidding their admission; the choirs, therefore, were filled only by men; the *soprano* and *alto* parts were assigned to *falsetto* voices, for which the Spaniards in the Pontifical chapel were remarkable. Lodovico Viadana, in the preface to his *Concerti* (1602), observes, that these songs of his were "better adapted for *falsetti* than for *soprani naturali*," because the latter (namely, *putti*, boys) sang carelessly, without expression, and were too weak. He does not allude to female voices, and seems to have known nothing of eunuchs. In the *History of Art* notice is also taken of the circumstance, that there were none of these in the Pontifical Chapel before the year 1625.

The introduction of monodies and of concerti (as they were called), as well as of dramatic music, singing, cantati, and the aria in operas, first made evident the necessity of fine voices being employed, and of the performance being of superior quality.

The success of the opera depended as much on the accomplishments of the singer, as on the successful composition of the author's music; and the managers were no less interested in procuring good singers by liberal terms, than the composers were in drawing out their full powers in the execution of their art. In Eastern countries there had been eunuchs for many centuries; it is well known that they were engaged in the harems as slaves; but it is nowhere mentioned that they were employed there as singers. However, it was an accredited fact, that they possessed to the latest period of their lives a fine and, comparatively speaking, even a strong *soprano* voice. Thus, it was not very difficult to conceive that, by a clever surgical operation, boys could be made *soprano* singers; and as the opera became more highly cultivated, that disgraceful custom soon came into use, which has so often been deplored by philanthropists, and the suppression of which appears to have been again reserved for our own age.

From this time forward there came into note, particularly towards the end of the seventeenth and the beginning of the eighteenth centuries, those celebrated singing-schools, which contributed so much to the advancement of music in Italy. During the epoch, of which we now speak, Pistocchi, himself one of these unfortunate beings, had founded such a school in Bologna; Fedi had introduced another at Rome, and Redi at Florence. Naples produced at that time excellent singers of both sexes; and the most distinguished composers willingly employed themselves in bringing to perfection any extraordinary talent, which their cultivated ears enabled them to discover. Italy had already produced for foreign courts many singers of the greatest merit.

Thus the art of sound, especially the department of the musical drama, appeared, even in Scarlatti's time, as if it could scarcely arrive at a higher degree of perfection.

CHAPTER XIV.

EPOCH OF THE MODERN NEAPOLITAN SCHOOL.

LEO AND DURANTE.

1725 TO 1760.

It was reserved for the Neapolitan school to give to music a still more elevated position, and to change, in a certain degree, its whole formation. Its founders are considered to have been Leonardo Leo and Francesco Durante, to whom may be added Gaetano Greco, all of them pupils of Scarlatti. The composers of this school were not only well versed in, but had a marked respect for, all harmonic and contrapunctic science; they understood both how to take advantage of every source of aid which had been handed down to them, and how to employ those modern and extended means which were presented in the skill of the dramatic singers, now arrived at the highest perfection, as well as in the great improvement of musical instruments which resulted from it.

But the most essential improvement, of which this school can boast,—for no school may be said to bestow on its pupils either grace in melody or fertility of invention,—consisted in the production of rules for the rhetorical part of melody, and the better construction of the aria. Rhythm especially had been hitherto subject to few, if any regulations; it seemed as though the necessity for it had never been clearly felt. Until that time the musical phrase, as the member of a supposed musical period, was commonly too short, and the cadenza therefore too frequent, and out of all proportion; the aria itself was also too short, and consequently of too fleeting a character for strengthening and confirming the impression which it might easily have created on the mind of the audience, by appropriate repetitions of the principal ideas. The modern Neapolitans, while they lengthened the phrase, as well as the aria, appear to have derived their plan of remodelling it, from architecture, in which there is not only a necessity for beauty of outline in the conformation of each separate part of the building, but for a proportionate symmetry also of the separate parts in relation to one another.

These composers generally lengthened the ritornelle, when the outbreak of passionate declamation in the poetry did not otherwise forbid it;

the object of this being to prepare the listener for the coming melody, and even to raise his expectation concerning it. They opened the aria with the principal melody; which was followed by a second, and sometimes a third, appropriate idea as an accessory; these were conducted into related keys, and performed with various modifications; then repeated again in the original key, in which, after the so-called cadence had been made, came a suitable piece for the instruments, taken mostly from the motive of the opening symphony, and thus concluded the first part. The second part consisted of a short piece, frequently taken from the idea of the first; from which, however, it was distinctly separated, and was characterized by being performed in a related but perceptibly different key. After the cadence, with which the second part concluded, there followed the *da capo*, or repetition of the first part, from which in general it only varied in some slight abbreviations of the symphony.

This form of the aria was, with very trifling exceptions, the model which all composers, both in Italy and elsewhere, very soon adopted. It long maintained its ground, and may be said still to exist, with some unimportant deviation, in the real aria of our own times. For the sake of variety, there were arias composed also without the second part, as above described; these were of a less formal character, and were even then known under the name of *cavata* or *cavatina*.

In the orchestra, where bow-instruments had been hitherto exclusively employed, with the occasional assistance of a single wind instrument in concert with the voice, an addition was now made of two oboes, two horns, sometimes also a couple of flutes and fagottas, and now and then of trumpets. Limited, however, as was the use made at that period of the above instruments by the composer, their effects being little understood, and perhaps in no degree appreciated, there was gained, nevertheless, by the employment of them, not only a new shade of sound, but a stronger body of tone, where they were used, which increased the effect to be produced in the ritornelles and intermediate pieces.

Whether it was owing to this higher flight of art, the encouragement given to the composers of the school in question, the honour with which they were everywhere distinguished, the excitement produced by the lofty example of their teachers, or the presiding genius of the art which threw its "inspiring mantle" over Naples in this interesting epoch,—certain it is, that, neither in any other country nor at any subsequent period, were so many celebrated masters at one time in the field, the whole of whom belonged to the Neapolitan school. To the government of these was entirely submitted the opera of Italy and of other nations, and for many successive years the well-earned reputation of their school was maintained by their pupils.

From the above school,—to mention only the most familiar names even at an early period of its celebrity,—we derive a Porpora, Sarri, Carapella, Vinci, Pergolesi, Duni, Perez, Teradeglias, Feo, Sala; somewhat later, Traetta and Jomelli; soon after whom we have Sacchini, Piccini (the inventor of the Italian opera buffo, with *ensemble* pieces and finales); Majo, Anfossi, Caffaro, Guglielmi the elder; and lastly, Guglielmi the younger, Cimarosa, Paesiello, and Zingarelli, the last four belonging more properly, however, to a later period. To these must still be added from our own country (Germany) the name of Hasse, who in 1720 enjoyed the friendly and paternal instruction of the patriarchal Scarlatti, and also acknowledged himself to be of the same school. Moreover, even our own illustrious Joseph Haydn is said to have studied under Porpora, a circumstance which the Neapolitans feel pleased to mention, that they may wind up the long list of masters whom their school produced, and who adorned their century, with a name so much renowned at the later period of their splendour.

There can be no doubt but that the style of the Neapolitan school was universally adopted by composers in Italy and other countries, and that the music of the present day is still essentially that of Naples. The lively and elegant style of this school could scarcely fail to find admission into Church music, which, in fact, was consequently rendered far too similar to the music of the theatre, especially in Italy, where there was scarcely any perceptible difference between the opera and the sacred mass, with the exception, perhaps, of some fugued pieces, by which it was meant to stamp on the latter the seal of Church music. The organ, however, continued in use throughout Italy, as an accompaniment for serious and elaborate compositions, and the organists never suffered themselves to be led away by the luxurious style of the period.

Instrumental music, even from the best composers of the Italian opera, cannot be said to have possessed altogether much brilliancy in its department, as may be proved by the overtures which preceded their masterpieces. For the chamber, however, Dominico Scarlatti was the author of a great many compositions (sonatas) which are still valued by the true and more erudite admirers of the piano-forte; and there are some excellent quartettes for bow-instruments by Sacchini. The art of using the bow was brought in this epoch to a state of inconceivable perfection by Tartini, by his pupil Nardini, and also by Pugnani. The admiration for bow-instruments having increased by means of these masters, it became requisite, as a matter of course, that the same should be maintained and fostered by new compositions, no small number of which were the result of such admiration. Wind instruments also had their share of increased attention, to their evident improvement; and many virtuosi distinguished themselves equally at concerts in this department, as others did in the use of bow-instruments.

It was soon after the commencement of this epoch that Rameau made his appearance in France as a composer for the French grand opera, disputing the palm with the long-admired Lully, and gaining, like his predecessor, the favourable report of all the musicians, connoisseurs, wits and literati of Paris, who now swore by Rameau with the same orthodoxy and perseverance as they had manifested during four prior decennia in the case of Lully. Rameau's operas also found their way into some towns of northern Germany, where they were represented in a

German translation; and in some musical periodicals of that country the question was actually discussed, whether the preference should be accorded to the Italian opera or the French! Nevertheless, the lively genius of the French nation very soon gave encouragement to the occasional introduction of songs into their comedies, whence arose a peculiar kind of composition, the French operetta, in which, since the year 1740, Monsigny, Philidor, and after them Grétry, were particularly famous, and towards which the better educated portion of the public, if not the most eminent in rank, became always more and more inclined. France accomplished nothing in Church music, during this epoch, worthy of being recorded. The organ appears not to have been altogether neglected, though a Marchand could have but little chance in competition with a Sebastian Bach. Instrumental music for the chamber seems to have been cultivated there with success at this time; the musical journals of northern Germany have spoken frequently in its praise, and have even adduced it as a model; but it has long since died away, and its effects appear equally to have perished with the compositions, so that it would be futile to give it any further notice.

In England, Dr. Arne was much esteemed in

the department of the English opera, or rather operetta; and about his time, Handel, and afterwards Gluck, Hasse, and the Italians, wrote for the Italian opera in London.

Let us now turn our attention to Germany; but in so doing we ought not to omit giving a retrospective glance to a somewhat earlier period than that of which we are now treating. In Germany, about this epoch, or somewhat prior to it, several persons appeared who attracted the notice of the world, and whose names are still mentioned with pride by the people. Shortly after the Reformation, there had arisen in that country, through the introduction of popular melodies into the Church, a species of metrical choral music quite new at that time (sixteenth century), and perfectly original. The practice of harmonically accompanying this choral music on the organ, and the endeavours of the organists to attain an intellectual and varied accompaniment, materially assisted in promoting and perfecting the harmony, and scientific counterpoint upon the choral. Germany could always from that period, and especially at a later date, in the seventeenth century, boast of having possessed the greatest masters in organ playing. A complete mastery of this instrument, which presupposed an acquaintance with all that was known of the higher departments of counterpoint, tended likewise to secure a deeper study of it; and the facility of displaying this study extemporaneously gave the most immediate encouragement to such compositions as distinguish this period, and which were multiplied in print as well as in manuscript by the ablest masters. In order to satisfy the demands of their genius, it is evident that as the study of art advanced, the organ must also have received an improved practical temperament, or tuning,* in order to facilitate its modulation into every

* For those but slightly acquainted with the nature of keyed instruments, such as the organ or piano-forte, it may be of use to state that, if either of these instruments were tuned exactly perfect in any one key, this perfection would be confined to that particular key; and so soon as an attempt was made to modulate into a different one, the whole instrument would be found to be out of tune, the disparity of tune becoming greater in proportion as the modulated key was distant from the one to which the instrument had been tuned. To correct this imperfection, a method has been adopted, by which a certain number of fifths can be tuned in some degree higher than the ear would actually require, and a similar number in a corresponding degree lower, but which is nevertheless so minute, and so equally distributed throughout the whole of the keys, as to be scarcely perceptible even to the most sensitive ear; and by these means the perfection and imperfection are so balanced as to neutralize each other. For example, F♯ and G♭, though one and the same note on the organ or piano, are not so on the violin, or any other perfect in-

conceivable key; and when we consider that, at the same time,—in the thousand varieties of combinations which were produced in the fugued piece by the obligato—harmonies must have arisen which were not previously known, but which it became necessary to regulate according to some prescribed rule, we can readily conceive how the organists alone must have extended the limits of harmony, and have been regarded as lawgivers and authorities in its mysteries,

"Quos penes arbitrium est, et jus et norma loquendi."

Since the time of Rameau (1722) and that of D'Alembert, who first developed a proper system of harmony, no labours were so industrious and so successful, either in Italy or France, in regard to the theory of accompaniment, counterpoint, and composition in all its parts, nor was so much printed on the subject, as in Germany; it will suffice to call to our recollection, from that comparatively early time, the names of Mattheson; Carl Phil. Emanuel Bach; Marpurg; Kirnberger; Sorge; Daube, etc.

From such schools for organists as we have

strument; and the above method of tuning, which seeks to bring the imperfect to an equality with perfect instruments, is denominated the temperament or tempering of the tuning of the instrument.—*Translator*.

recently described, there sprung up, early in the eighteenth century, the German heroes of this universally wondrous epoch, Handel and Joh. Sebastian Bach, who to all likelihood will for ever remain as unapproachable as they are unrivalled ; no country, no school, no age, has produced anything that can equal the oratorios of the one, or the fugue-works of the other. They stand in these respects so distinctly alone, so peculiarly isolated, that I could not prevail upon myself to place them at the head of an epoch, the succeeding one of which cannot be regarded as a continuation, far less as a perfection of their own. HANDEL and BACH *began and ended their own peculiar epoch.* The higher cultivation of music subsequently regards the species or kinds alone, and depends in a great measure on the tastes of the times, which, devouring the old *(tempus edax rerum)* and for ever insatiate, is constantly requiring something new.

In regard to instrumental music, during this epoch, the Germans were certainly in other places far from being idle: it is well known, however, that no kind of music depends so much on the partial taste of the nation, and is so much swayed by fashion as the instrumental; thus the fact can be readily accounted for, that, while we can listen, at the present day, even with pleasure, to the melodies contained in the operas or cantatas of Cavalli, Cesti, Carissimi, and others who flourished in the middle of the seventeenth century, the would-be "gallant" style of instrumental music in all countries from the first half of the eighteenth century appears to us deplorably insipid, if not ludicrous; so that the more enlightened amateurs of the violin seek for and collect the works of Corelli for the year 1690, while the chamber music of a much later period has long been disregarded and almost forgotten; and out of the works belonging to the epoch of which we are now speaking, only such have been preserved as, like the quartetts, trios, and concertos of Handel, or the fugues and preludes of Johan Sebastian Bach, were written either in strict counterpoint, or at least in a more serious (studied) style, the compositions of others in the esteemed "gallant" style of that period being scarcely ever mentioned; and those even which can be discovered being saved from oblivion merely by some collector of antiquities, or in a library, where they run the risk of being treated as waste and useless paper.

No opera essentially German can be mentioned as the production of this epoch. The Italian opera was patronized at all the leading courts; and this was partly composed by Italian, and partly, as was often indeed the case, by German masters: at other courts and cities, where the scenic art was encouraged, there was only a demand for translated Italian operas, or French operettas; but in 1760, and afterwards, original operas in German, or, properly speaking, comedies interspersed with songs, after the manner of the French operetta recently introduced, were written by Hiller, Geo. Benda, and others.

In the department of the sacred cantata and the grand oratorio, Stölzel of Gotha, and Telemann of Hamburg, were distinguished among various composers; but above all the rest, Graun, whose *Tod Jesu* is justly regarded as a classic work, especially in respect to recitative and chorus. This composer also produced a great number of Italian operas for Berlin, and his Italian chamber cantatas are not inferior to the best in this species of composition.

CHAPTER XV.

EPOCH OF GLUCK.

1760 TO 1780.

As, according to Solomon, nothing is perfect under the sun, there must sooner or later have been perceived some deficiencies, of more or less importance, which had either originally existed, or in the course of time had crept in, and adhered to the forms introduced by the Neapolitan school.

If we examine at the present day the works which this school produced, the observation forces itself upon us, although we live in an age when popular favorites give us a taste for repetitions and prolongations in music, that the arias of the Neapolitans, and of the composers who wrought in their style during the epoch just described, were valued beyond their merits;—that the repetitions exceed *æsthetical* "raison";—that their middle piece, or *seconda parte*, as it is called, is too insignificant and out of all proportion, when compared with the principal idea, or the aria previously developed and concluded;—that, finally, the simple *da capo*, that is, the repetition of a complete aria which has just been heard, and scarcely to all appearance interrupted by the *seconda parte*, cannot well be tolerated according to the principles of philosophical criticism.

Still these prolongations and repetitions were not the only faults of the Italian opera in those days; a greater evil consisted in the introduction of the *aria di bravura*, that senseless piece of buffoonery, by which so many splendid works are disfigured, in all other respects acknowledged as most successful master-pieces; but the greatest evil of all was coldness of manner,—the destruction of all art.

Whether similar reflections were made at that time on the Italian opera, we cannot tell. The mere title, index, and contents, of the books or pamphlets which were published at that period in reference to the subject, exhibit no vestige of such; and it really appears that the authority of the masters, the force of custom, and the charm of the glorious melodies, added to the *virtuosité* of the eminent singers who flourished in this epoch, as well as the pride felt by the nation in its opera, had blinded the critics; but in France and Germany criticism was employed only upon the operatic works produced at their respective theatres.

It was owing, however, to these considerations, that Gluck,* after having laboured with success in London and Italy in the style hitherto received, determined on endeavouring to create some reform in the opera, by laying aside that vain formality of manner. He communicated his ideas to men of genius and taste, who could not but think them reasonable, and he consequently felt more encouraged by their judgment in accomplishing his design; he was fortunate enough also to enlist in his views several poets, who, on their part, assisted in the reform which Gluck projected. Thus prepared, this tasteful composer made his first attempt at innovation in 1764 at Vienna, with the opera of *Orfeo*, the text of which, written under his direction by Calsabigi, was immediately received with the greatest applause; and a like attempt, with the same result, was afterwards made, in the same city, with the *Alceste* and the *Elena e Paride.*

In 1772, Gluck was invited to the grand opera in Paris, where the works above mentioned were represented with a French translation, and where he composed his *Iphigenia in Aulis*, *Iphigenia in Tauris*, and the *Armida*, works that crowned

* Born in 1714, at Weidenwangen, in the Upper Palatinate of the government of Prince Lobkowitz, and died at Vienna in 1787.

his triumph not only over the former idols of the Parisians, Lully and Rameau, but also over a contemporaneous and powerful rival, Piccini, after an immense number of treatises had been published *pro et contra.*

"When I undertook to compose the music of this opera," observes Gluck, in the Italian dedication of his *Alceste* to the Grand Duke Peter Leopold of Tuscany, "my object was, to clear it of all those abuses which had been introduced by the ignorant vanity of the singers, or by a too ready acquiescence on the part of the composers, and which had so long disfigured the Italian opera, making it the most ludicrous and tedious of all spectacles, instead of being the most sublime and beautiful.

"I wished to limit music to its true aim, that of assisting poetry in giving expression to the words and subject of the poem, without interruption of the plot, or any diminution of its interest by useless and superfluous decorations; and I fancied that it would have the same effect as liveliness of colouring and well selected contrast of light and shade in a correct and properly defined picture, enlivening the figures without disturbing the *contour.*

"I have been desirous, therefore, not to impede the singer during the greatest fervency of the dialogue, by causing him to wait for a tedious symphony (ritornelle), nor did I wish him to make a pause on any favourable vowel in the middle of a word, in order to display his execution and beautiful voice in a long passage, or wait until the orchestra gave him time to collect force for a particular cadence. I did not approve of hurrying through the *seconda parte* of an aria, how passionate soever and important it might be, merely to afford an opportunity of repeating in order the words of the first part four times over, and of making the aria conclude at a point where, perhaps, the sense of the words did not admit of such conclusion, or of allowing the singer the means of showing that he was really capable of varying a passage according to his fancy as often as he chose; and, generally speaking, I was anxious to banish all those abuses, against which sound common sense and just feeling had so long combated in vain.

"I conceived that the overture should, in some degree, prepare the audience for the nature of the plot, or, if I may so speak, that it should announce its contents; that the instrumental part should accommodate itself to the proportionate importance or passion, without manifesting any divisional section between the aria and the dialogue; that it should not interrupt the course of the poem in an unseasonable manner, nor mar the force and interest of the story.

"I further conceived that my greatest exertions should be directed to the study of a beautiful simplicity; I wished to avoid dazzling with difficulties at the expense of perspicuity; the introduction of any novelty appeared to me only valuable, so long as it emanated naturally from the situation and expression; and I never particularly hesitated in sacrificing a rule for the sake of effect. Fortunately for me, the poem itself assisted me greatly in my design; the celebrated poet, Calsabigi, had struck out a new path in the working of dramatic scenes, owing to which, in place of flowery descriptions, superfluous comparisons, and erudite but cold moral sentences, there now appeared the language of the heart, powerfully depicted passion, affecting situations, and a constant change of scene.

"The result verified my general theory; and the unequivocal success which attended these efforts, in such an enlightened city, has clearly proved that simplicity, truth, and nature, form the real basis of the beautiful in all works of art."

So far Gluck; his delicate æsthetic tact and refined taste happily led him aside from the rock on which these maxims, so excellent in themselves, might have caused him to split, if all considerations for the demands of the music, which must exist in the opera as an independent art, were to be sacrificed to the poetry and the "situation." His genius knew how the independence, as well as the beauty, of his music was to be maintained, with all due regard for the poetry; music with him was by no means the handmaid of poesy, but a loving sister, appearing, indeed, almost too considerate in not manifesting her superiority beyond measure, but still too charming in herself not to be able, if she chose, to carry off the palm.

Gluck's melodies, in accordance with the words, delight us by the truth of their musical expression; but even if divested of the poetry, they would be regarded as beautiful and characteristic. If these melodies, indeed, produce their whole effect only when combined with scenic representation, and apart from this may not be appropriately produced in concerts, still they are by no means destitute of form, and their leading ideas stand forth so distinctly in their charms, as to enable us, after listening to his operas, to repeat them mentally, as it were, with the same ease and willingness as we have ever repeated, in like manner, those of any Italian opera.

In no place, perhaps, was music so prepared for Gluck's reform as in Paris, where the grand opera, hitherto governed by Lully and Rameau, had always remained ignorant of the Italian forms, and more than probably of every other kind of form; whilst, on the other hand, the Parisian public, from the less pretending, yet natural and agreeable forms of the operettas of Gretry, already at that time admired, could more readily enter into the simple style of Gluck, which united justness of expression with the charms of melody.

Gluck's influence on the opera in Italy was not very material; still it was a considerable step gained, that even there, towards the year 1780, the composers began to deviate from the aria in two parts; renounced the convenient *da capo;* no longer separated the second part from the first in the middle of the aria, but interwove them one with the other, imperceptibly returning to the first idea, and conducting it with some few variations to the conclusion; and thus the aria formed at least a connexion, or, if I may so express it, shaped itself into a whole by one process, though the bravura embellishments were even still regarded as being, in certain places, an essential or integral part of the aria.

Far more considerable, however, was the influence which the reform of Gluck had upon the nature of the opera in Germany, where the composers became, from his example, particularly assiduous in the study of expression, without entirely disregarding the form, and made a most happy application of the means of aid which they found in the instrumental music cultivated by them at that period, of the grand effects of which upon the opera, Gluck had given them an admirable foretaste.

Thus may be said to have been prepared by Gluck the epoch of Haydn and Mozart, to which we shall now proceed; but it would scarcely be proper to conclude the present section without mentioning the meritorious son of the great Johan. Sebastian Bach, Carl Philipp Immanuel, who, without forsaking the school of his father, was able nevertheless to unite its seriousness and solidity with the gracefulness of the more modern compositions. His works in the department of Church music, the grand sacred cantata, and oratorio, are quite as valuable as his numerous instrumental productions. He was in some measure the precursor of our celebrated Haydn, of whom he was the personal friend, and who declared more than once, how deep were his obligations to him in this department of music. By his famous work, *Die wahre Art das Clavier* *zu Spielen*,* as also by his solid piano-forte compositions, he had laid the foundation for a better and more tasteful use of this instrument, which was afterwards brought by Muzio Clementi and W. A. Mozart to that degree of perfection which excites at the present day such deserved admiration.

* The true Art of playing the Piano.

CHAPTER XVI.

EPOCH OF HAYDN AND MOZART.

1780 TO 1800.

JOSEPH HAYDN, who was born at Rohrau, in Lower Austria, in 1732, and died at Vienna 1809, had at the latter place, so early as the year 1770, acquired, by his instrumental compositions, a most distinguished reputation, which extended throughout Europe; yet his most brilliant period is principally from 1780 to 1800, during which time he composed the greater number of his very excellent quartetts and symphonies, his glorious masses, and, finally, his grand, imperishable oratorios, *The Creation*, and *The Seasons*. It was Joseph Haydn who invented that most interesting kind of chamber music, the scientific and intellectual quartett, who gave a form to the "grand symphony", and who brought combined instrumental music to a degree of perfection which had never been foreseen. Possessed of an inex haustible fund of invention, having the most extraordinary facility in conducting his subjects through manifold changes in a manner surprisingly charming; having also a perfect knowledge of instrumental effect, he has stamped upon each of his works the seal of genius, and long will they be referred to as models of the "truly beautiful."

Wolfgang Amadeus Mozart (born at Salzburg in 1756), while yet a youth, made his *debut* as an opera composer contemporaneously with Gluck, during the year 1770, in Italy; and the most brilliant period of his career may likewise be said to have commenced at Vienna in 1780. Unfortunately for the art and its worshippers, his existence was prematurely brought to a termination by "inexorable fate" in that capital in 1791; but not before his works had already secured for his genius an imperishable fame.

In the composition of instrumental music, Mozart's paternal friend Haydn was his type and model, as Gluck was in the dramatic department, and Handel and Bach in the walks of higher counterpoint, all which masters were held by young Mozart in profound veneration. In the first two departments of composition, he soon raised himself to the same elevated position as had been attained by those regarded as his models; nay, he may be said even to have excelled them in the fertility of his genius, the wonderful accuracy of his natural feeling with regard to æsthetics, and by the happiest application of contrapunctic facility which he had early acquired. In operatic composition he has never been surpassed; in a different age, and with other tendencies, he might have been a Handel or a Bach ; but perhaps it is better as it is.

By Haydn and Mozart the art of sound was raised in all departments to the highest perfection; their style was the exclusive model for all the composers of Germany and France; and whatever has been produced in later times, deserving of being called grand and beautiful, owes its origin to this epoch. We must, therefore, characterize these two eminent composers as the founders of a new school, which may be called that of Germany, or more properly the Viennese school, seeing there has since arisen a sect in Germany who claim the former title for themselves.

Inspired by the works of Haydn and Mozart, the French opera composers, so early as the year 1790, produced masterpieces in their department; and France, towards the end of this epoch, beheld the dawn of her most brilliant era with regard to the art of sound.

In the reminiscences of that splendid period, from the year 1780 to 1790, and of those impressions which are wont to be produced by an art lately renovated and invigorated,—impressions as difficult to pourtray as to be again excited,—my contemporaries, with all respect for eminently modern composers, will, I feel assured, agree with me in pronouncing the epoch of Haydn and Mozart the "golden age" of music.

In alluding to the most remarkable characters of this time, let us here pay the tribute of respect which we owe to the excellent Naumann, well known to us by several compositions for the Church, and especially by his "*Vater unser*" (Lord's Prayer), which may be classed among the best productions of his day, and by the opera of *Cora*, which, to our misfortune, we have only heard in a German translation from the Swedish, with a pianoforte arrangement.

In the department of instrumental music, next to the quartetts and quintetts of Haydn and Mozart, those of Bocherini were deservedly held in estimation among the more scientific and not too fastidious amateurs of this style of music.

The works of Cimarosa, Paesiello, Sarti, Salieri, Zingarelli, and others, in the department of Italian opera, are still vividly impressed on our remembrance.

CHAPTER XVII.

EPOCH OF BEETHOVEN AND ROSSINI.

1800 TO 1832.

If the epochs into which this history of Music has been divided may be said with justice to have derived their names from those masters who have at any time succeeded in improving their art, and who have gained for themselves over others the applause of their contemporaries, the more recent decennial periods of our own time may be correctly denominated the epoch of Beethoven and Rossini, although the latter belongs properly to a still more advanced decennium, and the former has already ended his earthly career.

As the one, formerly the most celebrated pupil of the Viennese school, shines pre-eminently in his instrumental compositions, so have the lively and expressive operas of the other, aided equally by vocal and instrumental art, won for him, without opposition, the undivided approbation of his time.

I must forbear, however, to expatiate on this

part of my subject, inasmuch as it is far from my intention to characterize the abilities of the favourite composers of our own day, and much less to hazard a critical opinion with regard to their style. Future ages will on some occasion pronounce an unbiassed judgment on their works. It is, comparatively speaking, the same thing with the music of an entire period, as with objects spread on all sides over a wide range; we can only appreciate their merits at a certain distance both of time and space: the following remarks, however, are, in my opinion, necessarily called for, in reference to the condition of the art during the present epoch.

The masterpieces of Haydn and Mozart had, since the preceding epoch, given a fresh impetus to every description of music: the novelty of ideas, the boldness of execution, the manifold nature of their harmony, and the freedom, nay, often the apparent want of continuity in the modulation, presented to composers a new model; and more particularly the manner and way in which these genial masters had employed the instruments in the orchestra, in which, it would appear, the most powerful lever for their effects was thought to have been discovered, were all looked upon as the pattern which ought to be imitated, and, if possible, excelled.

The progressive improvement of instrumental music more especially, occasioned by the admirable compositions of these masters, and the predilection which everywhere has increased for music of this kind, would also necessarily awaken the zeal of instrumental performers, whose powers in the course of this our last epoch have actually reached to such a degree, as almost to preclude the possibility of farther advancement. It was therefore very natural that composers should now take into consideration, more than ever had been done before, the effects produced and to be produced in instrumental composition. In this respect Beethoven has accomplished what was formerly not even thought of, and he has considerably enlarged the path previously pointed out by Mozart. By these means of help, the lively French composers, towards the end of the last and in the first years of the present illustrious epoch, succeeded in giving a new and powerful inpulse to their opera; and even the great matador of the more recent Italian opera seized on the now perceived effects of German instrumental music (which he thoroughly understands), and which he has transferred with incredible success into the operas of Italy, overcoming the prejudices of his country and the vanity of its vocal performers; although Ferdinand Paer and Simon Mayer may nevertheless be mentioned as having introduced before him (still, however, with a praiseworthy moderation) the instrumental style of Mozart.

Meanwhile the capabilities of instruments, and their power of creating astonishment, gradually became overvalued,—composers endeavoured to surpass their predecessors, and even themselves, in striving after effect,—a most dangerous extravagance crept into use. . . . .

Under the direction of Genius, however, every kind of music prospers in its own style, but its example is not, on that account, always profitable to the art: the immoderate use of artificial means spoils very soon the taste of our contemporaries; the effect on repetition is not always the same, and at length two and two cease to be four.

Justice, however, obliges us to admit, that in the present epoch, there have been produced many excellent works of every kind, the authors of which may worthily take their rank beside the greatest masters of past times; and that music has made a rapid progress, particularly in bringing to perfection the appliances of the art, and the knowledge of their use, whereby much advantage may be anticipated for the opera, as well as for instrumental music, in future.

The art of counterpoint and fugue (now exclusively so called), confined, as it is at present, according to the standard of our music, almost entirely to the Church and the oratorio, and consequently not perhaps so easily attainable, or so much practised, by performers as in earlier years, must not, on this account, be deemed a lost art; neither are there wanting persons to maintain this unceasing fire, and often enough to give convincing proofs of its existence; so that very lately, even, and especially among the Germans, a fresh ardour for the study of it has been excited.

In the department of Church music more particularly, that noblest and most exalted of the kind,—which we have never been able, however, to bring back to the simplicity it displayed in the time of Palestrina,—this our last epoch can boast of a considerable number of meritorious works in the grandest style of composition; and there have lately appeared performers on the organ, who would have been acknowledged as thorough masters of that instrument in the most illustrious epoch during which it formerly flourished.

Let us now bestow a glance on those centuries which have passed since the origin of the Art of Harmony, in the course of which it is delightful to observe how this fairest of the arts has, through a series of epochs, with slow yet certain progress, gradually arrived at that perfection which we all believe (and I think with great justice) that it has now attained. But the boundaries of an art, which does not, like the plastic arts, find its object, its model, or even its limits, prescribed by nature; springing, on the contrary, into existence in new and unimagined perfection, from the unfathomed depths of the feelings, and from the mind of some genial spirits, raised up providentially at intervals of more or less duration,—the boundaries of the art of music, I say, no one has ever defined; and it would be disgraceful, if not almost sacrilegious, were we to reckon the works already produced as the *ne plus ultra* of musical achievement.

And yet, whether we will or not, the questions forcibly arise,—if this art may not at length have its appointed limits?—if, among the sister arts, whose highest beauty and gradual decline mankind have witnessed in the course of ages, this one alone is to enjoy the privilege of an ever blooming, ever ripening youth?—if this, at last, must not itself also yield to the destiny, which has attested its power, in the history of the human race, over all that is fair as well as all that is great and mighty?—if we are not already, indeed, aware of the sad symptoms of its decay, perhaps even of its approaching destruction?

The historian, who has only to deal with the past, can readily avoid an answer to such captious questions; still it is his province to recall to mind, that lamentation has, in every age, been heard over the decline, and even the absolute loss, of the "good old music"; while, nevertheless, at the same time, every age has imagined itself to have attained the utmost summit of perfection in the art. Thus it was in the epoch of Palestrina, Carissimi, Scarlatti, and that of the Neapolitans, down to the times of Haydn and Mozart: the productions of our own time we, indeed, denominate as "classic"; but, after the lapse of another century, history will most probably decide upon such a claim. Meanwhile, we shall hope the best for this beautiful art. Should it sink, the oft-repeated proverb must be verified, that "*wherever an art has fallen, the blame must rest with the artists alone*"; but we would willingly persuade ourselves that so deplorable a result is still far distant.

Our circle of vignettes, representing the historical epochs of the art of music, may here be brought to a close. It might not have been difficult for the artist (so called, to preserve the metaphor), to have added to the groups in the foreground a considerable number of individuals more or less famous in the several Schools: these, however, he must omit, from a dread of injuring the distinctness of the picture, were he to cover it over with heads which, with the exception of some important physiognomies, would generally have borne a family likeness to the common stem, especially in the perspective of the background.

Still I shall, in some measure, atone for this deficiency in the following catalogue of names, which, whilst its aim, in one respect, is to review the epochs described, contains, moreover, a list of many composers, teachers, and writers, who have nearly equalled the most renowned of their times, without considering too closely the claims of several others, whose names, perhaps, may not be included.

My contemporaries must excuse me for not having filled up the sketch of this final epoch, as I have already mentioned my reluctance to make any particular remarks upon the illustrious authors of our own time, and their respective merits; since their most distinguished works are everywhere to be heard, and their celebrated names are continually on the lips of all real friends of the art.

REVIEW OF THE EPOCHS

OF THE

MUSIC OF WESTERN EUROPE,

WITH A LIST OF THE

COMPOSERS, TEACHERS, AND AUTHORS,

WHO MADE THEMSELVES DISTINGUISHED

IN EACH EPOCH.

ABBREVIATIONS.

Comp. . . .	Composer.	Fr.	French.
Theo. wr. .	Theoretical writer.	Mil.	Milanese.
Flor.	Florentine.	Ferar. . . .	Ferrara.
Belg. . . .	Belgian.	Parm. . . .	Parma.
Sch.	School.	Crem. . . .	Cremona.
Pont. chap.	Pontifical chapel.	Pad.	Padua.
Ven.	Venetian.	Mod.	Modena.
Germ. . . .	German.	Sicil. . . .	Sicilian.
Eng.	English.	Franc. . . .	Franconian.
Port.	Portuguese.	Sel.	Selissian.
Span. . . .	Spaniard.	Ham. . . .	Hamburg.
Bolgn. . . .	Bolognese.	Neap. . . .	Neapolitan.
Ital.	Italian.	Aust.	Austrian.
Veron. . . .	Veronese.	Bohem. . .	Bohemian.
Car.	Carniol.	Vien. . . .	Viennese.
†	Died.	Berl.	Berlin.
Neth. . . .	Netherlands.		

REVIEW OF THE EPOCHS

OF THE

MUSIC OF WESTERN EUROPE,

ETC.

I.

EPOCH OF HUCBALD.

The Tenth Century—901 *to* 1000.

Hucbaldus of St. Amand in Flanders, † 930, first who described the attempt of accompanying a given chant with one or more voices, *i. e.* with the intervals of the fourth, fifth, or eighth in similar motion; also in two parts, with other intervals not consonants; all very rude experiments. Tone-writing: Syllables of the text placed in parallel lines, or a method of notation invented by him, after the ancient Grecian, by means of an alphabetical letter; never came into use.

II.

EPOCH OF GUIDO.

The Eleventh Century—1001 *to* 1100.

Guido of Arezzo, Benedictine monk of Pomposa, Flor., 1020 to 1040; revived the study of the Organum. Tone-writing: The neumata, or *nota romana* of the earlier periods, improved by the aid of lines, and also by means of the seven Gregorian letters of the Latin alphabet.

III.

EPOCH NOT DISTINGUISHED BY THE NAME OF ANY PARTICULAR INDIVIDUAL.

The Twelfth Century—1101 *to* 1200.

Invention of the note. Continued and more successful experiments in counterpoint, almost to the time of the discovery of the mixed species, in aid of which the invention of notes of different time-value, or mensural notes, called also figures. Thence the origin of mensural and figural music.

Originators, teachers, and first improvers unknown; no existing monuments.

IV.

The Thirteenth Century—1201 *to* 1300.

Continued experiments in the composition for several voices. Improvement of the mensural theory. Discantus.

Franco of Cologne; the oldest known writer in this department. He must have flourished in the early part of the thirteenth century.

Walter Odington, monk of Evesham in England, Theor. wr., 1240.

Hieronymus de Moravia, in France about the year 1260, Theor. wr.

Pseudo-Beda, country and time of his existence unknown, Theor. wr.

Adam de la Hale, of Arras, lived at the courts of the Counts of Provence about the year 1280, Comp. Specimen of a three-part composition.

V.

EPOCH OF MARCHETTUS AND DE MURIS.

1300 *to* 1380.

Gradual extension of the knowledge of Discantus and Mensura. Low state of the practical department.

Marchettus of Padua, Theor. wr., 1309.

Joannes de Muris, Fr., 1323, Theor. wr. and Comp. Specimens are given.

Guillaume de Machault, Fr., about the year 1340.

Franc. Landino, Florent., about the year 1360.

Anonymous in the *Cantu et Mus. Sacra* of Prince Abbot Gerbert.

VI.

EPOCH OT DUFAY.

1380 *to* 1450.

First or ancient Netherland school. Improved and more regular counterpoint.

Brasart.

Binchois (Egidius).

Dufay, of Chimay in Hennegaw, singer in the Pont. chapel.

Eloy (*id est* Eligius; probably one and the same as Egidius)

Faugues (Vinc.), and others.

VII.

EPOCH OF OCKENHEIM.

1450 *to* 1480.

Second or modern Netherland school. More artificial (learned) counterpoint. Commencing fame of the Netherland school.

Ockenheim vel Ockeghem, chief of the school.

Basnoys, Neth.

Carontis, Neth.

Hobrecht, Neth.

Regis, Neth., &c., &c.

Celebrated Teachers in Italy.

Johannes Tinctoris, Neth.
Gulielmus Guarneri, Neth.
Barnardus Hycaert, Neth.

Celebrated Organists.

Sguarcialupo (Antonio degli Organi), in Florence.
Bernardus (called the German), inventor of the Pedal, in Venice.

VIII.

EPOCH OF JOSQUIN.

1480 *to* 1520.

Flourishing condition of the Netherland school over the whole of Europe. Native contrapunctists arise in Germany. Excellent teachers in Italy. Some Frenchmen distinguish themselves in foreign countries.

Authenticated Pupils of Ockenheim.

Agricola.
Brumel.
Gaspard.
Loyset Compère.
Josquin (*des Prés.*)
Prioris.
De la Rue.
Verbonnet.

Aaron (*Petr.*), Ven., Theor. wr.
Adam de Fulda, Germ. wr.
Bassiron, Neth.
Carpentras, Fr. in Rome.
Craen, Neth.
Dygon, Engl.
Fevin (Rob.), Fr.
Fevin (Ant.), Fr.
Gafurius (*Franchinus*) of Lodi, Teacher and Theor. wr.
à Goes, Port.
Goodendag, Germ. or Neth.
Hofheimer, court organist in Vienna.
Isaak (Heinr.), Neth.
Lapicida, Neth.
Mahu, Germ.
Mouton, Neth.
De Orto, Neth.
Ramis (de Pareja), Span., Theor. wr.
Spataro, Bologn., Polem. wr., and many others.

IX.

EPOCH OF WILLAERT.

1520 *to* 1560.

Netherland masters teach in Italy, where their art takes root and flourishes. Madrigal of the Venetian school.

Animuccia, Bologn. in Rome.
Arcadelt, Neth.
Cambio (Perisson), It.
Canis (Corn.), Neth.
Certon, Fr.
Clemens non Papa, Neth.
De Cleve (Joa.), Germ.
Crecquillon, Neth.
Deiss, Germ.
Ferabosco, Rom.
Festa (*Cost.*), Flor. in Rome.
Giacchetto de Mantua, Neth.
Glareanus, Theor. wr.
Gombert, Neth.
Goudimel, Neth., Teacher of Palestrina.
Guerrero, Span.
Henry VIII, King of England.
Jannequin, Fr.
Maillart, Fr.
Manchicourt, Neth.
Morales, Span. in Rome.
Moulu, Fr.
Paminger, Germ.
Payen, Neth.
Pevernage, Neth.
Phinot, Neth.
Porta (*Cost.*), Cremona.
Regnard, Neth.
Richefort, Neth.
De Rore (*Cypr.*), Neth.
Senfl, Germ.
Sermisy, Fr.
Utendaler, Germ.
Della Viola (Alfon.), Ven.
De Waert, Neth.
Walther (*Joh.*), Germ.
Willaert, Neth.

X.

EPOCH OF PALESTRINA.

1560 *to* 1600.

Commencing sway of the Italian masters. Close of the great period of the Netherlanders.

Aichinger, Germ.
Anerio (Fel.), Rom.

Asola, Veron.
Bennet, Engl.
Betti (called il Fornarino) Rom.
Bird, Engl.
Calvisius, Germ., Theor.
Dentice, Neap.
Donati, Ven.
Dragoni, Rom.
Falconio d'Asolo.
Le Febvre, Neth.
Felis, Rom.
Gabrieli (*Andr.*), Ven.
Gabrieli (*Gio.*), Ven.
Gallus, Carniol.
Gastoldi, Milan.
Gatti, It.
Giovanelli, Rom.
Hasler, Germ.
Ingegneri, Rom.
Isnardi, Ferrara.
Lassus (*Orlando*), Neth.
Lejeune (Claude), Neth.
Marenzio, Rom.
Mayland, Germ.
Merulo (Claude), Parm.
De Monte (*Phil.*), Neth.
Nanini (Gio. Maria), Rom.
Nanini (Bern.), Rom.
Nocetti, Parm.
Osculati, It.
Palavicini, Crem.
Palestrina, Rom.
Prætorius (*Hier.*) Germ.
Ponzio, Parm.
Rota, Bolog.
Rubini, Ven.
Scandelli, It.
Schöndorfer, Germ.
Stabile (Annib.) It.
Tallis, Eng.
Valcampi, It.
Vecchio (Orazio) Moden.
Vecchio (Orfeo) Mil.
Venosa (Gesualdo, Principe di) Neap.
Vittoria, Span. in Rome.
Vulpius, Germ. Theor. wr.
Zang, Germ.
Zarlino, Ven. Theor. wr., and many others.

XI.

EPOCH OF MONTEVERDE.

1600 *to* 1640.

First attempts at a recitative style; origin of the opera; of the monody, and the concerted style (Church concerts).

Agazzari of Siena.
Agostini, Rom.
Allegri, Rom.
Bateson, Eng.
Buel, Germ.
Caccini, Rom.
Casciolini, Rom.
Catalani, Sicil.
Cavalieri (*Emil. dei*), Rom.
Cifra, Rom.
Cima, Mil.
Croce, Ven.
Erbach, Germ.
Faber (Bened.), Frank.
Franck, Sel.
Frescobaldi, in Rome, celebrated organist and comp.
Gagliano, Flor.
Giacobbi, Bolog.
Gibbons, Eng.
Grandi, Ven.
Gumpelzheimer, Germ.
Heredia, Span. in Rom.
Kapsberger, Germ. in Rome.
Landi, Rom.
Leoni, Ven.
Mazzocchi (Dom.), Rom.
Mazzocchi (Virg.), Rom.
Monteverde, Ven.
Peri (Jacopo), Flor.
Pacello (Asprilio).
Prätorius (Mich.) Germ. Theor. wr.
Philipps, Engl.
Prioli, Ven.
Quagliati, Rom.
Selle, Ham.
Soriano (Rom.).
Turini
Ufferer, Germ.
Ugolino, Rom.
Viadana of Lodi.
Walliser, Germ.
Ward, Engl.
Wilbie, Engl.
Weelkes, Engl.
and many others.

XII.

EPOCH OF CARISSIMI.

1640 *to* 1680.

First improvement of recitative and dramatic melody; cantate; introduction of instruments in concert with the voice.

Abbatini, Rom.
Benevoli, Rom.
Bockshorn (Capricorn), Germ.
Carissimi, Rom.

Cesti, Rom.
Cavalli, Ven.
Corso of Celano.
Corvo, Crem.
Durante (Silv.), Rom.
Federici, Rom.
Ferrari, Ven.
Foggia, Rom.
Graziani, Rom.
Hammerschmidt, Germ.
Legrenzi, Ven.
Monferrato, Ven.
Rovetta, Ven.
Schütz, Germ., Opera Comp.
Stadlmayer, Germ.
Stradella, Neap.
Ziani (the elder), Ven., and many others.

XIII.

EPOCH OF SCARLATTI.

1680 *to* 1725.

Essential improvement of the recitative and dramatic melody. First formation of independent instrumental music.

Agostini (Piersimone), Rom.
Aldobrandini, Bologn.
Alessandri (Giul. Canon d').
Astorga (Sicil.)
Bach (*Joh. Christoph.*), Germ.
Badia, It.
Baj, Bologn.
Bagliani, Mil.
Banner da Padova.
Barbieri, Bologn.
Bencini, Rom.
Berardi, Theor. wr.
Bernabei, Rom.
Biffi, Ven.
Brossard, Fr. Lexicogr.
Buononcini, Bol., Theor. wr.
Caldara, Ven.
Calegari (P.), Ven.
Caniciari, Rom.
Caresana.
Casini, Flor., Org.
Clari, Rom.
Colonna, Bologn.
Conti (Franc.), Ven.
Cordans, Ven.
Corelli, Rom.
Costanzi, Rom.
Dedekind, Germ.
Dalla Bella, Ven.
Fux(*Joa.Jos.*),Vien.,Theor.wr
Gabuzio, Bologn.
Gasparini, Ven.
Gonella, Bologn.
Geminiani, Lucca.

Keyser, in Hamburgh. Germ. Opera Comp.
Lotti, Ven.
Lully, Fr. (Italian origin)
Marcello, Ven.
Pacello (Ant.), Ven.
Pacchioni, Bologn.
Pasquale, Bologn.
Passerino, Bologn.
Perti, Bologn.
Pistocchi, Bologn.
Pittoni, Rom.
Palaroli (sen.), Ven.
Palaroli (jun.), Ven.
Porsile, Bologn.
Predieri, Bologn.
Scarlatti (Dominico), Neap.
Scarlatti (Alessandro), Neap.
Steffani (Abb.), Ven.
Vinaccesi, Ven.
Vivaldi, Ven.
Ziani (the younger), Ven., and many others.

XIV.

EPOCH OF LEO AND DURANTE.

1725 *to* 1760.

Neapolitan school. Reform of melody. Instruments more numerous in the orchestra.

Abos, Neap.
Avossa, Neap.
Adolfati, Ven.
D'Alembert, Fr. wr.
Bach (Joh. Seb.), Leipzig.
Bergamo, Trevis.
Brusa, Ven.
Beretti.
Caffaro, Neap.
Carapella, Neap.
Carpani, Rom.
Casali, Rom.
Ciampi (Franc.), Neap.
Ciampi(Vinc-Legrenzio)Neap.
Ciampi (Fil.), Rom.
Chiti, Rom.
Conti (Nic.)
Cocchi, Ven.
Cotumacci, Neap.
Couperin, Fr.
Durante (Franc,) Neap.
Eberlin, Germ.
Feo, Neap.
Ferradini, Neap.
Galuppi, Ven.
Gozzini, Bergam.
Grassi(called il Bassetto),Rom.
Graun.
Greco (Gaetano), Neap.
Händel.
Hasse (called il Sassone).
Halzbauer, Austr.

Jerace, Neap.
Jomelli, Neap.
Lampugnani, Mil.
Leo (Leonardo), Neap.
Mancini, Neap.
P. Martini, Bologn., Hist. wr.
Mattheson, Germ., Theor. ästh. and polem. wr.
Nardini (Viol).
Palotta of Palermo.
Paradies, Neap.
Perez, Span. in Neap.
Pera (Sen.) Ven.
Pergolesi, Neap.
Piticchio, Rom.
Porpora, Neap.
Porta (Gio) Ven.
Pugnani (Viol).
Ragazzi, Neap.
Rameau, Fr. wr.
Reuter, in Vienna.
Riccieri, Bologn.
Ristori, Bologn.
Sala, Neap.
Salinas (Gius.) Sicil.
Saratelli, Ven.
Sarri, Neap.
Scarlatti (Domen.) Neap. comp.
Speranza, Neap.
Stölzl, Germ.
Tartini, of Pirano in Istria.
Telemann, Hamb.
Teradeglias, Span. in Neap.
Tinazoli, Neap.
Traetta, Neap.
Tuma, in Vienna.
P. Valotti, Pad.
Vinci, Neap.
Wagenseil, in Vienna.
Zelenka, Bohem., and many others.

XV.

EPOCH OF GLUCK.

1760 *to* 1780.

Reform of the operatic style. Introduction of ensemble-pieces and the grand finale. Increased perfection of instrumental music.

Basili (Sen.) of Loreto.
Bach (Carl Phil. Eman.), Instr. comp. and Theor. wr.
Bach (Christian, called the London, and also the Mayland Bach).
Bach (Friedemann), son of Sebastian Bach.

Benda (Geor.), Bohem.
D. Eximeno, Span. wr.
Fenaroli, Neap.
Fioroni, Mil.
Gassmann, Vienna.
Gluck, Germ.
Grétry, Belg.
Guglielmi (the elder), Neap.
Hiller, Germ.
Homilius, Germ.
Kirnberger, in Berlin, Theor. and polem. wr.
Majo, Neap.
Marpurg, Berlin, Theor. and polem. wr.
Misliweczek, Bohem.
Mondoville, Fr.
Monsigni, Fr.
Piccini, Neap.
Philidor, Fr.
Prati, Ferrar.
Rolle, Germ.
Rousseau (Jean Jaques), Genev., Comp. auth. and lexicogr.
Sacchini, Neap.
Scarlatti (Gius.) Neap.
Schuster, in Dresden
Stomitz, Bohem.,
etc. etc.

XVI.

EPOCH OF HAYDN AND MOZART.

1780 *to* 1800.

Viennese School. Perfected instrumental music.

Albrechtsberger, in Vienna.
Anfossi, Neap.
Bertoni, Ven.
Burney, Engl. Hist.
Catel, Fr.
Cherubini, Flor. (in Paris.)
Cimarosa, Neap.
Clementi.
Dalayrac, Fr.
Dittersdorf, Sel.
Eybler, in Vienna.
Fasch, Berlin.
Forkel, Germ. Hist.
Furlanetto, Ven.
Gazzaniga, Ven.
Guglielmi (the younger), Neap.
Gyrowetz, Bohem.
Haydn (Jos.), in Vienna.
Haydn (Mich.) Austr.
Jannaconi, Rom.
Krauss, Germ.
Lesueur, Fr.

Lorenzini, Rom.
Martin (Vinc.), Span.
Mattei, P. Bologn.
Mortellari, Neap.
Mayer (Sim.), Germ.
Mozart, in Vienna.
Nasolini.
Naumann, Germ.
Paesiello, It.
Pleyel, in Vienna.
Portman, Germ. Syst.
Quaglia, Mil.
Righini, It.
Radewald, Selis.
Sabbatini, Ven.
Salieri, Ven. in Vienna.
Sarti, of Faenza.
Tarchi, Neap.
Tritto, Neap.
Vogler (Abb.), Germ. Theor. wr. and Syst.
Weigl, in Vienna.
Winter, Germ.
Zingarelli, Neap., etc. etc.

XVII.

EPOCH OF BEETHOVEN AND ROSSINI.

1800 *to* 1832.

APPENDIX OF NOTES.

APPENDIX OF NOTES.

I.

Key, containing an Epitome of the Theory of Ancient Greek Music.

SINCE the Theory of Ancient Greek Music is by no means generally understood, I may be excused for endeavouring to comprise, in a very narrow compass, such knowledge concerning it as appears indispensably requisite; the more especially as I feel satisfied that the reader will have but little cause to regret his possible ignorance, or even his total forgetfulness of the same. My sole inducement in doing so is, that he may be spared the trouble of consulting commentators, in order to assist his memory with regard to names and circumstances, not easily borne in remembrance even by those who have given to the subject their deepest study. I have been guided chiefly by the opinion of Marpurg (*Krit. Einl. in die Gesch. und Lehrsatze der a. u. m. Mus.*) and also of Forkel, who has treated this complicated subject, in the first part of his *History of Music*, with as much clearness as the most fastidious inquirer can in any way desire.

FIRST.—INTERVALS.*

The greater intervals were—

1. Diatesseron, the perfect fourth.
2. Tritonus, the augmented fourth, or diminished fifth.

* Notwithstanding the very great labour and care with which Burney has compiled and written his able work, there are to be found in it omissions and imperfections; this may be said to be particularly the case with reference to the Greek intervals, no explanation of which occurs in his treatise; for, although it is true that in the rubric affixed to one of his chapters this subject is included, not a word appears respecting it in the text.—*Trans.*

3. Diapente, the perfect fifth.
4. Tetratonus, the augmented fifth or minor sixth.
5. Hexachordum, the major sixth.
6. Pentatonus, the minor seventh.
7. Heptachordum, the major seventh.
8. Diapason, the octave.
9. Diapason cum diatesseron, the eleventh.
10. Diapason cum diapente, the twelfth.
11. Bisdiapason, the double octave, &c.

The lesser intervals were :—

Diesis enharmonica,
Diesis chromatica,
Hemitonium, semitone,
Tonus, whole tone (major 2nd).
Triemitonium, minor third.
Ditonus, major third.

The consonant intervals *(symphona)* were, according to the ideas of the Greeks, the perfect fourth, the perfect fifth, the eighth, the perfect eleventh, the perfect twelfth, and the double octave. All other intervals, the third and sixth not excepted, were esteemed dissonant *(diaphona)*.

Strangely enough, the consonant intervals were particularly distinguished according to the position of the semitones situated in the series. For example :—

b c d e

a b c d

g a b c

are with them three different kinds of fourths, although the extreme notes of all the three kinds are at equal distance one from the other.

SECOND.—SYSTEMS.

A system was a series of tones composed of different lesser intervals.

The received system, regulating all the rest, was that of

the tetrachord, and consisted of four notes, in which the semitone lay at the under part, between the first and second degree, thus:—

But the whole cohering system consisted of eighteen notes, which were divided into five tetrachords, as follows:—*

	GREEK NAMES.			LATIN NAMES.
18	Nete hyperbolaeon . . .	$\bar{a}$	. . . . . .	Ultima excellentium.
17	Paranete hyperbolaeon, or Hyperbolaeon diatonis	$\bar{g}$	Tetrachord hyperbolaeon.	Excellentium extenta.
16	Trite hyperbolaeon . . .	$\bar{f}$		Tertia excellentium.
15	Nete diezeugmenon . . .	$\bar{e}$	. . . . . .	Ultima divisarum.
14	Paranete diezeugmenon, or Diezeugmenon diatonos	$\bar{d}$	Tetrachord diezeugmenon.	Divisarum extenta.
13	Trite diezeugmenon . . .	$\bar{c}$		Tertia divisarum.
12	Paramese	*B* ♮	. . . . . .	Prope media.
11	Nete synemmenon . . .	$\bar{d}$	. . . . . .	Ultima conjunctarum.
10	Paranete synemmenon, or Synemmenon diatonos	$\bar{c}$	Tetrachord synemmenon.	Conjunctarum extenta.
9	Trite synemmenon . .	*B* ♭	. . . . . .	Tertia conjunctarum.
8	Mese	*a*	. . . . . .	Media.
7	Lichanos meson, or Meson diatonos . . .	*g*	Tetrachord meson.	Mediarum extenta.
6	Parypate meson	*f*		Subprincipalis mediarum.
5	Hypate meson	*e*	. . . . . .	Principalis mediarum.
4	Lichanos hypaton, or Hypaton diatonos . . .	*d*	Tetrachord hypaton.	Principalium extenta.
3	Parypate hypaton . . .	*c*		Subprincipalis principalium.
2	Hypate hypaton . . .	*B*	. . . . . .	Principalis principalium.
1	Proslambanomenos . . .	*A*	. . . . . .	Adsunta seu adquisita.

* Or rather of fifteen notes and eighteen names, which, for the sake of being

THIRD.—GENERA.

The Greeks had three kinds of genus,—the diatonic, the chromatic, and the enharmonic,—each distinguished by the division of the tones which are situated between the two extreme notes of a tetrachord.

The diatonic tetrachord progressed with a half tone and two whole ones, thus :—

b c d e

---

rendered more clear, are here subjoined, in order to compare with the above.

1 2 3 4 5 6 7 8 9 10 11

A B c d e f g a b $\bar{c}$ $\bar{d}$

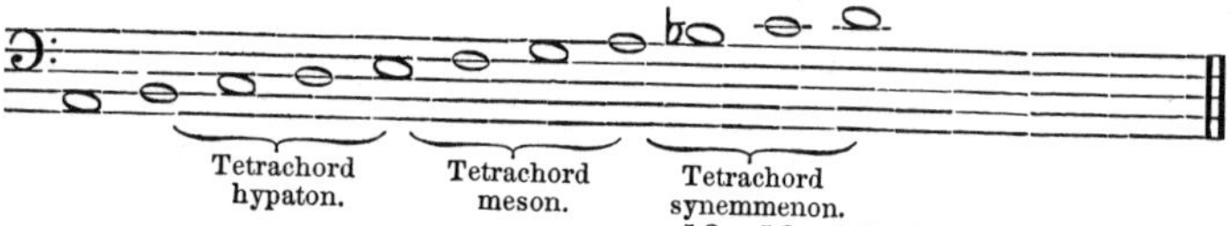

12 13 14 15 16 17 18

b $\bar{c}$ $\bar{d}$ $\bar{e}$ $\bar{f}$ $\bar{g}$ $\bar{a}$

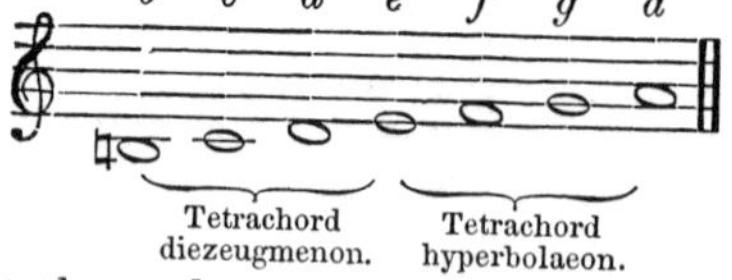

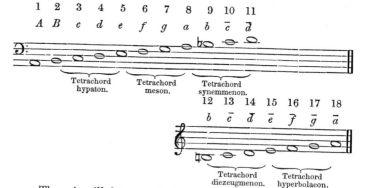

Thus, it will be seen that the scale consisted indeed of eighteen names, but in reality only of fifteen sounds, if we reckon B flat and B natural as one note; but as it goes back again to B natural at the fourth tetrachord, the three first notes of this tetrachord *(Diezeugmenon)* received again fresh appellations, and hence the eighteen names.

With reference to the Greek scale, Burney, vol. i, p. 12, states, that " their most extensive system or scale did not exceed *two octaves* or *sixteen sounds*" : again, at p. 18, he says, that " to complete the *three octaves and one tone*", &c. ; and, at p. 26, he adds, " Our compass is indeed much more extensive than that of the Greeks, but if we confine it to *three octaves* only, which was the extent of the whole range in the system of the ancients", &c. So that we find, in this esteemed author, no fewer than three distinct and contradictory accounts of the Greek scale.—*Trans.*

The chromatic consisted of two half tones and a minor third, thus:—

b c ♯c e

The enharmonic progressed through two quarter tones and a major third; but we are as incapable of expressing these proportions by our own notes as with our voices; nevertheless, they may be understood somewhat after the following way in writing:—

b $\frac{1}{4}$ *b* $\frac{1}{4}$ *c e*

This genus was at one time much esteemed, but it had fallen into disuse during the most flourishing period of Greek music.

It may, however, be observed, from this very brief representation, that in our modern music we have neither a chromatic nor an enharmonic *genus*, and we express by these words totally different ideas.

FOURTH.—MODES (KEYS).

Most of the Greek authors are agreed as to the number of fifteen keys *(modi)*. They consisted of five original ones, which had their position, that is, their principal note, in the middle of the system, each of them being always higher by half a tone than the other. These five original modes corresponded to five in the under fourth and five in the upper fourth, as exhibited in the following plan, wherein the tones and keys with which they would probably agree in our own system are also represented.

High or Acute modes.	11. *G* minor. Hyperdorian or Mixolydian.	12. *G* sharp minor. Hyperiastian or Hyperionian.	13. *A* minor. Hyperphrygian. or Hypermixolydian.	14. *B* flat minor. Hyperæolian.	15. *B* minor. Hyperlydian.
Middle or Original modes.	6. *D* minor. Dorian.	7. *D* sharp minor. Iastian or Ionian.	8. *E* minor. Phrygian.	9. *F* minor. Æolian.	10. *F* sharp minor. Lydian.
Low or Grave modes.	1. *A* minor. Hypodorian or Locrian.	2. *B* flat minor. Hypoiastian, Hypoionian, or Grave Phrygian.	3. *B* minor. Hypophrygian.	4. *C* minor. Hypoæolian or Grave Hypolidian.	5. *C* sharp minor. Hypolidian.

According to the arrangement of the scale, the fifteen modes are represented in the following table :—

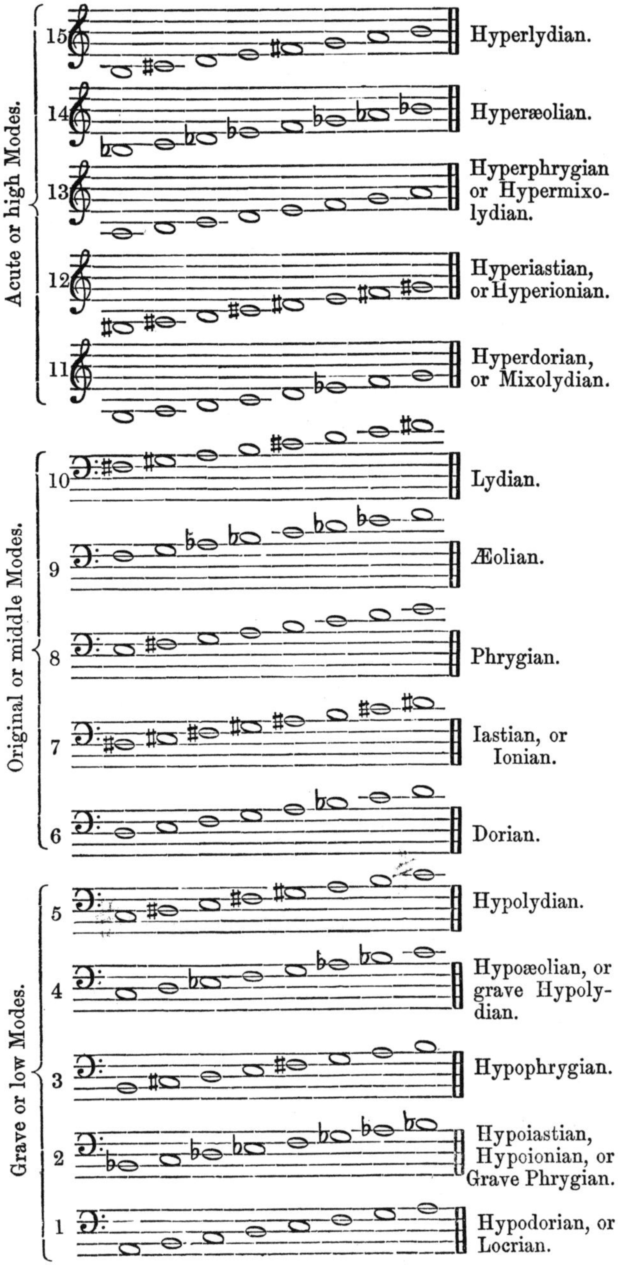

From the above sketch, it will be perceived that the three numbers 13, 14, 15, are properly mere repetitions of 1, 2, and 3, so that we can freely coincide with those writers who admit only twelve of the fifteen, especially as the numbers 13, 14, 15, having gone beyond the whole tone-system assumed by the Greeks, could not on that account be performed at all.

It is further to be remarked, that (according to our ideas) we have not before us fifteen keys, but only fifteen transpositions of one minor scale, in which the sixth and seventh degrees are never raised in ascending, although from custom and the feeling of harmony our ear demands this.*

From these keys *(modi)* the octave species must be carefully distinguished *(species diapason)*, the difference consisting in the fact, that the distance of the intervals situated in the compass of an octave is altered in each of these species of diapason. For example :—

A B c d e f g a
B c d e f g a b
c d e f g a b c

are octave species of one and the same key *(Hypodorian)*; on the other hand,

B ♯*c* . *d e* ♯*f g a b*
c d ♭*e f g* ♭*a* ♭*b c*

are keys or modes. It is scarcely necessary to remind the reader that in one key there can only be seven octave species.

* It certainly is a curious circumstance, that the Greeks were totally unacquainted with our major key.

FIFTH.—PROPORTIONS OF THE INTERVALS.

The proportions of the intervals were first taught to the Greeks by Pythagoras; but since this great philosopher gave numerals (as Marpurg expresses it) the preference to the ear, it is not surprising that he could never arrive at their true natural measurement.

According to his theory, the ear must be corrected by calculation; and since he followed the prejudice in favour of the quaternion (1 : 2 : 3 : 4 :), esteemed so sacred by the Greeks, and by which they were accustomed to swear, resolving to recognize all simple ratios which passed over this limit as dissonant, it was only the ratio of the octave, as 2 to 1, the fifth, as 3 to 2, and the fourth, as 4 to 3, which had the honour of being esteemed consonances; the numbers 5: 4: 6: had the misfortune to be excluded, and he invented amplicated ratios for the thirds and sixths, with which they were necessarily thrown aside among the dissonances. At the period of the rapid decline of Greek music (B.C. 38), Didymus first, and after him Claudius Ptolemæus (A.D. 125-161), discovered the correct ratios for both thirds, as 5 to 4 and 6 to 5; but still they were not recognized as consonant. The prejudice against the thirds and sixths was naturally inherited by the Hellenizing musical pedants of the middle ages; and at the time when these intervals in counterpoint had in fact already long acquired the right of citizenship, Faber Stapulensis (A.D. 1514) showed them to be dissonances, although Franco of Cologne, about the year 1220, had previously held the thirds as imperfect concords. Glarianus also *(Dodecachordon*, 1547) pointed them out as "imperfect" consonances;

but may not this blot of *imperfection* be nothing more than a small remnant of the old leaven, which our musical grammarians would at the present day attribute to them?

Zarlino (in 1558) was the first to discover and represent the true proportions of all the intervals of our scales.

SIXTH.—TONE CHARACTERS.

The number of characters required in the old Greek semiography may well excite our wonder; the reason is, as Forkel very justly observes, that "they overlooked all similitude in those things which were to be marked, and gave separate signs to each of them, as if they were in themselves distinctly different."

Thus the instrumental part is, beyond all comprehension, quite differently marked from the vocal, and the eighteen notes of the system received marks totally distinct in each of the three genera, although the names of the notes in the tetrachord were left the same. Thus, too, the number consisted of 1620 tone characters with which musicians were compelled to burden their memory; for instance, fifteen keys in each of the eighteen tones required 270; this being multiplied by the number of the three genera of sound, the vocal part alone would require 810 marks, and the instrumental as many more, giving the number of 1620 above mentioned, and this number is actually laid down by Alypius; it is, however, somewhat reduced according to Forkel's very correct remark, that the two extreme notes of the tetrachord, in all keys and in all genera of sound *(soni stantes)*, retain their marks, so that only 990 marks remain, actually different from each other.

These tone characters consist of the capitals of the Greek alphabet, which, in order to attain the necessary multiplication, are represented sometimes upright, and at other times inclined, flat, oblique, contracted, elongated, &c. &c. It would, nevertheless, have been impossible, even by these means, to have gained the whole number, had not another meaning been given to one and the same mark in each key, but which contributed indeed very slightly to assist the memory.

For the duration or value of the notes the Greeks had no marks, nor did any appear to be required by a people with whom poetic rhythm alone had weight, and it was solely on this that the excellence of their music essentially depended. Notwithstanding their intellectual merits, they had not yet fallen upon a method of notation which could raise in the mind of the beholder an idea of the ascent or descent of the voice,—a discovery which was reserved for the middle ages, so often pronounced to be barbarous.

I shall here close this brief sketch of the rudiments of ancient Grecian music, sufficient no doubt, in its present shape, for enabling my readers to understand the references which appear in the introduction to this work. I shall only add, that, according to Forkel, (*G. D. M.*, part i, page 314), the Grecian music began to decline soon after the death of Alexander the Great (B.C. 330), and that it was at a very low ebb when it reached the Romans, whose inclination for this art was either too feeble, or too much repressed by the spirit of warfare, again to revive it. What Forkel has further added to the passage above noticed, is a matter of opinion in which I confess that I do not exactly coincide.

II.

NEUMATA.

The Neumata, in which the oldest Chant-books of the Latin Church now extant are noted, consist of points, little hooks, strokes, and flourishes, in different shapes and directions; these represented to the singer by their position the height of tone, and by their shape the inflexion, *i.e.* the rising or falling, of the voice.

In order to afford the reader a better notion, I subjoin on the opposite plates a *fac simile*, which Padre Martini has represented in his *History of Music*, with a decyphering in choral notes, which he has added.

The notation, marked No. 1, although the idea is undoubtedly well-founded, has one important defect, inasmuch as it is scarcely possible for the writer to put down a mark so correctly, that the reader (singer) may not take the sound one or more notes higher or lower than the one intended. This was in some degree remedied during the ninth and tenth centuries, when a line was drawn parallel with the words of the text, above and below which the Neumata or marks were inserted. (See Nos. II. and III.) A still greater improvement was, the use of two lines, one red and the other yellow, which served at the same time as the *F* and *C* keys; between these two lines, in the interstice higher or lower according to the eye, the notes lying between *f* and *c*, namely *g*, *a*, *b*, were inserted. (See No. IV.) In this condition Guido found the writing of Neumata, and he materially improved it by drawing a line under *F*, with one in the middle between red *F* and yellow *C;* whilst in this system of four lines, he now taught the use not only of the lines, but also of the spaces between them; so that each tone at length held its appointed place, which could not be mistaken, and all ambiguity was prevented.

This system of lines was still retained, when, at a later period, the note or point-writing was introduced.

Nº 1.

Original neumata
Celi celoy laudate deum
The above marks represented by notes
Ce li Celorus laudate deum.

Nº 2.

Original neumata
Per sice gref sus me os mse muis tu is
Interpretation
Persi ce gres sus meos in se mi tis tu is

N.º 3.

Original neumata
Desiderium anime eius tribuisti ci &c.
Interpretation
De si de ri um a nimę e ius tribuis ti e i et.

N.º 4.

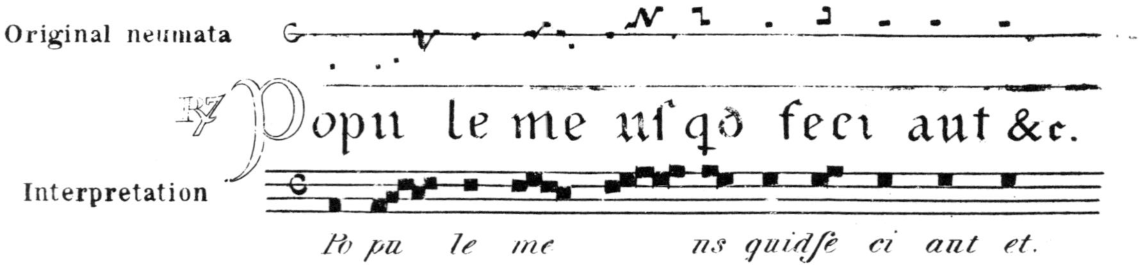
Original neumata
℟ Popu le me us qd feci aut &c.
Interpretation
Po pu le me us quid fe ci aut et.

The word Neuma has, moreover, a meaning totally different from that attributed to it with regard to the tone-marks just described. For instance, in choral chants, by Neuma is understood a melodious phrase at the end of a verse (Melisma), which is merely vocalized without text, as it were, *per metonymiam*, an aggregate of Neumata or tone-marks. Finally, Guido of Arezzo, in many parts of his treatises, uses the word Neuma even for a written chant.

The Latin Neumata writing gained no footing in the East, where the people were already in possession of different kinds of notation. The most ancient codices have accents by which scarcely anything more than a kind of collect-chant or slow reading could have been marked. In the fifth century, we find fourteen prettily-formed marks, which are said to have been introduced by St. Ephraim (see Gerbert's *ält Lex.* Art. Ephraim); but their meaning has long been lost. This notation, at a later period, gave place to a third, which the Greek Church is said to have received from St. Joannes Damascenus, who died A.D. 766, and which is used exclusively in the books of their Liturgy even to our own day. It is equally distinguished from the Neumata and note-writing which point out the height of tone from the higher or lower position of the marks, as from the tone-writing of the ancient Greeks, or the letters of St. Gregory, where each mark at least showed with certainty a determinate tone; it is a species of writing which commands, as it were, how many steps the singer should ascend or descend from the tone which he had last in his throat. It resembles, therefore, the tone-writing invented by Hermannus Contractus (an author of the eleventh century) *per intervallorum designationem.* (See the note immediately following.)

Its marks, if not so numerous as those of the ancient Greek music, are still complicated; partly owing to particular rules for their use, and partly by the mingling together of a considerable number of marks without reference to sound (*aphona*), which have an effect only on the manner of delivery and the formation of the voice; furnishing a notation beset with ambiguity, and very difficult to be understood. Moreover, the Christians of the separated Greek Church have certainly not only retained the eight Church Keys of St. Gregory, but many other and different chants (for they sing incessantly), which had their origin partly from St. Johannes Damascenus, and partly at a later period (the thirteenth century) from Joann Lapidarius, Manuel Chrysaphus, Joasaph Kukuzele, Joann Kukugell, and others.

Whoever may desire to become more closely acquainted with the now obsolete Byzantine notation, will find some information, although not of the most satisfactory kind, in Burney, in Forkel's *G. I. M.*, in P. Kircher's *Musurgie*, and a little more in a treatise of Villoteau, which is to be met with in his comprehensive description of Egypt. The latest source of information is probably the *Isagoge* of Chrysanthos, in the modern Greek language (printed at Paris, 1821), vol. viii. p. 56; which for my own part I have found quite as unintelligible in an attempted German translation as in the modern Greek tongue, a language wholly unknown to me.

III.

HUCBALDUS AND HERMANNUS CONTRACTUS.

Hucbaldus invented a method of tone-writing in imitation of the ancient Grecian, with a curiously-formed and differently-placed letter *F*, for as many tones as were in use throughout the whole of the tone-system. It has nowhere been brought into use; and I have never found it except in a treatise of Hermannus Contractus (see Gerbert, *Script. de Mus.* part i. p. 145); again, in the *Dialogus qui et Enchiridion vocatur*, and very frequently appended, under the name of *Domni Oddonis*, to the treatises of Guido (see Gerbert, *Sammlung Script. de Mus.* part i. p. 252); but erroneously, as I imagine, admitted among the treatises of St. Oddo of Clugny.

Hermannus Contractus also attempted a peculiar tone-writing, or rather tone-marking, in which he only marked the interval above the text, where the singer should join in; for example, e for *equalis;* s *semitonium;* t *tonus;* ts *tonus et semitonus;* tt *duo toni vel ditonus*, &c.

IV.

HEXACHORD.

The Hexachord is a companion to the Tetrachord of the ancient Greek theory. Whoever may wish for further information on this point, will find an account of it, amongst other matter, in Koch's *Mus. Lex.* Art. Solmisation, p. 1407. It appears rather to have originated with the scholars and commentators of Guido (who spun it out from his syllables *ut re mi fa sol la*), than with that author himself. It is neither introduced nor alluded to in the works of Guido ; and his most famous commentator, *John Cotton, makes no mention* of it.*

---

* Subjoined is a plan of the Guidonian hand, and a table of the Hexachords.—*Translator.*

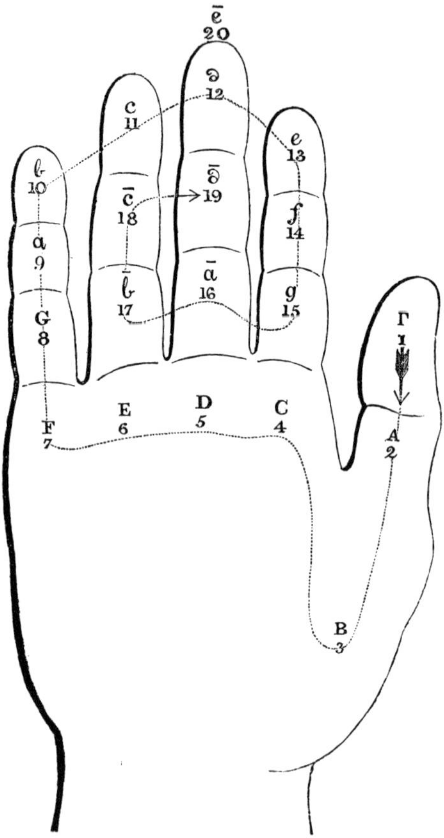

TABLE OF THE HEXACHORDS

OF THE GUIDONIAN SCHOOL, WITH THEIR SYLLABLES.

e e							*la*
d d						*la*	*sol*
c c						*sol*	*fa*
b vel ♮						*fa* (b)	*mi*
a					*la*	*mi*	*re*
g					*sol*	*re*	*ut*
f					*fa*	*ut*	
e				*la*	*mi*		
d			*la*	*sol*	*re*		
c			*sol*	*fa*	*ut*		
B			*fa* (b)	*mi*			
A		*la*	*mi*	*re*			
G		*sol*	*re*	*ut*			
F		*fa*	*ut*				
E	*la*	*mi*					
D	*sol*	*re*					
C	*fa*	*ut*					
B vel ♮	*mi*						
A	*re*						
Γ	*ut*						
	G	*C*	*F*	*G*	*C*	*F*	*G*

Mi meant everywhere the position of the half-note, or more

V.

HARMONY, MELODY.

Harmony among the Grecians signified a succession of single notes, according to their scale; and Melody, a succession of these harmonic sounds, according to the rules of rhythm.

That which the ancients called Harmony signifies with us Melody, which comprises at the same time within itself both the Grecian Harmony and Melody.—Forkel, *Gesch. d. Mus.* part i. p. 401.

VI.

ELOY, EGIDIUS BINCHOIS, VINCENTIUS FAUGUES.

Eloy is evidently only the Christian name of this writer, and means the same as Eligius.

Egidius I cannot help supposing to be merely a change from Eligius, and that Egidius Binchois is identical with Eloy. Time, however, will elucidate the fact. That Binchois, too, was a Belgian, and not a Frenchman, appears to be confirmed by many circumstances; at all events, France was not in his days the country where counterpoint was studied.

Tinctoris, who erroneously assigns Dufay and Binchois to France, may be equally presumed to have fallen into a mis-

---

properly the *subsemitonium modi*, which received at every such place the syllables *mi fa*. The so-called B rotundum (*B* flat) appears only in the hexachord of the scale of *F*, which was in consequence called *Hexachordium molle*. With this exception, *B* natural (namely *B quadratum*, the English *B* natural, or French *Si*) is always understood. The tones *E F* being semitones contained in our natural scale, are therefore *mi fa* in themselves.—*Translator*.

take with regard to the latter, as he is proved to have done in respect to the former; or he may have meant by the term "*Gallia*" the southern provinces of the Burgundian territory (Hainault, Cambresis, Southern Flanders, &c.), where the Gallic tongue was the native language, in contradistinction to the northern provinces, where the low German in different dialects was generally spoken.

Faugues, according to Baini, was called by the prænomen of Vincentius, more than one of whose compositions he had before his eyes. Tinctoris, in a treatise A.D. 1476, speaks of a Guillermus Faugues as contemporary with Joannes Ockeghem, Joannes Regis, Antonius Busnoys, and Firminus Caron, who flourished about that period, and who "boasted of having had as teachers in this divine art the lately deceased Johannes Dunstable (?), Egidius Binchois, and Guillermus Dufoy" (? ?).

I have no doubt of the identity of this Faugues mentioned by Tinctoris, with the one referred to by Baini, although there are evidently in his account several anachronisms. But there appears in the publications of Petrucci, in the *Motetti della Corona*, 1519, a La Fage, or La Faghe, without any prænomen, who probably was a different person from this ancient Faugues.

CORRESPONDENCE WITH THE AUTHOR.

In the following correspondence with the author, the translator thinks it unnecessary to quote his own letters; the replies of the former to his remarks, (a translation of which is here given) being sufficient to lead the reader to a knowledge of the subject treated of.

Note to Guido's Scale (page 12).

"Your projected note to explain the scale of Guido I find quite appropriate. It is, properly speaking, the system of Pope Gregory exactly as we know it through Guido, for the originator himself left nothing behind him on this point that we know of; (a treatise by him is said to have been lost), but in Guido's system the note C is the principal note, as the *Ut queant laxis* demonstrates (of which more in another place), and this system, founded on the note C, is what the moderns have retained."

Ut queant laxis (page 57).

"That you give in this place the familiar *Ut queant laxis* is quite right, only it might be as well for less instructed readers to remark, that Guido took the beginning syllables of each line in the hymn written in honour of John the Baptist

(Ut, re, mi, fa, sol, la), which he (or his pupils) introduced for the appellation of the first six tones of the scale instead of the alphabetical letters, and which are still used by the French and Italian schools. In the school of the Guidonians, however, these six syllables were not, as at present, united to certain notes, as C, D, E, F, G, A, but were used in such a manner that the half tone, which, as we know, occurs twice in the scale, should necessarily fall between the syllables *Mi, Fa.* The syllables had, therefore, to be changed at each variation of the melodic modulation, and this was called mutation. This process was not without difficulty, which, in the course of time, was attempted to be obviated for the student. In the schools in France, the syllables were (as far as is known at least) first immutably fixed; Ut was, once for all, substituted for C; Re for D; Mi for E; Fa for F; Sol for G; and La for A. Now, however, arose a dilemma, from the circumstance of there being no seventh syllable. Various of the learned proposed a new syllable for the seventh, or else seven entirely new ones; but at last it was agreed to retain the seven original ones, and to add for the seventh the new syllable Si, which the French and Italians still use; the English and Germans, however, had given up the old solmisation, and returned to the alphabetical letters C, D, E, F, G, A, B.
1 2 3 4 5 6 7

"The curious reader might very naturally inquire why Guido himself did not invent a seventh syllable. He did not require it; the mutation of the syllables made this superfluous, as he had only to change his hexachord in such a manner as to produce a new *mi fa* in its proper place."

The table of the hexachords in the appendix will be sufficient to explain this. The reader who may wish for more information on the subject, is referred to the author's work, entitled, "Guido von Arezzo—sein Leben und Werken."—*Translator.*

Walter Odington.—Burney's General History of Music, vol. ii, p. 155, *et seq.*

"But concerning the obligations which music has had to Franco, as I shall have occasion to speak more fully in the next chapter, I shall take my leave of him for the present, and introduce to the acquaintance of my readers an Englishman, of whose writing a treatise is preserved in the library of Benet College, Cambridge,* that is so copious and complete with respect to every part of music which was known when it was written, that, *if all musical tracts hitherto mentioned, from the time of Boethius to Franco and John Cotton, were lost, our knowledge would not be much diminished, provided this manuscript were accessible.*

"Walter Odington, monk of Evesham in Worcestershire, the author of this work, was eminent in the early part of the thirteenth century, during the reign of Henry III, not only for his profound knowledge in music, but astronomy and mathematics in general. As Walter of Evesham lived at a period which furnishes but few records concerning the abode of music in England, and as I am unacquainted with any other copy of his manuscript than that which subsists at Cambridge, I shall be somewhat the more minute in describing its character, and pointing out its peculiarities.

"The first page only has been injured by time, and some vacuities have been left by the scribe, which seem intended to have been filled up with red ink. The work is divided into six parts or books." Here follows an enumeration of the contents of the book.

"The musical examples, however, as usual in old manuscripts, are incorrect, and frequently inexplicable, owing to the ignorance of music in the transcribers; but if this tract

* Hawkins says Christ College.—*Translator.*

were corrected, and such of the examples as are recoverable, regulated and restored, it would be the most ample, satisfactory, and valuable, which the middle ages can boast; as the curious inquirer into the state of music at this early period may discover in it not only what progress our countrymen had made in the art themselves, but the chief part of what was known elsewhere."

So far Burney, now for Kiesewetter.

"You are right to copy Burney at the place in question, regarding Walter Odington. With my remarks (which, by the way, did not arise on my part) you may do as you think proper.

"In the paragraph which offends you, I have found nothing to alter. Our musical historian Forkel (vol. ii, p. 415, *et seq.*) has given the whole passage, which Burney has extracted from Walter's manuscript, word for word literally translated. The whole communication consists of an *enumeration of the chapters*, and a very *meagre summary of their contents.* I find, therefore, that a German author can conscientiously say, that *we know scarcely anything more of him than the name, and the existence of a treatise said to be his, but nowhere published.* I challenge all English critics to confess, that they know nothing more of the monk of Evesham, if they know him only through their Burney. The praises which the Doctor lavishes upon him are by no means conclusive. He is dazzled by patriotism, and his object can only be to flatter his countrymen, when he says of the treatise in question, that *it would have made all works, from the time of Boethius to Franco, (!) even had they been collectively lost, (!!)* unnecessary to the world. If Dr. Burney had allowed his conscience to express an opinion, he would have been obliged to confess, that *Walter Odington is far behind Franco in knowledge*, and indeed belongs more to the time of the neumata than to that of *mensural* and *figural music*, and that his work could be as well dated 1140 as 1240."

On the origin of the German H, as name for the second note of the alphabetical series.

"The B has also with the Germans as many significations and employments as with the English, with the exception only that we never understand it to be H (English B natural, or French Si). For the rest, I have long been of your opinion, that our old teachers would have done better had they retained the B for the natural succession of the series, namely for the tone which the Germans call H, the English B; it would not have prevented them from appending the *is* and *es*, which is introduced to express a note being raised or lowered a semitone. But as we have had it so long, we neither can nor desire to divest ourselves of it.

"It appears that we were also in some perplexity with regard to the appellation of the seventh note of the scale, and that the difference of the already existing signs b and ♮, occasioned the introduction of the H, because the sign ♮ in itself could be taken for H by drawing the stroke downwards from the right side, in the same way that out of 𝔟 we procure an *h* by the prolongation of the stroke to the right, namely 𝔥.

"The appellation of B rotundum (b), and B quadratum (♮) have long since become obsolete everywhere, and in the course of time the ♮ has even been introduced as a sign to restore a note to its natural state which had been made either sharp or flat; a very clumsy invention, because it would have been better to have taken this sign to raise a note a semitone which had accidentally been made flat, and to have introduced another new sign to lower a note a semitone which had accidentally been made sharp, instead of using, as we do now, ♮

to lower C sharp into C natural, and the same ♮ to raise A flat into A natural, a course of great annoyance in transposing at sight on an instrument.

"I always regard, however, the German elementary school as the best of any, because any sound in the scale can be pronounced with one syllable, without trouble and without ambiguity. Our boys sing the notes with their names as quick as lightning. For example,

German—A.	H.	C.	D.	E.	F.	G.
English—A.	B.	C.	D.	E.	F.	G.
German—Ais.	His.	Cis.	Dis.	Eis.	Fis.	Gis.
English—A sharp.	B sharp.	C sharp.	D sharp.	E sharp.	F sharp.	G sharp.
German—As.	B.	Ces.	Des.	Es.	Fes.	Ges.
English—A flat.	B flat.	C flat.	D flat.	E flat.	F flat.	G flat.

"Take, for instance, the scale of A flat major, and let us consider how other nations would pant for breath were they to *solfa* this scale. The English would say A flat, Bi flat, Ci flat, Di flat, E flat, Ef, Gee, A flat. The French, Labemol, Sibemol, Ut, Rebemol, Mibemol, Fa, Sol, Labemol!! The Italians even go so far as to name the notes of the scale Cesolfaut, Delasobre, Elami, Fefaut, Gesolfaut, Alamire, Befami!!! Besides this, how difficult do other nations find it to distinguish by words the precise note in the whole system of the octaves which may be required to be described, whilst we express it by one word *eingestrichen, zweygestrichen,*" &c. —*(See Translator's Note concerning the System of the Octaves,* page 12.)

"Perhaps it would be sufficient in this place, where it certainly does not require a profound discussion, simply to remark that the name of the second note of the scale was twofold: one with a ♭ called B rotundum, and one with a ♮ called B quadratum, which last agrees with the H of the Germans, the B of the English, and the Si of the French." . . . . .

"I have thought of writing to you for some time past, having been requested by my publisher to revise my *History of Modern Music* for the purpose of publishing a new edition, and a few days ago I at last dispatched the manuscript to Leipzig. I cannot exactly make anything new of it, which perhaps I would have done were I twenty years younger; but I confess that in the revisal I found more places to draw my pen through than to add new matter. That which, however, has long oppressed my conscience, and which makes the appearance of a new edition much to be wished for on my part, was the circumstance that I did not do proper justice to the English. To correct this was my peculiar aim, and is almost the only new matter which I have added. I here send you, on another sheet, the small but—in respect to the above subject in the first edition—important additions, and with much pleasure empower you to make any use of them you please in your work, as my new edition may not appear for months yet. . . . . .

"The period of my musical and musical-literary activity is now passed. Released from the fatigues of office,* I could now give myself up entirely to music; but we have been so blessed (!) with concerts of the Virtuosi, that I can find no evening, unoccupied by artists, to produce, as usual, specimens of ancient music, and the musical institution here has been dumb for at least five years. But in regard to musical-literary authorship, the age of nearly seventy-three years is

* Kiesewetter was many years at the head of the war department in Vienna,—a singular occupation to unite with musical pursuits,—and was in the habit of giving annually, at his own residence, private historical concerts, commencing with the first experiments in counterpoint down to the elaborate compositions of the greatest masters.—*Trans.*

no longer that of productiveness." [This letter is dated 29th July 1846.] . . . . .

I have to thank you for the honour you have conferred upon me by your translation of my 'History.' The feebleness of this work I am well aware of, and peculiar circumstances alone could have induced me to publish it. It has met, however, with success in Germany and France. The only merit it possesses consists in the plan: its feebleness is evinced by the superficial method in which the subject-matter is worked out, but this may almost be urged as a point in its favour, from the cursory and general view which it gives of the whole progress of the science; because many amateurs or professional musicians would summon courage for the study of the present work, few of whom would have the patience to wade through the voluminous histories of Forkel or Burney. . - . .

"You are surprised, dear friend, at my musical-literary activity during the last ten years. I am surprised myself when I look at the collection of music, theory, and literature, which I have written, and when I reflect that I have produced all this, independent of the fully occupied time which the labours of office required. But for me it was recreation, and it is easy to imagine that the composer or practical musician cannot give himself up to such pursuits. This belongs to the dilettante who has a calling for the thing, and can easier find time for musical authorship, since he generally can produce but little in the practical department.

"Without venturing, in the most remote degree, to compare my insignificant efforts with the solid productions of the ablest writers in this department, I beg merely to remind you that the most diffuse amongst them,—such as Matheson, Marpurg, and Rochlitz in Germany,—D'Alembert, Brossard, and others in France,—and Hawkins and Burney in England,—were either amateurs, or, at all events, more to be regarded as such than as practical musicians.

"In fact, my *soi-disant History*, imperfect and superficial as it may be deemed, has the advantage of brevity, in which respect it will suit the convenience of readers in general; and this may be regarded as its principal, if not its sole merit, whilst at the same time it constitutes its foible.

"It may not, perhaps, be uninteresting to you, in a spare hour, to look over the catalogue of my published works. Should the experiment with my *History of Modern Music* succeed, and you might be inclined to attempt another, I would recommend No. 4 or No. 6. The latter would probably interest the many orientalists in England, who would there find a few hundred of Arabian and Persian words, possibly to them unknown or unexplained. It is to be observed, however, that the names and technical words of art must be arranged according to the English orthography, on which subject there is, unfortunately, no agreement among the different orientalists of Europe."

CATALOGUE

OF THE

PUBLISHED WORKS OF THE

BARON AND IMPERIAL CHANCELLOR, R. G. KIESEWETTER.

Treatises which have appeared separately.

1. Die Verdienste der Niederländer um die Tonkunst. Von dem Königl. niederländischen Institut zu Amsterdam gekrönte Preis-schrift. Amsterdam, 1830, in 4to.

2. Geschichte der europäisch-abendländischen, das ist, unsrer heutigen Musik. Leipzig, 1834, 4to.

3. Ueber die Musik der Neugriechen, nebst freyen Gedanken über altegyptische und altgriechische Musik. Leipzig, 1838, 4to.

4. Guido von Arezzo, sein Leben und Wirken. Mit einem Anhange über die dem heil. Bernhard zugeschriebenen musicalischen Tractate. Leipzig, 1840, 4to.

5. Schicksale und Beschaffenheit des *weltlichen Gesanges* vom frühen Mittelalter bis zu der *Erfindung des dramatischen Styles.* Leipzig, 1841, 4to.

6. Die Musik der Araber nach Original Quellen. Leipzig, 1842, 4to.

7. Ueber das *Leben und die Werke des Palestrina, nach dem grossen Werke des Ab. Baini.* Aus dem Nachlasse von F. S. Kandler, mit einer Vorrede und mit Anmerkungen begleitet herausgegeben. Leipzig, 1834, 8vo.

Treatises and Essays which have appeared in different Journals.

1. Ueber den *Umfang der Singstimmen in den Werken der alten Meister.* 1820.

2. Ueber die Tonschrift P. Gregors des Grossen. 1828.

3. Ueber Franco von Cölln und die ältesten Mensuralisten. 1828.

4. Nachricht von einem noch *unangezeigten Codex aus dem* XVI Jahrh. 1830.

5. Die *Tabulaturen der älteren Practiker* seit Einführung der Figural und Mensural Musik.

1st Art. Die Deutsche Tabulatur.

2nd Art. Die Lauten Tabulatur.

3rd Art. Orgeltabulatur (vorgebl. in Italien).

4th Art. Italienishe Tabulatur oder die bezifferten Bässe.

5th Art. Die Notentabulatur oder Partitur der alten Contrapunctisten. 1830.

6. Ueber die *Herkunft Josquins des Prés.* 1835.

7. Ueber den *weltlichen und volksmässigen Gesang* im Mittelalter. 1838.

8. Ueber die Lebensperiode Franco's (Duplik). 1838.

9. Ueber die Tonschrift S. Gregors, M. Eine *Duplik* aus Veranlassung der Briefe des Hrn. Fetis über seine Reise durch Italien. 1843.

10. *Randglossen zu den Artikeln des Hrn. Fetis* in der Revue et Gazette Musicale, v. J. 1843, No. 21 and 22, Ueber *die Tonschrift* deren sich *S. Gregor* für den Gesang seines *Antiphonars* bedient hat. 1845.

The above works appeared in the Leipzig Allg. Mus. Zeitung.

11. Ueber *Tonmessungen und Temperaturen.* 1842.

12. Recension. Tonarten des (römischen) Choral-gesanges. 1842.

13. Ueber die *Musikalischen Instrumente im Mittelalter* bis zur Gestaltung unsrer dermaligen Kammer-und-Orchester-Musik. 1843.

14. Recension. Notice sur les Collections Mus. de la Bibl. de Cambray, par E. de Caussemaker. Paris, 1843. Cæcilia, 1844.

15. Ueber die historische Novelle, oder das Capitel von den falschen Säeleuten.

[The above appeared in the Cæcilia of Mayence.]

16. Ueber die verschiedenen Methoden die Harmonie zu studiren. Carlsruher Zeitschr. 1843.

17. Sur l'analyse que *M. Fétis* a faite de l'ouvrage de M. R. G. Kiesewetter; *La Musique des Arabes* d'après les sources originales. Par l'auteur du livre. Paris, 1846.

18. Recension. *Ottaviano Petrucci da Fossombrone, der erste Erfinder des Musiknotendruckes mit beweglichen Metalltypen,* und seine Nachfolger im XVI Jahrhundert. von A. Schmid, Wien, 1845. In den Oesterreichischen Blättern für Literatur und Kunst. Jahrgang 1846.

19. Im Manuscr. ein grosses Werk über die *Accordenlehre* (Studien des Verfassers von J. 1811). Drey Foliobände mit unzähligen Notentafeln. (Nicht zur Ausgabe bestimmt.)

Ausser obigen, verschiedene minder bedeutende Gelegenheits Artikel in verschiedenen musical. Zeitschriften.

"I beg to announce to you, with this opportunity, that the second edition of my *History of Modern Music* has just appeared. Any alterations in the text are not worth speaking of. The most important are those which regard the labours of the English, and those I gave you in my last letter.

"There has also just appeared a small book of mine, under the title, 'Der neuen Aristoxener zerstreüte Aufsätze über das Irrige der musicalischen Arithmetik und das Eitle ihrer Temperatur-rechnungen; gesammelt und mit einer historisch-kritischen Einleitung als Vorrede. Leipzig bey Brietkopf und Härtel, 1846.'"

NOTE.

Supplementary explanation by the Author to the second edition of the *History of Modern Music*, in reference to the *Kyrie* and *Christe*, from the mass *Gaudeamus*, which is printed in the musical examples of the first edition under the name of Joannes Ockenheim.

On the testimony of a valuable manuscript codex existing in the Imperial Court Library, the author selected for the collection of examples in the first edition these two pieces, as compositions of the patriarch Joannes Ockenheim, and they have been likewise introduced under his name into the text of the new edition. Too late to correct the press, he has since discovered, by a mere accidental comparison made in the library with a mass noticed among the printed works of the celebrated Josquin des Prés, under the exactly same title *Gaudeamus*, that an error or mistake has been committed by the transcriber of the above-mentioned codex, and that the *Missa Gaudeamus* alluded to as being by Ockenheim, is no other than the precisely same *Missa Gaudeamus* by Josquin des Prés.

The author considers it his duty to apprize the possessors of the present, as well as the former edition, of this circumstance. Regarding the error which has crept into the text, he consoles himself in thinking that, instead of a composition of Ockenheim, of whose talent they already possess a specimen, they will receive one of his equally great pupil Josquin, from whose works the author would from the first have communicated some specimens, had he not considered that he was obliged to restrict himself in the number of musical examples.

FINIS.

Richards, Printer, 100, St. Martin's Lane.

SUPPLEMENT

TO

Kiesewetter's History of Music.

Containing the most

Ancient Monuments,

OF

FIGURED COUNTERPOINT.

The most ancient remnants of figured Counterpoint.

Remark – The accidental ♯, ♭, and ♮ are supplied in the score by the collector, and in order to keep the original unchanged, these symbols are placed not before but above the notes: on the contrary, the few which the author has expressly introduced are placed before the notes on the stave.

Nº 1.

Old French chanson for three voices, composed by Adam de la Hale about the year 1280: communicated by M. Fetis in the Revue musicale.

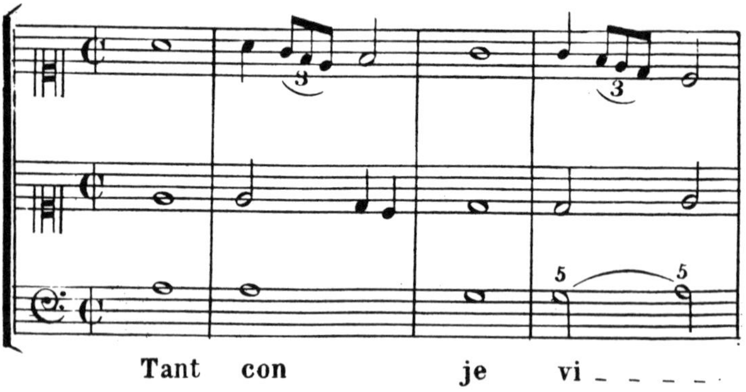

_ vrai n'a _ _ me _ _ _ _ _ rai au _
_ _ _ _ trui que vous.
je n'en par _ _ ti _ _ _ _ _ rai.

No. 2.

Facsimile communicated by Kalkbrenner in his Hist: de la Mus.

Triplum.
Et in ter--- ra pax ho - mi - ni --------- bus
Motetus.
Contratenor.
Tenor.
bonau vo --- lun ta tis landa mus te

No. 2.

Fragment of a Gloria from a Mass which was performed at the coronation of Charles the V of France in the year 1364, composed by Guill. Machault. Deciphered by R. G. Kiesewetter.

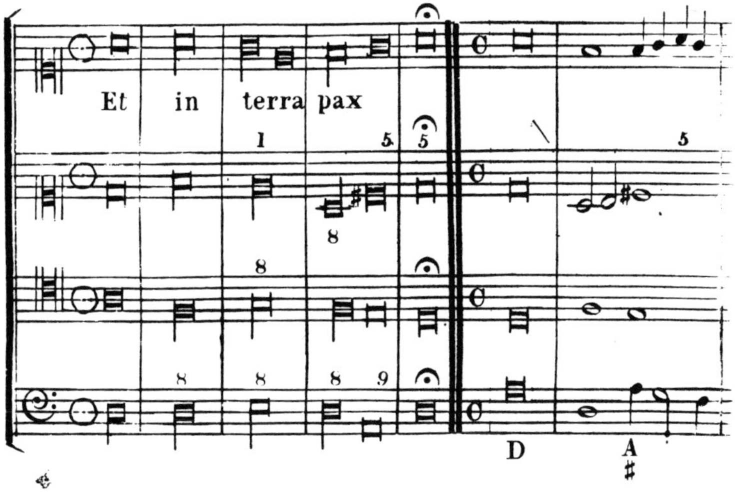

N°. 3.

Old French Chanson for three voices discovered and communicated by the Prince Abb. Gerbert in his historical work "De Cantu et musica sacra." Tome II, Tab XIX.

*) Ochetus.

**) Unexpected change of clef.

Here for the first time interpreted.

Superius.
Contratenor.
Tenor.
Mais qu'il vous vien_ne a plai _ _ sance da _ _ _
me en por ter pi _ _ tié; donnez moi par ca _ _ ri _
_ té de ma douleur ai _ _ san _ _ _ _ ce:
76 76

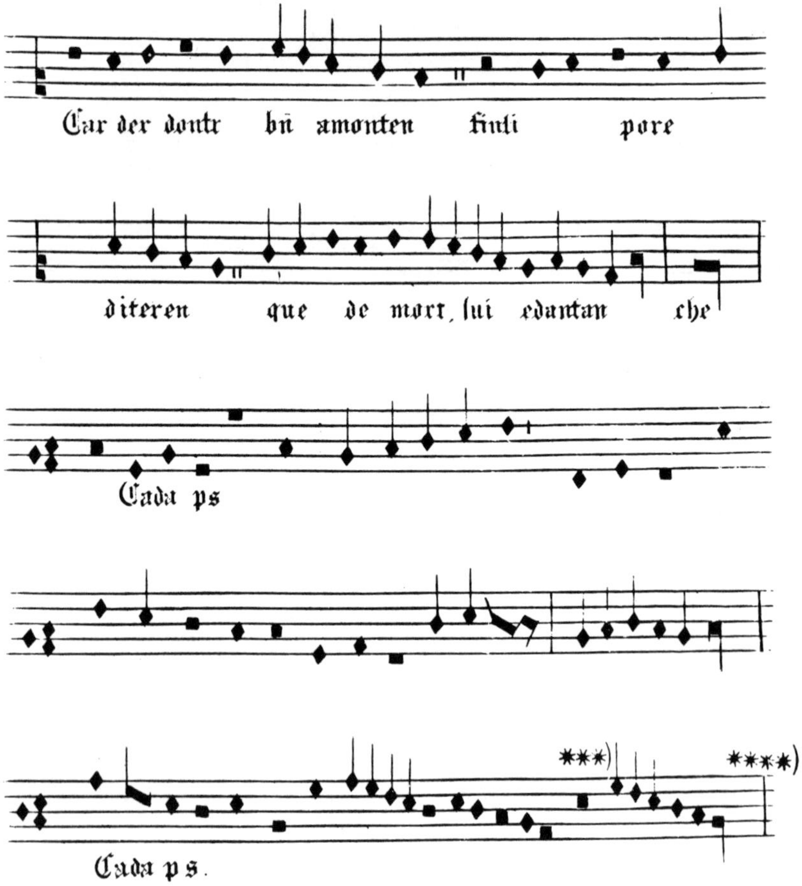

***) In this place two Temporas are wanting.

****) Hiatus in the manuscript.

Dots or Points are wanting in several places which in the original may probably have got rubbed out.

The text has manifestly been copied by an illeterate person; the attempted translation here giving may perhaps express the literal meaning.

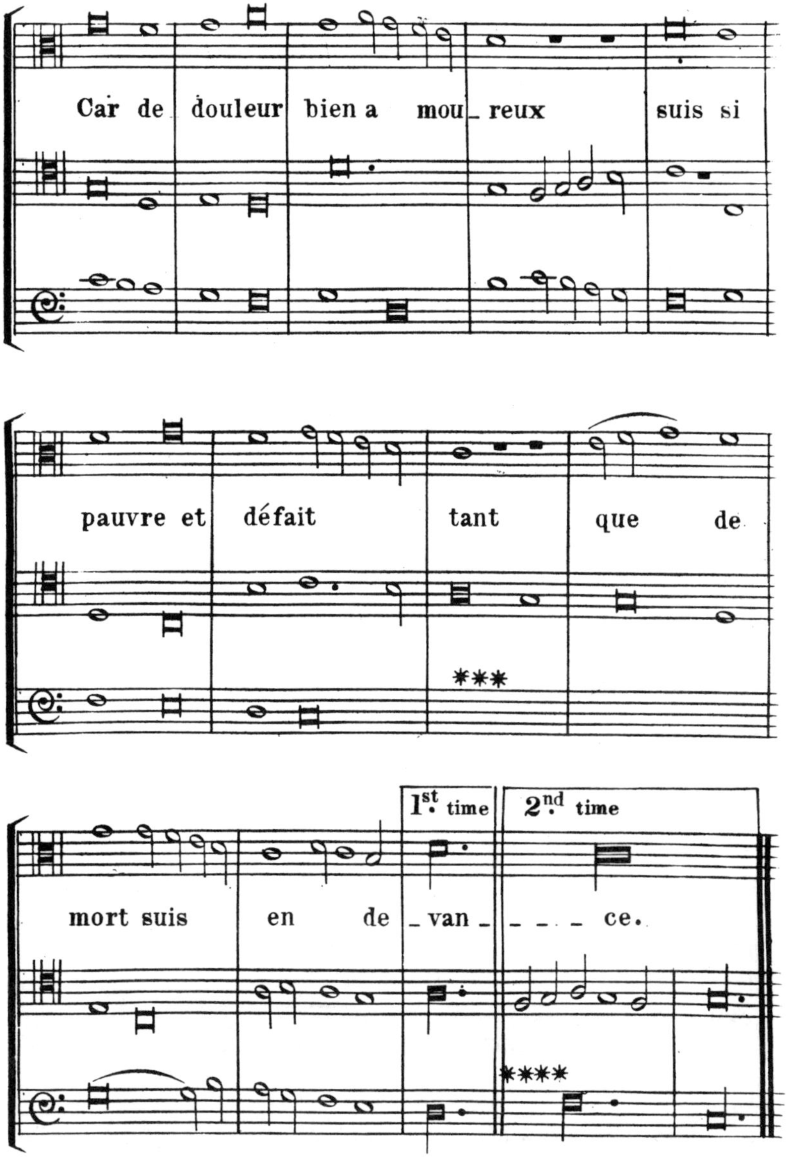
Car de douleur bien a mou_reux suis si
pauvre et défait tant que de
1st time
2nd time
mort suis en de _van_ _ _ _ ce.

Nº 4.

Italian Canzone for three voices from a volume of Songs by Florentine composers, communicated by M. Fetis in the Revue musicale Composed by Francesco Landino about the year 1360.

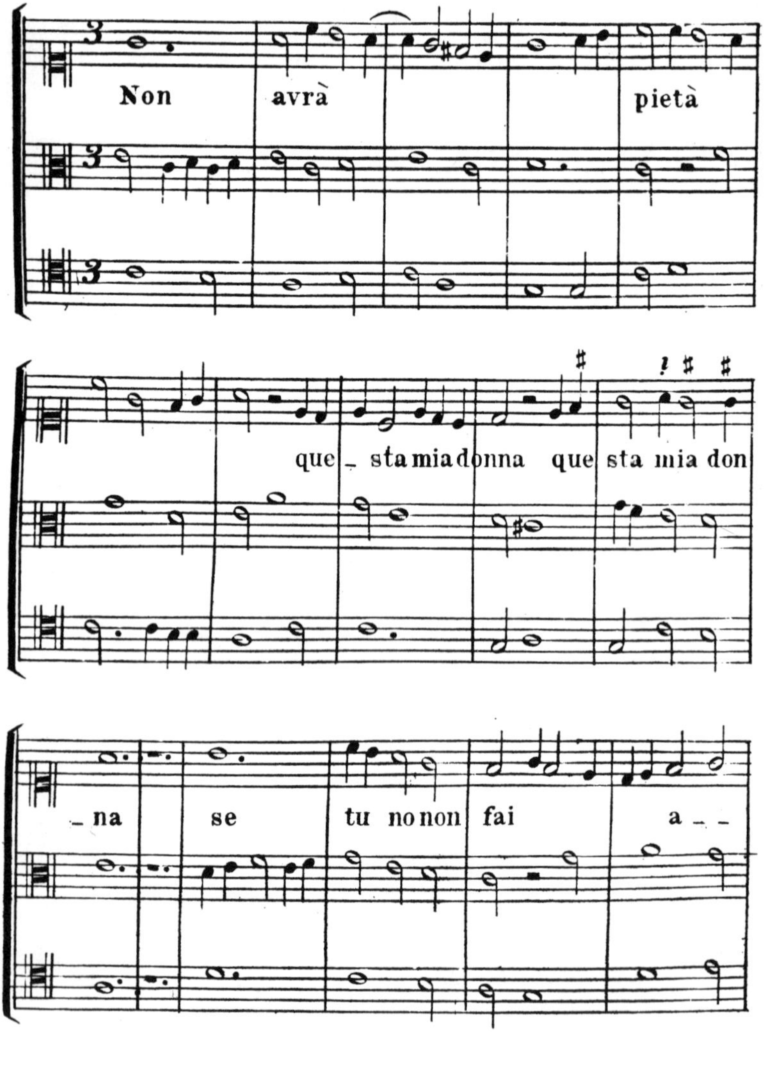
Non avrà pietà
que _ sta mia donna que sta mia don
_ na se tu no non fai a _ _

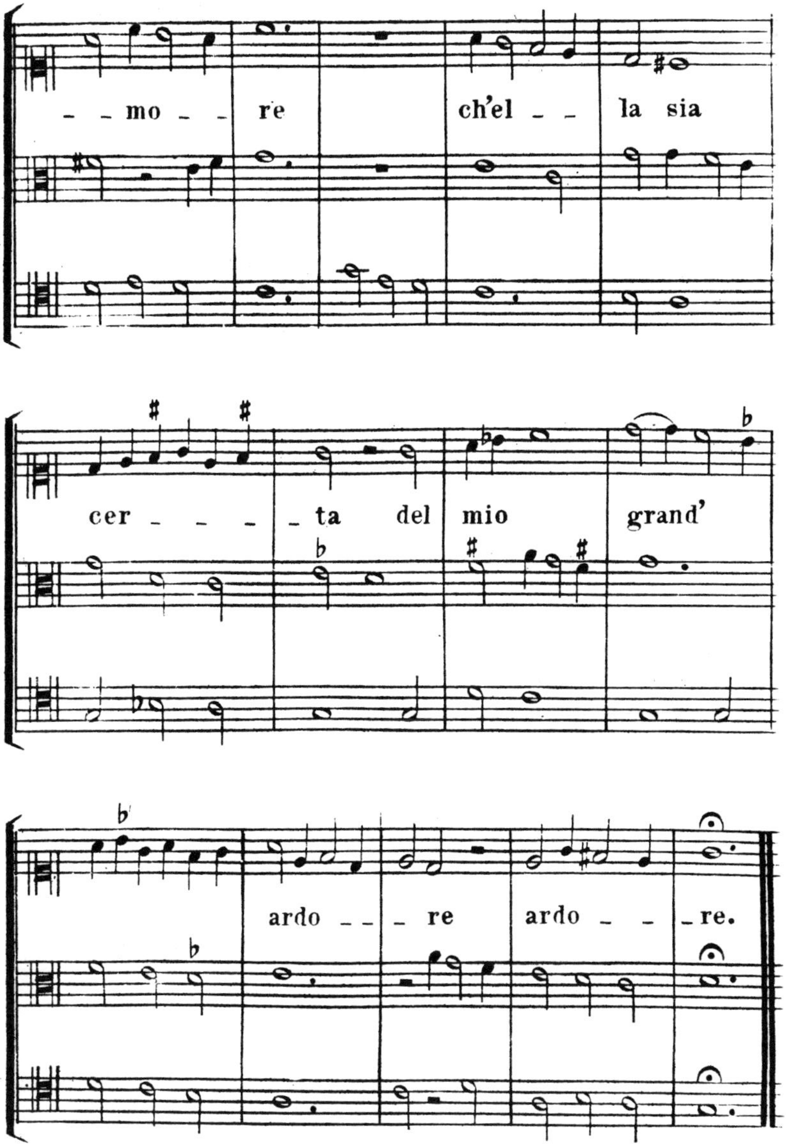
– – mo – – re ch'el – – la sia
cer – – – – – ta del mio grand'
ardo – – – re ardo – – – re.

No. 5.

Here follow several examples from the works of the masters of the ancient Belgian School, of which nothing has hitherto been made known.

Guilelmus Dufay (*Flor:* 1380 *to about* 1432)

a). ***Ex Missa se la face ay pale, 4 vocum.***

Interpretation.

Eleison
NB
Kyrie
eleison
eleison
Kyrie.
eleison
e _ leison
Kyrie.

NB
7 ♯6

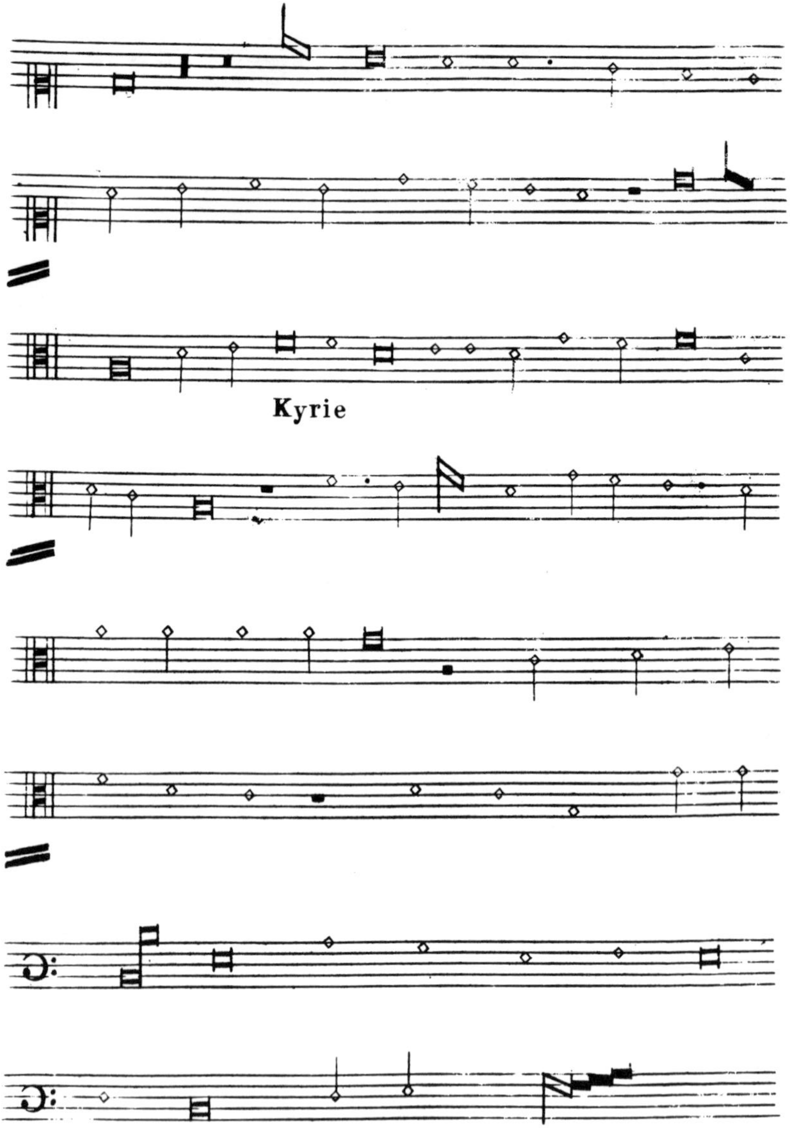
Kyrie

7 ♯6

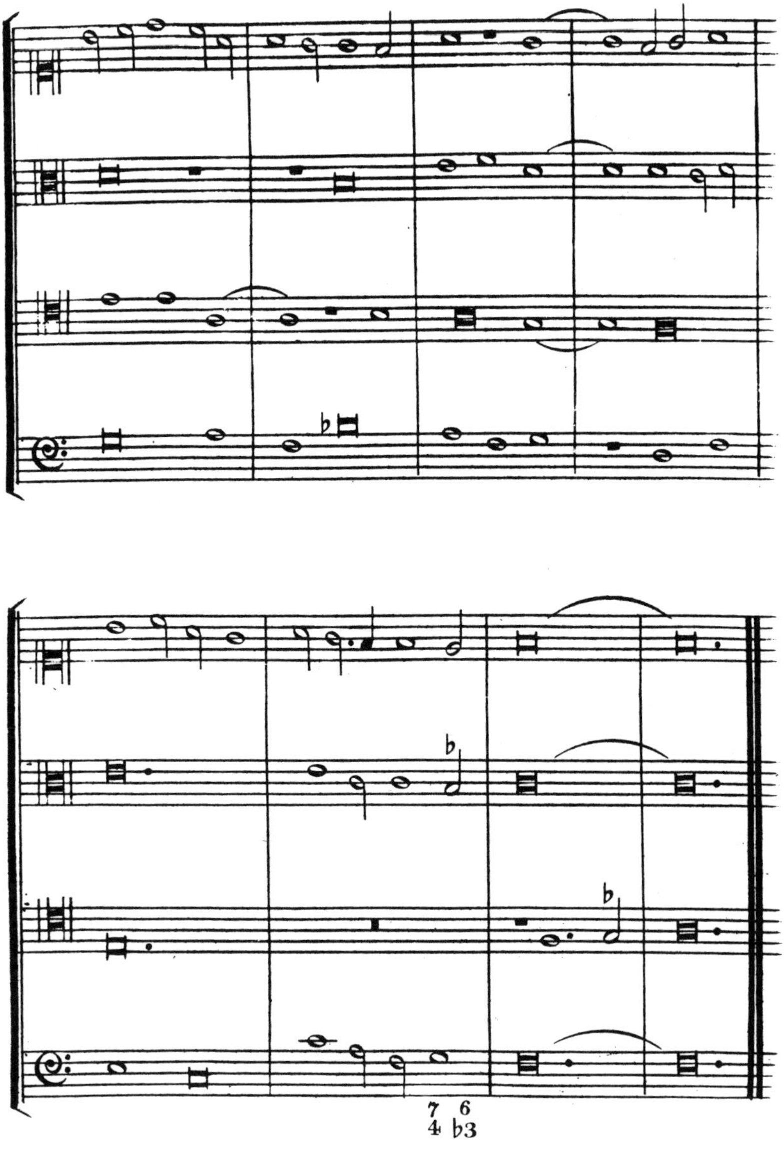
7 6
4 ♭3

b.) ***Ejusdem Guil. Dufay Benedictus ex Missa: Ecce ancilla Domini: a duabus vocibus.***

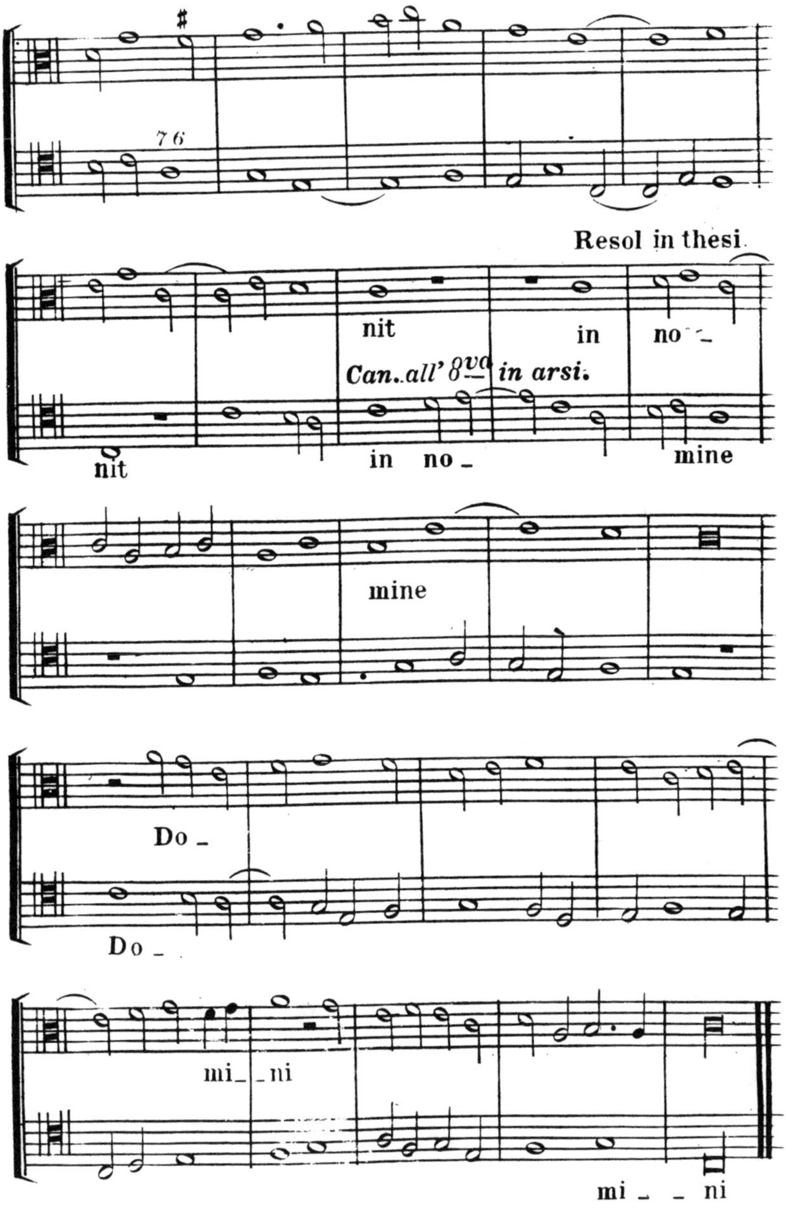
7 6
Resol in thesi
nit
in
no
Can..all' 8va in arsi.
nit
in no
mine
mine
Do
Do
mi_ni
mi_ni

c) *Ejusdem Guil: Dufay Kyrie ex Missa L'omme armé, 4 vocum.*

Remark – In the original the ♭ is only written in the Tenor part
Kyrie
(L'om – me l'om me ar – me)

№ 6.

Eloy. (Flor: about 1400)

a) *Kyrie ex Missa: Dixerunt discipuli.*

Canon Tenoris pro tota Missa: Non faciens pausas super signis capiens has, tempora tria prima semper bene pausa, sex decies currens cuncta que signa videns.

Tenor

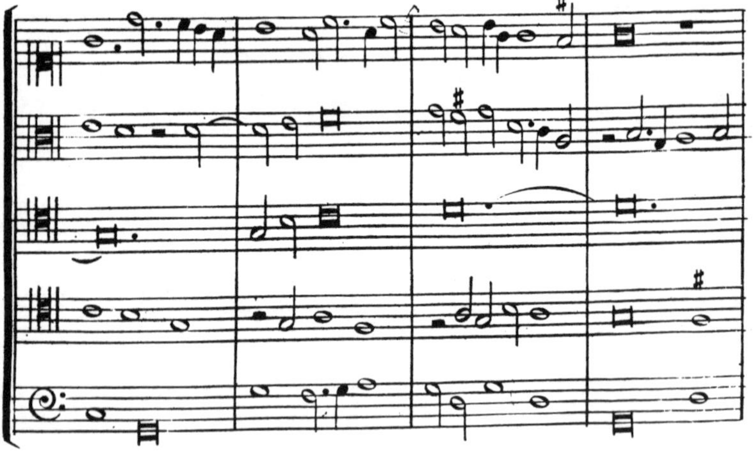

b. *Ejusdem Eloy ex eadem Missa.*

5
4 3
5
4 3

N.º 7.

Vincentius Faugues. (*Flor: in the first half of the XV Century.*)

Kyrie secundum ex Missa L'omme armé. 3 vocum.

*) In this place the substituted Mezzo-Soprono-clef (C on the 2nd line) is wanting.

Interpretation.

Remark. In the original the ♭ is not written in any of the parts, but must be so much the more un derstood (subintelligirt) as the known Tenor "L'omme arme" is written in the key of G with minor third.

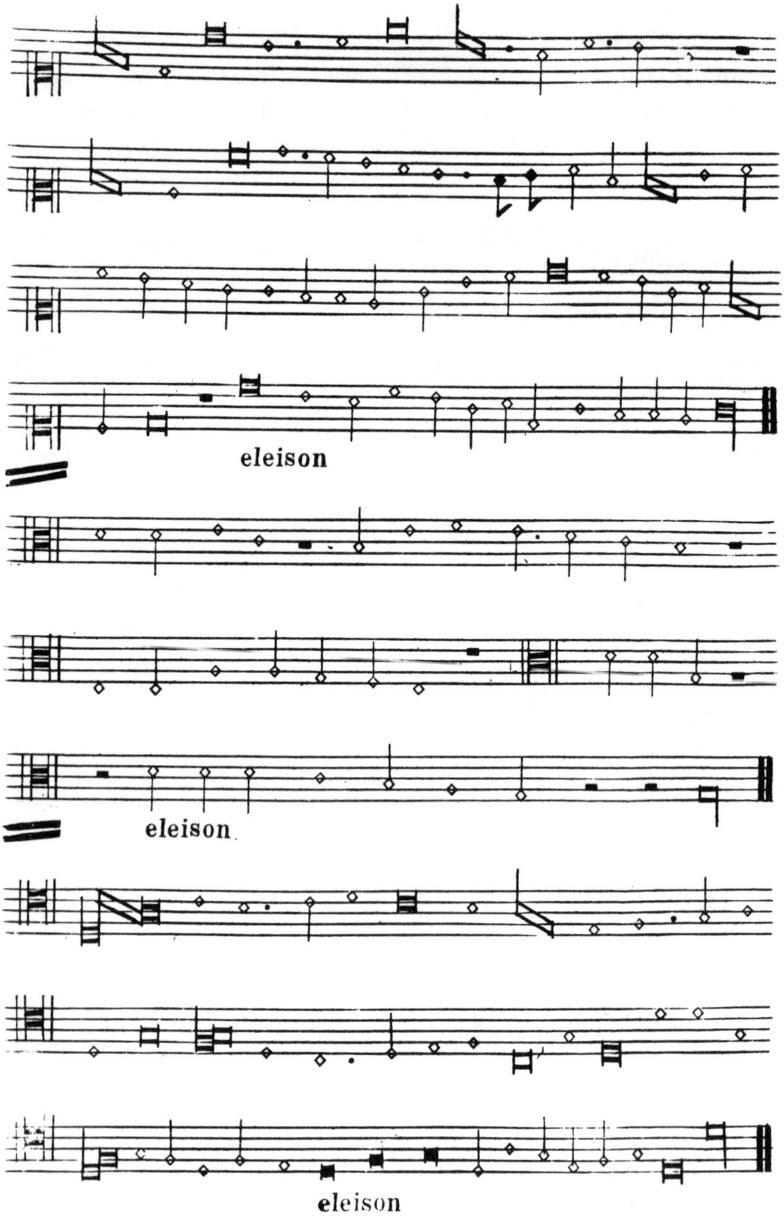
eleison
eleison
eleison

7 6

No. 8.

Joannes Ockeghem vel Ockenheim, chief of the second or modern Belgian School.

(Flor: about the year 1450.)

Kyrie from his celebrated *"Missa ad omnem Tonum"* which can be sung with any clef and in any key.

(In qua aures habeas oportet, says Glareanus)

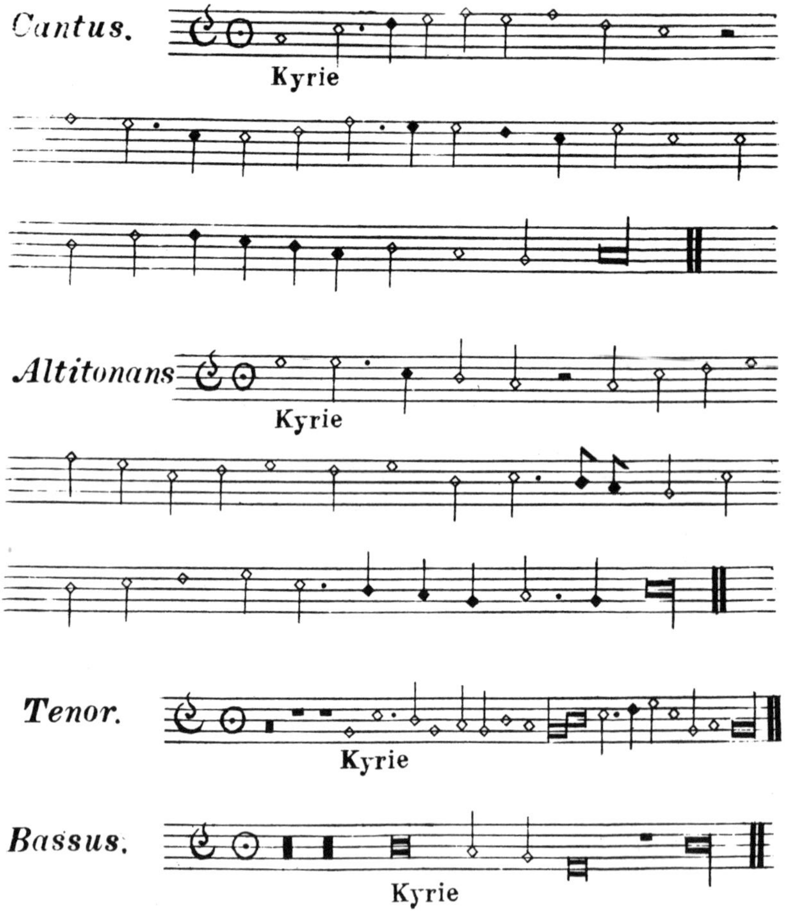

Interpretation.

Nº 9.

Josquin des Prés. *Flor:* 1480 to 1520.

Kyrie et Christe ex Missa Gaudeamus.

3
3
3
3

Christe ex eadem Missa.